MW00979604

L E A V E N
A Black and White Story

Douglas Blackburn was born in the East End of London in 1857, and from his teens he was a working journalist. He arrived in South Africa in 1892 to report for *The Star*, but soon launched various pro-Transvaal scandal-sheets. His first novels were published anonymously. His early work, *Prinsloo of Prinsloosdorp* and his first major novel, *A Burger Quixote*, have been republished.

Leaven – first published in 1908 and never reprinted – deals with his later experience in Natal where he worked as a parliamentary reporter on the *Natal Witness* in Pietermaritzburg. When *Leaven* was published in the U.K., Blackburn was widely hailed as the founder of the modern South African novel. One reviewer described it as 'the very best novel on South Africa . . . A magnificent story, written with a sense of humour, combined with a sense of honour.'

Stephen Gray's introduction appraises *Leaven* afresh as a unique and pioneering work of fiction well worth rediscovering in a changing South Africa. He is the author of the only book-length study of the writer to date, *Douglas Blackburn* (Boston, 1984).

LEAVEN
A Black and White Story

DOUGLAS BLACKBURN

With an Introduction by
STEPHEN GRAY

'It is like the leaven which a woman took and hid in three measures of meal till the whole was leavened.' – St Luke.

UNIVERSITY OF NATAL PRESS
PIETERMARITZBURG
1991

ISBN 0 86980 803 6

Cover designed and drawn by B.J. Heath

Typeset in the University of Natal Press
Pietermaritzburg
Printed by Kohler Carton and Print
Box 955, Pinetown 3600, South Africa

CONTENTS

CHAP.   PAGE

     Introduction by Stephen Gray   vii

    I   THE LURE OF THE CONCERTINA   1
    II   THE ROAD PARTY   7
    III   TOLD TO THE MISSIONARY   13
    IV   BULALIE UNDERTAKES A TRUST   25
    V   THE LIONS IN THE PATH   31
    VI   THE OFFICIAL VIEW   42
    VII FOLLOWING THE STAR   53
  VIII 'THE MISSIS'   60
    IX   FOR THE DEFENCE   71
    X   MERCY AND JUSTICE   78
    XI   THE PROGRESS OF ANNA   85
    XII THE PREPARATION OF THE LEAVEN   94
   XIII FREEDOM   100
   XIV THE EDUCATION OF BULALIE   106
    XV THE BLACKBIRDER   113
   XVI TO THE MINES   119
  XVII A MODEL COMPOUND MANAGER   123
 XVIII IN THE COMPOUND   130
   XIX THE IMPEACHMENT OF THE MISSIONARY   137
   XX THE UNFINISHED SERMON   144
   XXI CAPITULATION   152
  XXII THE CHRISTIANISED KAFIR   161
 XXIII CONVERTING THE MISSIONARY   170
 XXIV THE BACKSLIDING OF BULALIE   177
  XXV A HEATHEN DEATHBED   186
 XXVI REGENERATION   195

INTRODUCTION

The purpose of this introduction is to raise some of the questions that should be asked before reading Douglas Blackburn's magnificent novel, *Leaven* – reprinted here for the first time in over eighty years.

Not that it needs any outside support. *Leaven* may stand on its own as a fine fictional achievement. Those who like to grapple with the text without having their minds made up for them should proceed there directly.

Those who are little less certain of how to tackle this extraordinary work may first take advantage of the information offered here. The 'problem' of *Leaven* – the issues it raises, and the reasons why they are not raised more often – does perhaps require some far-reaching background knowledge. Not much work has been done in the field that *Leaven* covers.

What follows is divided into three broad categories: the circumstances of *Leaven's* publication and how it fits into Blackburn's career; the crucial place the novel holds in the history and development of literature in English in South Africa; and then an account of how it was originally received in London and in South Africa.

When Douglas Blackburn's *Leaven: A Black and White Story* was first published by Alston Rivers in London in 1908, it carried the following blurb:

> The author of *Prinsloo of Prinsloosdorp* has more than once proved his ability to write a sustained and serious story, and though certain aspects of life in South Africa are so absurd as to be merely amusing, there is no question that the native problem with which he has chosen to deal in his latest book is sufficiently grave. So far the Kafir in fiction has either been a farcical chatterbox or an object lesson of futile humanitarianism. Witty and pathetic as Mr Douglas Blackburn can be on occasion, he indulges in neither low comedy nor sickly sentimentality in *Leaven*. He traces the young Kafir from leaving his native kraal in guilty haste to the luxury of a good position in a mining compound. Incidentally young Bulalie is cast into prison and treated with the grossest brutality, and the characters who

vii

are concerned in his abasement and rescue are altogether original: the unconventional missionary, the Pietermaritzburg landlady and the compound manager are only a few of the admirable sketches which make *Leaven* a novel of remarkable and original merit.

Remarkable and original, yes . . . although we may feel that the blurb-writer has not quite presented the book squarely. His terms were designed to make the novel acceptable to the British readership of the day. We in South Africa may now see it in different terms.

Together with *Leaven*, in the same year Rivers reissued *Prinsloo of Prinsloosdorp* – a 'new edition of a South African Classic', the first one to be signed by Blackburn as the author. *Prinsloo* had been Blackburn's first publishing success, and on its first appearance had been hailed in these appreciative terms (in a lengthy review in *The Spectator*, 26 August 1899, p. 288):

> A new satirist has arisen, and appropriately enough, from Africa, the home of surprises. The anonymous author of *Prinsloo of Prinsloosdorp*, a true disciple of Swift, has not only levelled a trenchant indictment against Transvaal officialdom, but he has given us within the compass of a hundred and thirty pages as brilliant and sustained an essay in political irony as we can remember to have appeared in the last thirty years.

After an extremely lengthy summary of the work, the review concludes:

> This is hardly the place to attempt to solve the political equation of the book. It is enough to commend it to the reading public as a first-rate work of art, which deserves a permanent place amid the literature of social and political satire.

This glowing recommendation was frequently used to boom the value of *Prinsloo* in 1908 and, by implication, to invite readers to take *Leaven* just as seriously as a literary accomplishment.

In the same year Rivers also published a third novel by Blackburn, *I Came and Saw*. This was the work which completed his Sarel Erasmus trilogy, begun in *Prinsloo* (1899) and continued in *A Burgher Quixote* (1903). The latter had also been frequently reprinted (by Blackwood of Edinburgh). Blackburn had had other works published by Blackwood, but by 1906 when he made a brief return to Britain he had in some way fallen foul of them. As a result he must have arranged to transfer himself to Rivers with a three-book arrangement. When this eventuated in the triple publication of 1908, Blackburn made his final return to the U.K. to enjoy the attendant fame and rewards.

He was interviewed several times, and frequently referred to as the leading South African writer of his day. One example to illustrate his success will suffice: in *The Bookman* (in an article entitled 'The Literature of Greater Britain' by A. St. John Adcock, September 1912, p. 248), Stanley Portal Hyatt's opinion is endorsed that, after the Schreiner generation, Blackburn is 'the father of the modern school of South African novelists.' His place in Britain was secure, his reputation made.

The publication of *Leaven* itself was problematic, however. On 15 July 1908, Blackburn wrote from London to William Blackwood in Edinburgh:

> My dear Sir,
> You will probably have noticed that Alston Rivers Ltd is publishing a novel by me.
> I should not like you to think me ungrateful or discourteous after all the important assistance you have given my work.
> The M.S. of *Leaven* was with the copyright of my *Prinsloo of Prinsloosdorp* sold in 1897 to a Mr Dunbar who published (through MacLeay) *Prinsloo*. His representatives have since transferred both to Rivers and I have no financial interest in either.

(Blackburn's entire surviving correspondence is reprinted in *English in Africa*, Vol. 5, No. 1, March 1978, pp. 1–47, together with many of his fugitive journalistic pieces, drawn from the collection of the National English Literary Museum, Grahamstown.)

This letter appears to establish that the manuscript of *Leaven* had been completed in 1897, and thus is at heart the early satirical twin of *Prinsloo*. Indeed, many of the elements of high comedy, the brutal caricatures and Swiftian absurdity of *Leaven* are akin to those same elements in *Prinsloo*. In terms of historical time, as well, the action of *Leaven* also stops at c. 1897. Although in the text the action is nowhere dated, the concluding chapters very specifically deal with issues, like the liquor trade, its temporary prohibition and the related introduction of the compound system on the Rand gold-mines, which do locate it in the mid-1890s in Johannesburg.

Today, with hindsight and the benefit of works like Charles van Onselen's brilliant *Studies in the Social and Economic History of the Witwatersrand* (particularly his Vol. 1, *New Babylon*, with its 'Randlords and Rotgut, 1886–1903' section), or even with its more popular version, the Junction Avenue Theatre Company's play, *Randlords and Rotgut* of 1978, we may firmly connect the last sequence of *Leaven* to a history most of Blackburn's readers would have found hard to believe or, worse still, unknown. Those scenes, however, are historically accurate. Refer to Paul la Hausse's *Brewers, Beerhalls and Boycotts* (1988) for further corroboration.

In 1911 Blackburn himself, in the joint social history of the Rand he wrote with W. Waithmann Caddell, *Secret Service in South Africa*, also gives us chapter and verse on the issues which he had dramatised in the novel *Leaven*. For example, Chapter 3 in the later work deals with the 'Illicit Liquor Trade', Chapter 8 with 'Native-Labour Agents' and the blackbirding system and Chapter 15 with 'I.D.B.' – all these topics are central to an understanding of the novel's text. (Whether or not they are suitable material for fiction is another matter.)

So *Leaven*'s action is set in the 1890s and the last third of the book, located over the border in the Transvaal, very obviously derives from Blackburn's first-hand experience there and then. His own involvement in the mid-1890s on the Rand, as an independent journalist based in Johannesburg and Krugersdorp – as an exposer of corruption, a socialist revealing to all the mining magnates' capitalistic manoeuvres to maximise the productivity of their abject labour force – is too burningly actual not to have come directly out of experience. The dialogue set up between the rival compound managers, the crooked Sid Dane of the New Yankee and the pragmatic Mr Fraser of the Belmont, which forms the near culmination of the work, is too fresh and too detailed not to have been written directly from life.

Yet, despite Blackburn's evidence to the contrary, it is hard to believe that *Leaven* as it now stands was actually completed, finalised and sold off to Dunbar by 1897, and Dunbar certainly did not see it into print. Perhaps a first draft was done, but then that first draft could only have dealt with matters on the Rand (the last third of the novel we have). From 1892 when he first arrived in South Africa from London until the outbreak of the Second Anglo-Boer War in 1899, Blackburn's sole focus was the Transvaal and he became known as a prolific press-correspondent specialising in 'Boer affairs.' Indeed, his first novel of all, *Kruger's Secret Service*, is set uniquely in Johannesburg and Pretoria, and his last novel for Blackwood, *Richard Hartley, Prospector* (1905), is nothing but a 'history' of Kruger's Transvaal Republic up to its demise.

Blackburn did not move to Natal until late 1899. After riding with the Boer forces during the opening months of the war at the Natal front as a special correspondent (the experience from which *A Burgher Quixote* is derived), he was expelled through Delagoa Bay back to British territory. While a non-combatant reporting from the other side he was badly wounded at the Battle of Pieter's Hill, and spent most of the first three years of the new century recuperating far from any battlelines, in the Loteni District tucked in the foothills of the Drakensberg, 120 kms west of Pietermaritzburg. For the *Times of Natal* he must have gone down from there to the capital to write and compile their 'war number' of late 1900, a scrupulously impartial record of the first phase of the war.

But the Loteni Valley was his base, 'hidden under the shadow of Giant's Castle', one of the 'richest and most fruitful, as well as the least known districts of the Colony. Crime in the Loteni district,' he wrote, 'has never soared to a greater altitude than sheep-stealing . . .' (these observations in a letter published in *The Natal Witness* of 6 June, 1902, refuting their premature report of his death as a war casualty!). The police-post where he lived has gone, but the remains of what became Father Hyslop's mission village are still there. Blackburn obviously grew hale and hearty in his Loteni retreat, and also extremely productive: he finished the massive *A Burgher Quixote* there before the war was over. Surely he also set about reworking *Leaven* there as well; he must have done, for the first third of the new *Leaven* is obviously set in the Loteni with Himeville and Underberg as the seat of its magistrate, just as the second third is set in the Pietermaritzburg to which he would gravitate (and where he would find employment as a parliamentary reporter on the *Witness* over 1903–06).

Anyone who has read *Leaven* may see that its real focus is not the Reef at all; it is the workings of Natal Colony itself. David Hyslop, Bulalie, Weldon the blackbirder and even Sid Dane are studied as Natalians, even when they are all drawn to and washed up on the Reef. Blackburn's interest had shifted wholly from the antiquated Transvaal to the more modern 'Garden Colony' of Natal. With the world's attention now off the 'Boer question', there is hardly a trace of Afrikanerdom left in the text – for example, only one Afrikaans word is used familiarly, 'klippie'. Now the world's attention is on the so-called 'native question', which in *Leaven* is one of Blackburn's main concerns as it manifests itself in Natal.

So it is safe to deduce that, during or after the Loteni years and his residence in Pietermaritzburg, Blackburn entirely recast the first two-thirds of *Leaven* and matched it to his previous ending set on the Rand. He then deleted any specifics of time and historical event, meaning the new *Leaven* to stand as a more or less timeless story of the black-and-white experience of colonisation and industrial-isation in Southern Africa, which after all by then was entirely British. In 1908, with the Union of South Africa in view, it went without saying that his was *the* story of the subcontinent. Blackburn had found his 'big subject'; accordingly, because of its continuing relevance to us, *Leaven* is the easiest of his works to read today.

Nor has it lost its bite. Blackburn's deployment of irony still cuts. The South Africa of *Leaven* is a modern South Africa, very recognisable to us. His themes are numerous: the way justice is stacked by one sector of the population against another, and looks a lot like legalised theft; the way crime pays and virtue is seldom rewarded; the way economic compulsion controls lives (Blackburn is as fierce a bookkeeper as Defoe); the way good laws are subverted by their upholders; the profiteering; the rape of a land, in short. None of these themes has gone away, become 'historical'.

Yet it would be foolish to decontextualise *Leaven* entirely and read it too flatly as some sort of prophetic critique of our present national malfunctions, injustices and dilemmas. Although it was very much in advance of its time − compare *Leaven* with some of Schreiner's essays in *Thoughts on South Africa* to see how Blackburn escaped some of the Victorian attitudes to which she remained attached − it is still very much *of* its time.

That time is not the rumbustious and witty *fin-de-siècle* of the 1890s to which *Prinsloo* and *A Burgher Quixote* rightly belong, but the first decade of the new century. During these years in Britain a rather more sober and sombre school of materialism was evolved in the novel − examples are Joseph Conrad's *Heart of Darkness* (1902), H.G. Wells's *Kipps* (1905), Arnold Bennett's *The Old Wives' Tale* (1908) and even D.H. Lawrence's *The Rainbow* (1915), all of which give weighty analyses of social problems in a manner not unlike Blackburn's in *Leaven*. That was the market within which Blackburn now competed and for which he now wrote. The extremes of rich and poor, the cutting edge of class and caste − and in Blackburn's case colour − are all typical issues of the novel of flamboyant and affluent Edwardian days. An analogous case is *Margaret Harding* of 1911, written by Blackburn's friend and colleague in Natal, Perceval Gibbon. Edwardian fiction normally probed the basic factors controlling society, even a society as remote from the metropolis as colonial Natal.

Blackburn's analysis of the colony, although it is confined to the inland sphere of influence, is thorough and even relentless. Perhaps no other novelist, before or since, has viewed that part of the British overseas world in such penetrating terms − cold, basic terms. Consider how in Blackburn's text the romantic myths about the white man's civilizing mission in Africa bite the dust. Bulalie, we know within a few pages of meeting him, has *no chance*; David Hyslop, too, is beaten *before* he can begin. Never for one paragraph does Blackburn let us feel that their stories will culminate in some romantic glow of resolution and togetherness. We are compelled to look head-on at an unromantic system, prepared to be bludgeoned with reality, as both Blackburn's leading characters are in the gruesome last sequence.

The tone of Blackburn's analysis is realism. Upright, tough Mrs Hopgood is not the simpering victim she pretends to be at Bulalie's trial during the Black Peril scare which so acts to her advantage – she is a greedy opportunist and an outright liar. Alice Lester may be 'sincere and ardent', but her treatment of her only convert amounts to persecution. Watch carefully how Blackburn uses the role of the press in Natal to give the official version of each event – for example, KAFIR OUTRAGE ON WHITE WOMAN!, a sensational headline which the text of the novel shows should have been reversed.

The bottom line of Blackburn's realism is his ironic attitude to the colony's labour policy – in 1908 the Natal government's labour laws were widely held to be an example of enlightened and civilised policy, yet as the novel shows Blackburn held the real situation to be akin to that of slavery. If exportation of labour to the mines is banned in Natal, then how do the agents, Weldon and Hacker, make £40 000 in five years (which at £2 a head means they alone have dispatched 20 000 people illegally over the border)?

What really happens in Blackburn's Natal is that, from the moment the sound of the concertina is heard in Bulalie's home, his life is determined, although in a random, picaresque way: road-gang, 'house-boy', convict, convert, 'mine-boy', 'boss-boy', accidental live sacrifice. Not that Bulalie is a passive, innocent victim, either. He is a vicious parricide, in fact, who goes unpunished. All the system sees to is that he is heavily punished for everything but his original crime.

In Blackburn's view Bulalie lives under the reign of the whip – the original edition of Leaven had an embossed, gold cat-o'-nine-tails as its only illustration on the cover. Bulalie is never smart enough to get hold of the whip handle, but he would have if he could; that is all. We are truly a long way from the world of H. Rider Haggard (from one of whose romances the name 'Bulalie' the killer is borrowed). In Haggard the savagery is always far from the Garden Colony over some fanciful border, but in Blackburn the savagery starts right at home, deep in the heart of every man, woman and child.

In Blackburn no one in Natal is exonerated; the system that involves all is diabolically clever; none can escape it. This is more than political satire, which is usually one-sided and partisan; this is the writing of a thorough, angry indictment of the whole. The leaven of righteousness simply cannot permeate this mess of meal, and during the course of the novel Blackburn more or less gives up on the idea. Hard to take, to be sure. Which is probably why Leaven has remained firmly out of print for over eighty years.

There are many good reasons, beyond its historical and political interest, for rediscovering *Leaven* today. Firstly, it is more than competently done: its double story is beautifully planned and executed, with the switch at the end when the hired killers get the wrong man being dramatically perfect – and absolutely heart-rending. Secondly, at the level of organisation of plot it is an extremely cunning achievement – while the rather old-fashioned sub-plot of Bacheta's diamond-cache is resolved, the newer style of plot – dealing with reciprocal malice and vengeance – overtakes it and silences it. Larger issues remain gapingly open.

Thirdly, Blackburn's realism introduces the reader to many areas of South African experience that had not been depicted before (but which since have become the staples of much South African fiction). The Pietermaritzburg jailhouse for a start – who can ever forget the horrifying vividness of the triangle there? (Blackburn had a great sympathy with the convicted – Sarel Erasmus writes the whole of *A Burgher Quixote* from those same dismal cells, and that is where Letty in his *Love Muti* of 1915 will end up, too.) The landscape of the Rand mines is another new area for fiction, with its deafening battery-stamps and the managers' monopoly over accommodation in those concentration camp-type compounds. There are many other examples of new settings.

A fourth observation to make is the following: at one single go, in the Bulalie story in *Leaven*, Blackburn discovered the essential features of what has become known as the 'Jim Comes to Joburg' trope of the South African novel. There were many of them, using the 'low life' trope in one way or another, to come: W.C. Scully's *Daniel Vananda* (1923), William Plomer's *Ula Masondo* (1927), Frank Brownlee's *Cattle Thief* (1929), R.R.R. Dhlomo's *An African Tragedy* (1931), Peter Abrahams' *Mine Boy* (1946), Alan Paton's *Cry, the Beloved Country* (1948), Peter Lanham and A.S. Mopeli-Paulus' *Blanket Boy's Moon* and Doris Lessing's *Hunger* (both 1953), while kraal-to-grave stories are still used in the media today, not to mention lived out by millions of South Africans in real life.

The features of this trope are well-established in Blackburn: the expulsion from the homesite, forced labour for the 'blanket-boy' (in Bulalie's case as a 'horse-boy'), in an urban area ruled by passes and the curfew, domestic service, convict labour, concealment, being compulsorily recruited, the transportation by railway to the wicked city, etc. To be sure, in *Leaven* the steps are worked out most consequently: Blackburn's basic pattern would become played out in many other variations by later writers. Because the 'Jim Comes to Joburg' story is *the* major South African story, it persists in our imaginations. Blackburn's founding version is by no means an underdeveloped, shadowy prototype; some may argue that no writer since has articulated the theme in such astute, driving detail.

A fifth observation about the value of rediscovering *Leaven* is this: a recently influential school of literary criticism has come to explain and assess the colonial novel as essentially 'dialogic'; that is, as an amalgam of mixed discourses and styles betraying all the stresses and fractures of a society not yet settled into one dominant mode. The dialogic text makes room for a wide variety of experiences without homogenising it – without *being able* to homogenise it. Nowadays this is interpreted as the inevitable product of a strained, mixed, transitional society in which gaping incongruities and vast social (and language) differences rub shoulders, as it were; in which the chasms between one character's version of an experience and another's are so vast that there is no bridging them; they co-exist, that's all. Like many later South African novels, *Leaven* is pre-eminently such a dialogical text and answers to the theory in an examplary way. Today critics may have a field day showing how typical it is of all novels produced in mixed colonial cultures.

Thus we may come to see aspects of *Leaven* which may previously have been considered crudities or uneasinesses as very revealing of the broken nature of Natal society in Blackburn's day. In Blackburn Natal was the very province of miscommunication itself. Consider merely the extended scenes of Bulalie's trial: the upshot rests not so much on the process of injustice as on mistranslation, on systematic misreading of the symbols. Hyslop's wonderful, unfinished sermon to the Nonconformists of Pietermaritzburg – believers in a new creed, 'blessed by residence in a country free from the intolerance, bigotry and narrowness that obtain in the older civilisations' – is more than just inappropriately ironic and bitterly satirical. Hyslop has indeed discovered a new language that he stutters out in the finest dialogical way . . . only to have it blotted out by organ-playing.

Blackburn may be seen to be making some significant stylistic breakthroughs in the text. The brief chapter entitled 'Freedom', one of the first in South African literature to deal in any detail with a black-black encounter (specifically the last between Bulalie and Bacheta), is an example. Here most of the material is 'translated' for the benefit of the English-language reader, and in stark contrast to Bulalie's usual awkward pidgin, set up for us so painstakingly in the early sequence with Gabriel Betts ('Baas said bring boy for sjambok', 'No, no, baas, give me half my money . . .'). In this chapter the language soars: a dignified, poetic cadence is achieved through subtle grammar, accumulating connectives . . . all interrupted by a bullet. Plomer and Paton used this effect later, and today the Old Testament-sounding rhythm of Zulu-in-English is thought of as Patonesque. In Blackburn this technique makes its first appearance.

The whole of *Leaven* is full of such dialogic effects – changes of register signify discourses in contestation. In fact, the scrupulous care Blackburn took with the way he wrote all his dialogue in the text – his perfect ear – suggests he *heard* Natal at the turn of the century as a Babel of competing voices. As a humorist he was long accustomed to catching exact nuances, every give-away turn of phrase; in *Leaven*, in his view, these voices are at war with one another, so the end result could hardly be a stable, unified text. (Indeed, much of *Leaven* is quoted from a wide variety of sources.)

The problem Blackburn presents in *Leaven*, then, goes far beyond the moral questions of good/bad magistrates, honest/dishonest landladies or straight/crooked lawyers like Mr Darter. In other words, it is not sufficient just to say of *Leaven*, well, it was a few right bad 'uns who soured the whole mishmash, but surely it wasn't as bad as all that. Blackburn sees beyond that position to the problem of a society which *cannot* find a common language . . . indeed, a society which *does not want* to find a common language. Not finding a common language – in which words like 'freedom' mean freedom (instead of death), 'mercy' and 'justice' mean mercy and justice and one's daily bread is leavened with plain righteousness – Blackburn shows, over and over again, means untold distortions may continue to hold sway; may flourish and be perpetuated.

In Blackburn these competing dialogues are never resolved. 'While the missionary discoursed on the wages of iniquity,' Blackburn tells us, at Bulalie's death-bed, all Bulalie comes out with is an incredibly astute: 'Tell them I said you are the preacher who never lies.' But there is no common agreement between them, no final locking together of their codes. They simply do not understand one another. Hideously, Hyslop is the one who says, 'I am content', and Bulalie the one who dies.

But to distil all of *Leaven* into an early 'Jim' novel – a fine social-realist example of the countryman goes (or is driven) to town story – is to do it a partial injustice, to read it askew. Blackburn's subtitle, *A Black and White Story*, insists on the interconnectedness of the two halves of the narrative. The figure of David Hyslop is given as much detailed attention as Bulalie. Today much of the theory of colonialism shows how the process has made 'others' of any (in our case) non-English-speakers. This 'othering' cuts so deep that many white English-speakers (both in South Africa and abroad) feel that the only

xvii

suitable characters in South African fiction are Afrikaners and blacks. When the
mirror is held up to themselves, they evade seeing their reflections; they resist
self-scrutiny and analysis, passing the springbuck – so to speak – down the
line. (The original blurb, quoted earlier, is a fine example of this tendency.)

But Blackburn's text does not readily allow such brushings off of
responsibility on the part of the English-speaking white; his plot involves them
equally and integrally with blacks; they are all co-responsible for the situation.
A correct reading of *Leaven* would stress that Blackburn himself sees colonial
society as a cohesive and integral whole.

Hyslop's story is another trope that Blackburn also seemingly found for the
South African novel at one go. That it has been rarely used by later South
African writers – perhaps only by Nadine Gordimer in *A World of Strangers*
(1958) – is merely an indication of how shy English-speaking South Africans
have become in portraying themselves. Hyslop's is the 'Johnny-come-lately'
story, the story of the newcomer, wet behind the ears, whom we watch as he
puts his foot in every cowpat, rubs everyone up the wrong way. The greenhorn
is of course an irresistible figure of fun in colonial fiction of the frontier days
(think of Mark Twain) and usually used by the novelist to instruct the reader in a
formative society's norms and conventions. But in Blackburn Hyslop is used
rather against the grain – we are now beyond the Allan Quatermain phase of
frontier didacticism. It soon becomes clear in Blackburn that Hyslop will not
become absorbed by the settlers; on the contrary, he is treated very vindictively
by them and eventually expelled from their midst. Blackburn exploits this
version of the story to expose how contradicted and closed his 'last outpost' had
become.

The 'Johnny-come-lately' trope is interesting for the comparisons and
contrasts it offers to the 'Jim' trope. Hyslop travels from the wicked city (in his
case, London) to the bundu. His first instructor is the 'superintendent of roads'
who advises him in the art of remaining 'a white man'. His mission field is
strictly defined as the reduction of the dispossessed indigenous population
through magistrates, taxes and the police into cheap labour units. He and his
ex-governess wife live the lie of their roseate press releases. The local press so
persecutes them that they are frozen out of normal commerce. After the disaster
of the unfinished sermon in Pietermaritzburg, he is dismissed and goes
freelance. On the Rand he is manipulated into supporting the most segregation-
ist and oppressive industrial policy yet, and when he still refuses to knuckle
down he is to be assassinated. There his incredible story ends rather
appallingly – he has not made *one* convert, but a fortune in ill-gotten gains.

In this story we are a hair's breadth away from one of Blackburn's favourite themes – the conversion of the missionary himself to non-belief. (Obviously in Pietermaritzburg Blackburn had been very moved by Bishop Colenso's dilemma.) One of Blackburn's last creative pieces to be published (in *The New Age*, 7 November 1912, p.9) was entitled 'The Converted Missionary' and begins:

> From the land of the White, to the Kraal of the Black,
> Came Bigsby the Missionman, hot on the track
> Of the Heathen in darkness all sitting.
> All sitting at ease, free from care or disease,
> With no want that their heathendom could not appease,
> And a pitying wonder that White men should please
> To consider hard labour more fitting.

Blackburn had long been of the opinion that missionary effort would be better directed to the populace 'back Home' in darkest Britain.

Be that as it may, like Bulalie, Hyslop is driven to live outside the law (surely Dickens is very influential here). In order to practise what he preaches he has to commit treason; in living his true faith he is harassed and blatant attempts are made to re-educate him. Nor is he offered sainthood as a way out; another being is uselessly martyred in his stead. Nevertheless he is as much a victim of the same system as Bulalie: in his case the 'freedom of speech' that the new Natalians wished to further as they found their South African feet never opened up to admit him. Plantation culture, the slave-holding mentality, religious 'euthanasia' – these prevailed. 'Johnny-come-lately', in this case, is their casualty.

Hyslop was never a 'good' preacher, defined as one who would serve the settler interest. So he is also a 'first' in South African fiction – the outsider figure, marginalised, finally set entirely against the monolithic system.

The play between the 'Jim' and the 'Johnny' stories in *Leaven* is perhaps its greatest achievement. Here is where Blackburn gets his greatest effects. One thinks of Hyslop going out into 'his' location, returning with a goat, and then a girl. One thinks of both Mrs Hyslop and Mrs Hopgood with their surrogate black children (Anna and the wickedly spoiled Dick). One thinks of how Mrs Hopgood's boarding-house establishment, painted with such loving care, is so connected through the kitchen to every detail of its own backyard. Old Boggis the prospector wanders so freely across the boundaries as if he knows no constraints. There are many other examples of crossing and connectedness.

Some critics have dismissed *Leaven* as a proto-apartheid novel advocating the separation of the races . . . but this is emphatically not so. The whole structure of *Leaven*, its very domestic geography, speaks of how the destinies of white and black are already interlocked, for ever intertwined. One rum-bottle up at Blue Krantz in the Drakensberg starts the action; rum-bottles bring about its closure. Blackburn's whole point is how *similar* the 'Jim' and the 'Johnny' stories are. And Bulalie is not 'othered' in *Leaven*; or, if you prefer, Bulalie and Hyslop are equally 'othered' . . . and Blackburn feels no essential difference between them as figures deserving attention in the South African novel.

In its time *Leaven* had a reception surely very different from the one it will receive today. In an article entitled 'Some South African Prejudices' (in *Chambers's Journal*, 22 November 1902, p. 815), Blackburn had set some of the guidelines for approaching a novel like this:

> Nowhere, not even in the most anti-negrophilist states of America, is the 'colour line' drawn more carefully than in Natal, and only a degree less strictly in the other colonies. The newcomer must never manifest any interest in the natives, except to abuse them; and he will not need a second warning against bringing up the subject of missionaries!

(The date of this quotation also incidentally adds evidence to the view that Blackburn must have been recasting *Leaven* after the war.)

The fiction-reviewer of London's *The Academy* (25 July 1908), although extremely complimentary, evades specific issues like the above:

> Great are the responsibilities and difficulties of the novelist who attempts a study of the relations between the white and black races, and if he succeeds his triumph is all the more noteworthy. Mr Douglas Blackburn is in the happy position of realising that he has given us the very best novel on South Africa that has yet appeared. *Leaven* is a magnificent story, written with a sense of humour combined with a sense of honour. The author touches on many of the gravest questions, moral and political; yet it is impossible to tell what his own private opinions are, for this book, though to a certain extent political, is quite unbiased . . . Anyone who knows good literature will find it in *Leaven*, even if he is not interested in 'South African problems', and that is high praise.

In *The Bookman* (August 1908) Blackburn provokes a more focused response by warning his readers through his interviewer that *Leaven* 'deals with certain pathetic and unguessed conditions prevailing among the black races that he thinks will come as a surprise if not a shock to the majority of British readers.' In September 1908 (p.231), their reviewer duly responds:

> Four things that become clear to any one reading *Leaven* are that the negro problem in South Africa is one of the most difficult, as well as one of the most momentous, problems of the day; that the brutal methods of treatment in favour with the majority of whites out there are not likely to solve it; that the kindly, humanitarian methods advocated by the minority are even less likely to do so; and that the safety, if not the existence, of the usurping population depends on its solution . . . This is in every way an original and an arresting story; it is alive with interest; its pathos and humour are unforced, and it is written by a man who brings to his work a profound knowledge of black and white humanity, and a big-hearted sympathy for both.

The reviewer of the London *Daily Mail* takes a slightly contrary view (15 August 1908, p.8):

> Mr Blackburn is emphatically a writer with a purpose, and perhaps his otherwise excellent story suffers just a little for that reason. His desire to prove that neither the black man nor the white man is improved by contact with the other has probably caused the writer to draw Colonial life somewhat darker than it really is. Or, at least, we hope so, for there is not much in this book to make us view with pride the progress of civilisation in South Africa . . .

By the time *Leaven* is distributed in South Africa its tendentious reputation has certainly spread ahead of it. Here is one very revealing response which may be considered typical, although in general the book was firmly ignored. It is headed: 'The Problem of Black and White: Hysteria from Basutoland' (*The Cape Argus Weekly Review*, 21 October 1908, p.8):

> *Leaven: A Black and White Story* by Douglas Blackburn will not greatly help either the Kafir's comfort or the author's literary reputation. It is one of the dreariest sermons ever delivered. It is a didactic essay in the form of a novel in 328 pages that could have been told to better purpose in twenty-eight . . . Mr Blackburn, we understand, is an invalid who lives in Basutoland [!]. He used to be a journalist in Natal. One can only regret that his newspaper training did not give him a better conception of South African life. *Leaven* is an open, loudly-shouted, almost hysterical attack on the Natal Government in particular, and South African white men in

general, for their treatment of the natives. There may be in it much of truth, and much of a praiseworthy earnestness to raise the native races. But Mr Blackburn displays utter ignorance of the methods of courts and newspapers in his book; and one of his stock arguments is that he understands these . . .

Even if Mr Blackburn made out a strong case against the manner in which Natal and the Transvaal administer justice to the native, he does not help us. He gives us a sermon in 328 pages; but he arrives at no conclusion. He tells us (in very feeble language, let it be said) that we are a most abandoned crowd; but he apparently arrives at the conclusion that the native is so bad that we could not be otherwise. He argues for total separation of white and black; and decides against it. He shows the Christianising of the Kafir to be folly; and he says go on Christianising. At least, those are what one gathers to be his conclusions.

His style has never before been so bad. His plot has never before been so flimsy. Here there is nothing but an air of utter provinciality, of hysteria, of unreality. There is nothing of what Kipling calls 'the power of the naked phrase'. On the whole, one has rarely read anything more illogical, more tedious and less literary than *Leaven*. The Natal people may be very bad and all that, but such arguments as those which Mr Blackburn uses are not going to make them better.

This reviewer's inability to come to terms with the novel – to give *Leaven* a fair reading for what it says and does, with all its subtlety and beauty – need not detain us today. Suffice it to say that the guilty, raw nerves the novel struck – those of labour and of Christian love – could jangle most unfairly in Colonial South Africa, to the distinct disadvantage of Blackburn's reputation in the land which produced his major work, his masterpiece.

Natal in 1908 had a population of 60 000 'Colonials', outnumbered twenty to thirty times by 'natives'. Only one of those human beings was a novelist equal to the task of describing them. His name was Douglas Blackburn; he was unique.

Read his testimony. Find the leaven.

STEPHEN GRAY
1991

Douglas Blackburn in Johannesburg, 1897.
This portrait was taken by Dunbar Bros.
who published *Prinsloo of Prinsloosdorp*
anonymously two years later.

Portrait used in the *Tonbridge Free Press* issue
which carried Blackburn's obituary in 1929.

Portrait used to illustrate an article in
Wide World Magazine, 1906.

Leaven :

A Black and White Story

BY

DOUGLAS BLACKBURN

AUTHOR OF "PRINSLOO OF PRINSLOOSDORP,"
"A BURGHER QUIXOTE," "RICHARD HARTLEY, PROSPECTOR."

" It is like the leaven which a woman took and hid in three measures of meal till the whole was leavened."—ST. LUKE.

LONDON: ALSTON RIVERS, LIMITED,
BROOKE STREET, HOLBORN BARS.
MCMVIII.

LEAVEN
A BLACK AND WHITE STORY

CHAPTER I

THE LURE OF THE CONCERTINA

Bulalie lay in a comfortable hollow, just big enough to fit his tall and shapely form, supporting his chin in both hands and watching the long wide valley below him.

He had been there since noon, and now the sun had nearly touched the blue hills many miles away, where he had seen it disappear every night that his memory could compass, perhaps fifteen years, when it had fallen into the great krantz where the hole was through which it rolled back under the rocks and the river to come up again behind the grey mountains in the morning.

Bulalie had been bidden to stay on and keep watching as much longer as it would take an ox wagon to travel between the two rivers, which he knew to be about one hour as the white men reckoned time. It was the nights of the dead moon, when even Bulalie, who had sight more keen than any one in the kraal, could see but a little way; therefore it would be foolishness to stay longer to watch for the police, who would not ride that way in the dark, not even to catch the kafirs sitting round the pot that held the sheep stolen that day.

Bulalie knew well the ways of the police, for as long as he could remember they had come much to his father's kraal, for old Tambuza was a bad kafir, on whom the resident magistrate kept strict watch and ward with his young policemen. Thrice had they taken Tambuza to Maritzburg to be tried for stealing sheep, or taking part in a tribal fight, and each time the old man had remained away for long, coming back with fresh marks of the cat, looking older, and more wrathful in his speech when talking of white men, whom he hated more than he feared.

Bulalie knew that it was vain to watch the road after the sun had fallen into the krantz, but the fear of his father's anger was stronger than his hunger, though not so great as his yearning to be free of a task that was unworthy of a young man old enough to be wearing the head ring. His heart was sore at the thought that he should be made to do the work of an umfaan, or even of a girl. It was no pleasure to him that he had been selected because of his greater wisdom in the ways of the police, neither did he give thought to the knowledge that an umfaan or intombi would be fearful of returning the long dark way to the kraal. He was sure that he had been sent to perform an unpleasant task not for these reasons, but because his father wished to show that his fourth son was still much under his authority, and to punish him for having often said he wished to go among the white men to get money that he might buy cattle and get a wife as his three elder brothers had done.

But there was another great cause for the discontent of Bulalie. That day there had come to the kraal, Sebaas, the son of his father's brother. He had been away four years, in Maritzburg and still farther away in Johannesburg where the gold was made, and had returned rich enough to buy cattle and take for wife a girl from a kraal by the Umvoti River.

Sebaas had bought many things that Bulalie had long hungered for, but best and greatest of all a concertina. Bulalie's heart had given a great thump when Sebaas had come out of his hut carrying the wonderful box that was louder and more beautiful than the mouth organ that was so common that even the youngest umfaans in the kraal possessed one. Bulalie actually envied the girls and married women who went to fetch water from the river, when he saw that Sebaas with his concertina accompanied them.

He had thought of this most of the afternoon as he lay watching the road, and his heart was full of the pain of envy.

It was to do honour to Sebaas that the sheep had been stolen. There would be a great feast as soon as it was dark, but Bulalie would arrive late, and perhaps have to share with the women the poor remains.

Just as the sun fell into the krantz Bulalie made the great resolution of his life.

He would leave the kraal and become as Sebaas. He would come back when the harvest was finished and kafir beer was in plenty in the kraals, and he would bring a concertina bigger and more loud sounding than that of Sebaas, if such there was; and the girls would crowd round him to hear him squeeze out the music, and he would be great in the kraal.

Thus without knowledge Bulalie justified the political economists of Natal who preached the gospel of forcing the native to work by fostering a desire for the luxuries and trivialities of civilisation.

He waited until the amber and gold dust had risen in smoke from the krantz which now hid the sun, and turned his face towards the kraal, walking leisurely at first, lest a too early arrival should prove that he had been an unfaithful sentry. But the thoughts of the feast and the memory of the four chords that Sebaas pressed out of the concertina made his feet move faster and faster till he began to run, and sing the song of few words wherewith the people of the kraals drive away the evil spirits that lurk after dark in the long grass and the gloomy places of the veld.

But he sang it in a new way — fitted to the music of the concertina, and to his surprise he remembered that while singing he had passed the stream where sometimes came the Togolosh that carried off maidens, and had felt no sinking of the heart. Truly the music of the concertina must be good and potent, for never before had Bulalie passed that spot after dark without feeling his heart thump and his blood turn to water.

'The music has made me very brave,' he said aloud, and jubilantly, for he knew he would have need of great courage that night when he carried out his resolve and spoke to his father.

When, an hour afterwards, Bulalie turned the corner of the hill and looked for the red glow of the fire that should be showing through the cracks in the low door of the big hut, he saw nothing. All was darkness and silence instead of firelight and the noise of feasting.

He stood still and listened, but heard only the river running among the rocks, and a child crying far, far away in the kraal beyond the mealie gardens.

Was it that the police had come suddenly upon the kraal from the other side of the river, and were now sitting waiting for him to come in? He listened for the sounds that police horses make when they champ their big bits and jingle the steel and brass that shine when the police trooper rides; but none came on the soft wind, that blew only the pleasant smell of smouldering cowdung from a fire that was dying.

Slowly Bulalie moved through the long grass towards the kraal till he came to the black ring where the grass had been burned to keep away veld fire, and it cracked and crinkled beneath his feet. Immediately came the barking of many dogs who rushed to meet him, ceasing their angry clamour when they knew it was Bulalie.

Then the dull red light from a dying fire in the large hut suddenly showed where the low door had been opened, and the voice of his mother called him.

Bulalie crawled into the hut and found it full of women.

'Where is the feast? Why are you not eating?' he asked.

'There is no feast tonight. Your father is angry with Sebaas that he should bring white men's things to the kraal. There was rum, which made Sebaas drunk, and white men's clothes which Sebaas put on because he was drunk, and forgot that your father hated that his people should go from their proper ways. So he beat Sebaas and bid him leave the kraal, and there has been no meat eating.'

She uncovered the pot where there was only cold mealie pap that she had saved for her son. He ate it, and crept into his father's hut to sleep.

Old Tambuza lay on the floor with his back uncovered, for the blanket had fallen away from his shoulders. The fire in the middle of the hut was not yet dead, and the wind that came in when the door was opened fanned the dying fuel into life.

As Bulalie lay down on the opposite side of the hut, he saw that the old man's back was bare, for the firelight shone on it, and showed the furrows old and new left by the cat that had cut into his flesh. Bulalie went gently across and drew the blanket over his father's shoulders, for he knew that it angered him that the marks should be seen.

Tambuza was not sleeping.

'Do not cover me,' he said. His voice was sad, not angry.

'Lie down as you were going to and look well at my back.'

'I have seen, father,' Bulalie answered, 'and it makes me angry with the Ingisi' (Englishmen).

Tambuza turned over and looked at his son across the red fire, which he fanned with a corner of his blanket and made glow bright for a space, so that he could see the face of Bulalie.

'Those are good words, if you speak truly, Bulalie.'

'They are true words, father.'

'Then why would you go and serve the white men who made these marks on your father?'

The heart of Bulalie grew large and tried to break out of his body till he was sick, for he knew that he dare not now speak the words he had framed while watching the sun die. So he was silent, and looked in the fire, knowing that the old man was watching his face and waiting for him to answer.

'Your eyes have been set on fire by the sight of the gold of Sebaas, and your ears made quick by the stories he has told of the towns and big kraals of the gold-mines. I have watched you when Sebaas talked. Is it not so?'

Bulalie could no longer be deaf and dumb before his father.

'I have only seen that he can now buy many cattle and take a wife,' he answered meekly, because he was fearful as to what his father would reply.

'I saw that you thought that way, Bulalie. But you need not leave the kraal to get money for cattle. Have I not enough for lobola for three wives for you?'

Bulalie was silent now from wonderment. Could he have heard aright? Was it that his father was offering to give him cattle to buy a wife? What strange change had come over the old man that he should talk of parting with cattle, that were as much to him as his life? 'You will take another wife, father?'

'Yes, for my son, if he will not stay in the kraal without one.'

'But I do not want to take a wife, father.'

'Then you want to leave the kraal.'

He paused, waiting for the reply that came not.

'You would go among the white men and learn their ways, you would come back, even as Sebaas did this day, and hurt the eyes of your father by doing white foolishness and wrong. You would forget that you are of your people, and would throw away the loin-cloth for the clothes of the white men. You wish to be no more of us.'

Tambuza rose to his feet as he spoke, standing tall and straight, a fierce and angry man.

Bulalie stood also, for it would be rudeness to lie down while his father spoke upon his feet.

'Tell me truly,' said the old man. 'Is not all true that I have said?'

Bulalie felt fear taking hold of him, for the wrath of Tambuza was terrible. He would have said, 'No, father,' but the words would not come. He looked into the fire and stirred the embers with his foot.

'Why do you not speak?'

Tambuza stooped forward that he might the better see the face of his son, and fell upon him across the fire, scattering the embers so that they filled the hut with a dull redness and smoke.

As Bulalie caught his father and bore him up, their faces touched, and the strong odour of a drink that was not kafir beer told Bulalie the truth.

He pushed the old man with all his strength, throwing him in a sitting posture to the ground, and, standing over him, spoke words such as never before had passed his lips.

'Father,' said Bulalie, 'you who reproach me for wishing to go to learn the ways of the white man. It is you who should be silent. Are you not now drunk with the white man's rum that Sebaas has brought – Sebaas whom you turned out of the kraal that you might drink and he not see?'

It was well that Bulalie had the keenness of sight which made him famous among his people, for even in the dull greyness of the smoke he saw the glint of the assegai which his father pulled out of the withes that bound the thatch of the hut.

Before its sharp point had lowered for the throw, he had lifted the big iron pot and hurled it with mighty force. He knew that it had smitten the old man on the head; he also knew by the silence that followed the fall of the body that a great hurt had been made, for the strongest and the bravest of his people always utter a cry of defiance and derision when receiving the blow of an enemy that does not kill; but Tambuza, the brave old lion of his tribe, had taken his hurt without a sound.

Bulalie stooped and gazed through the smoke, and it was as if his strong piercing eyes had the force of a blow, for the body of Tambuza fell sideways into the embers, and Bulalie saw that the eyes were wide open and he knew that it meant death.

Then a great fear came over him, and a shame and sorrow; but fear was the mightiest. It said to him, 'Go away, run away, go, go!'

He crawled through the low door, closed it after him, and walked quietly but quickly into the veld.

The bright big star which showed where Maritzbug lay shone out brightest of all the glittering lights in the dark violet sky. It said, 'Come this way,' as it often had in the nights when Bulalie had lain outside the hut to avoid his angry father. Tonight it spoke quite loudly.

His dog came up and put his nose in his hand, then gambolled away in the direction of his master's thoughts. It was an omen he dared not ignore. He looked once at the hut where his father lay silent in the smouldering fire, once at the hut that held his mother and his womenkind, then followed the dog into the quiet veld.

CHAPTER II

THE ROAD PARTY

Gabriel Betts, fair, fat, and forty, late of Hackney, London, at present a sojourner in Natal for the good of his health physically, morally and financially, was bossing a gang of semi-prisoners engaged in much-needed road-making in a remote and lovely district of Natal.

Local and official terminology did not describe him as a warder, but as superintendent of a road party; nor were the twenty or thirty kafirs who toiled under his incompetent direction either convicts or slaves. They were merely natives 'called out' *nolens volens*, to give one month's service to the Colony of Natal under the law which provides that the native chief who occupies a small slice of the land taken from him by his white masters may continue to live on it if, among other tributes and services, he supplies a certain amount of labour for the public roads. The Natal Government is careful to explain that the servitude is not obligatory, for the native 'called out' has perfect freedom of contract. He has the alternative choice of working for three months with pick and shovel on the roads for tenpence per diem or for an equal or longer period in preparing road material in the local jail in return for mealie pap and free water. Many of them prefer the alternative after one experience of the free and open life of the road gang.

Gabriel Betts being possessed of that flippant turn of humour which manifests itself in a habit of describing things as they are rather than as what they appear to be, always spoke of himself as a convict warder, and of his 'party' as 'my convict gang.'

It is a matter of statistical record that he so described himself in the Census paper – a piece of pleasantry which resulted in a peremptory order to interview the chief of his department at Maritzburg. The story goes that, with the aid of a dictionary, he convinced his chief that the description, if not technically correct, was much more accurate and true to the facts than the official title bestowed upon sundry dignified members of other departments.

When an amused and amazed community asked why he had not been dismissed, Betts suggested as the primary reason the inability of the department to find a successor less competent than himself.

To the everlasting credit of a Government frequently accused of seriousness, Betts was permitted to retain the position he had won as the most flagrant flouter of official dignity and authority in the public service.

He was sitting at the paper and food-littered table in his tent, marking with a blue pencil the grammatical blunders in an official letter just received from his immediate chief, the District Road Inspector, when his native foreman came to the door and in deferential tones and an injudicious admixture of English, Dutch and Zulu, nearly succeeded in making Betts understand that a strange kafir had come to the camp seeking work.

The unprecedented and extraordinary nature of the information distracted Betts from the congenial and absorbing task of literary censorship.

'What's that, you dunderheaded progeny of a Pretoria policeman?' he thundered.

'Yes, baas; good boy, baas.'

Betts threw the half-emptied tin of marmalade at the foreman.

'Pick that up. Chercher! Be quick, that means in your infernal lingo.'

The foreman picked up the tin, placed it carefully on the official foolscap letter where it made a jammy mess even more prominent than the corrective marks of the blue pencil, and proceeded to wipe from his coat the exuded marmalade and lick his fingers, calmly repeating, 'Yes baas, good boy baas, wants work, baas. Look, baas!'

He seized Bulalie by the blanket and pulled him within sight of his master.

Betts swung his big body round the whisky case that served as chair, and looked hard at the tall and shapely young kafir, who, with nothing but blanket and skin moocha (loin cloth) presented a pleasing contrast to the grizzled foreman – a spare half-starved, greyish, undersized figure in what had once been a large double-breasted overcoat of the narrow-waisted Newmarket type.

Bulalie grinned, showing his magnificent teeth, brought his hand to the salute and pronounced the Zulu salutation to a superior – 'Inkoos!'

'Who is he, what does he want?'

The foreman renewed his assurance that Bulalie was a good boy with the altogether superfluous addition that he was 'dam raw'.

'He may be raw, but he's clean, and that's more than you infernal antitheses of Keating's are.'

'Yes, baas,' the foreman assented.

'Know about horses?'

Mr Betts expressed the sentence by his own idea of its Zulu equivalent, which made the phrase more like tangled barbed wire than it would look if written.

Bulalie laughed the rich musical laugh that betokened intense amusement at the effort.

Mr Betts looked hard and angrily at the boy for a space. Then he smiled a fat good-natured smile. 'Well, I like that. Don't mind laughing to my face at my Zulu eh? You've a sense of humour. Pity you can't read my baas's letter. Never mind, I'll keep you amused. What does he want? How much money?'

The foreman interpreted to Bulalie and stolidly gave back the unsophisticated reply, 'Five pounds.'

'Dear me, so cheap! Ask him if he doesn't mean fifty.'

Mr Betts spoke as seriously as the foreman looked.

'Yes, he says he meant fifty.'

'I thought he had made a mistake. Tell him I'll give him five shillings a month if he's good, and the finest taste of the finest sjambok in the district if he isn't.'

The foreman interpreted fully.

'He says he will take five shillings, baas.'

'Of course he will, if he can get it. Perhaps he may. Now, you, what's your blessed name – show him my horse, tell him what he has to do, and send that blackguard to me who has been pretending to look after her. I owe him three hidings. I'll square it with one and call it quits. Chercher, you black brute.'

The foreman cherchered.

Betts returned to the study and correction of his chief's letter of instruction. The work interested him as it always did. He had a cigar box full of these sub-edited documents. He called it his Literary Museum, and cherished and added to it with as much zest and collector's joy as his colleague at the other end of the district derived from the accumulation of labels from the cigarette packets on which he expended as much of his £12 per mensem as was left after the whisky account at the distant store, and, incidentally the bill for necessaries, had been settled. One has to live the lonely life of the veld to realize to the full what simple pleasures can and do contribute to intellectual happiness.

Betts had been on this section a month, and during that period had had four opportunities of practising the art of conversing with white men. The road Inspector had spent part of one day in criticising the work done by the gang, and trying to calculate the cubic contents of a serpentine bank of earth having a height of two feet, fifty yards of length, and a base of six feet, narrowing to nothing. After exhausting their united mathematical knowledge and all the whisky, save the bottle which Betts had concealed in the flour bag, Mr Inspector decided that the account could be made to balance if he put down the labour on the embankment to time spent in transport, blasting operations, and 'et ceteras.' He then assured Betts in the strictest confidence, as had been his monthly custom since he first saw him, that he, Betts, was on the list for the next inspectorship and rode off, returning after riding half a mile to borrow a sovereign and impress upon Betts the imperative necessity of not mentioning his impending elevation to the man on the other section.

The other white humans who temporarily broke the maddening monotony were two farmers of the district who came over, one to borrow a few boys for a day or two to facilitate the progress of the farm work, the other to beg the loan of the only wheelbarrow fit for use. The third was a peregrinating stonemason whom Betts found one aftrernoon peacefully sleeping off the remains of a debauch. He had undressed and got into Betts's bed, where he lay for eleven hours, silencing the owner's remonstrances by the plea that he had not had his clothes off for a month, a statement more than verified by the appearance of the sheets.

The fifth visitor was expected that day in the person of a young and newly arrived missionary passing through to his station under the shadow of the wall-like Drakensberg forty miles way. Betts was looking forward to the event with peculiar satisfaction, for he would have a guest on whom he could and would offload part of his stock of Colonial knowledge gained during nearly a whole year spent in the country.

There is no more ardent instructor than the Englishman who has been out sufficiently long to learn that Durban is not a suburb of Cape Town or that the native is neither a cannibal nor a Christy Minstrel. Mr Betts having been for two months a billiard marker in Johannesburg, whither he had gone under the impression that he might work up a connection as agent for a London firm who were pushing an invention for warming conservatories, and nine months in the wilds of Natal at his present occupation of 'swearing and chucking things at niggers,' regarded himself as an old stager, and gave his advice and counsel to the inexperienced, freely and copiously. As opportunity had not been great, his reserve store was almost intact, and he could afford to be liberal to prodigality. He had made a mental note of some of the subjects he had determined to offer to the young missionary; the only fear he had was that the shortness of the stay would prevent his being as useful as he sincerely wished to be.

He had suspended operations on the Inspector's letter, not so much for want of material as for room on the margin for his comments. There was a long day before him; the traveller could not reach the camp till near sundown, so Mr Betts lay down to sleep.

He was awakened from his initial doze by the shaking of the tent pole and the voice of the foreman, 'Baas, baas! brought boy to be sjamboked.'

Mr Betts started and was on his feet instantaneously. His mind was on the expected visitor. He went out into the blazing sunlight and saw the foreman holding a native by the collar of his shirt.

'What's up?' he demanded.

'Baas said bring boy for sjambok.'

Mr Betts's red fat face grew apopletic. He snatched up an empty pail and threw it at the foreman who fenced it adroitly. 'You Basuto pig, you'd like to see me sjambok that boy, wouldn't you?'

Mr Betts added a few mispronounced abusive epithets from his limited Zulu vocabulary and was looking round the tent for something more convenient as a missile than the pail, when the foreman walked off.

'Hamba! Hook it!' he remarked to the frightened native and threw himself on the bed, talking to himself after the fashion of men who lead the solitary life.

'They're all brutes, never happy unless they see someone being knocked about. I'll punch his ugly head off if he makes me lose my temper again. I hate that beggar. He shan't be foreman any longer. Lazy as they make 'em.'

And Mr Betts went to sleep.

An hour later he was awakened by the entry of the kafir who acted as tent orderly. The boy was moving very quietly to avoid disturbing his master. Betts watched him with satisfaction, then got off the bed, and taking the marmalade tin he had thrown at the foreman earlier in the day, gave it to the boy.

'Good boy, you Thingammy, go lick this.'

Thingammy grinned his thanks and departed to lick the tin.

'After all, they appreciate kindness,' Mr Betts soliloquized.

Half an hour later he yelled for Thingammy. He could rarely remember the names of his boys or pronounce them if he did, therefore he labelled them all 'Thingammy' and 'the other Thingammy.' Three Thingammys responded to the call, including 'the other.' He dismissed two by projecting the washbasin at them, and proceeded to abuse the other for laziness, greed and ingratitude in sucking marmalade when he ought to be clearing the tent, and fined him sixpence, not for dereliction of duty, but for failing to understand that the present of the marmalade was intended as an incentive to prompt and immediate application to his duties.

Betts was always prepared to forgive such shortcomings as did not interfere with his personal comfort, but the obstinate refusal of the kafirs to understand his orders expressed in redundant sentences of intermixed Zulu and English irritated him.

'My Zulu, I know, is a bit shaky,' he would say, 'but, hang it, I *can* speak English.'

The dispassionate rebuking and punishing of the orderly, combined with the pleasing prospect of having some one to talk to in the evening, had an emollient effect. He strolled over to the working party, who, seeing him approach, put on a spurt with pick and shovel.

'Good boys!' he shouted encouragingly.

'You shall knock off an hour earlier tonight,' and he blew the whistle as a signal for 'cease labour'. The boys looked at the sun and knew that they still owed their paternal government a full hour's toil, but they manifested no surprise.

'I'm glad the baas is drunk,' commented the head boy; 'he don't know the time when he is thus.'

So Betts's generous concession was not accounted to him for righteousness.

CHAPTER III

TOLD TO THE MISSIONARY

The Rev. David Hyslop, B.A., arrived at the camp just before darkness – a tallish, slender young man with fair hair and a pince-nez, short black jacket, clerical collar, smasher hat and light cord riding breeches obviously bought at a wayside store; for they were of the universal fit pattern.

The young missionary was, physically, of the type easily sketched. A friendly artist would, or at any rate could, without undue flattery, depict him as an ascetic, oval-faced, saint-suggestive person. A frolicsome caricaturist could represent him as an Irvingesque Verdant Green, yet preserve his facial expression. Actually, Mr Hyslop was something between the two extravagances, with a leaning towards the guileless type, thanks mainly to his large earnest eyes and a suspicion of that Oxford drawl affected by, and associated with fledgling curates.

The young man arrived leading a saddled pony at the rear of a small wagon drawn by four oxen and bearing his baggage. Equitation not having formed a part of his college curriculum, he had found it less trying to lead his pony than ride it.

It was, therefore, a very sore and worn out missionary who limped into the tent of the Road Superintendent and gratefully accepted the cordial invitation to 'chuck yourself on the bed while tea is got ready.'

Betts, as a thoroughbred cockney who had never crossed a horse till he arrived in Natal, could heartily and wholly sympathize with a victim of 'saddle sick,' and a discourse on the trials and tribulations of horse travel in South Africa provided a convenient ice-breaking preliminary to future conversation.

While the kafir orderly was preparing the evening meal, Mr Betts had been timidly eyeing the whisky bottle he had left in its accustomed place on the table. Presently he gathered courage and boldly announced that he had always found a nip the finest curative after a long day on the road, and was more pleased than surprised when Mr Hyslop politely declined.

'I think you're right,' he remarked. 'You can't well preach teetotalism to kafirs if you drink. I find the little I take a stumbling block. I can't logically thrash my niggers for doing what I do myself, but they feel the evil consequences when I'm in liquor. Then I act, I don't preach; it's the only time I use the sjambok on the brutes.'

Mr Hyslop, being a very young and seriously disposed man, did not smile; on the contrary, he looked very grave.

Mr Betts improved the occasion to show that whatever his faults, hypocrisy was not one of them. He helped himself to an extra large tot. He had a presentiment that he would need a stimulant to carry him through an evening with this very serious and by no means loquacious visitor.

They talked generalities through the meal. When it was over the missionary did something that gladdened the heart of his host. He produced pipe and tobacco.

Betts beamed approval; the ice was broken. Before the second pipefull was half smoked he was addressing the Reverend David Hyslop as 'old man.'

'You'll do,' he asserted patronisingly. 'A parson, whether he chins religion to niggers or white men, must be a white man himself. Understand?'

Mr Hyslop thought he did.

'The fault of parsons in this country,' he went on, 'is that they put on frills, and though they don't exactly call us miserable sinners they look as though they would like to. What we want is men. You have begun well, you smoke like a sensible man. I only hope the next time you're underneath my tent you'll go for the whisky bottle as soon as you've said "good morning."'

Mr Hyslop expressed a hope that that was not the custom of other wearers of the cloth, whereupon Mr Betts accepted the remark as a request to be regaled with a selection from the mostly untrue and always silly Colonial stories about clergymen who have not maintained the dignity of their calling.

Had Mr Hyslop been more a man of the world, he would have recognised a strange familiarity and venerable antiquity about these narrations, which have been fitted on and told of different ministers in every English Colony for generations. Not being qualified in this respect, he could only give expression to his horror and regret, and hope that the stories were much exaggerated, which pious hope was promptly dashed to the ground by Mr Betts giving the customary Colonial assurance that he could vouch for their truth, by personal knowledge as a man who 'could lie with the best, but wouldn't.'

Mr Hyslop in an unguarded moment said he was glad that the isolated character of his work would remove him beyond the ken of such thinkers and suggesters of evil.

'That's just where you make a mistake, old man,' Mr Betts went on, his eloquence and fluency prompted by noting the effect of his revelations upon his unsophisticated auditor. 'These yarns are spread by the kafirs. There isn't much that escapes them. Although you will be fifty miles away, I shall know within a week through my boys when you have broken your teetotal pledge.'

'But the idea is absurd, impossible,' the missionary protested.

'Don't think I should blame you, old man. I know what it is to live with no one to speak to but kafirs. It's an awful life you're going to, and I can excuse you chucking your good resolutions overboard. All I say is, stick to one brand and see that you get it. Don't trust to labels – they're faked.'

Mr Betts proceeded to enlarge on this subject. He was qualified.

The missionary sat silent. His pipe went out, but he puffed it mechanically. He was not listening to the talker; he was passing through the soul-depressing stage that comes to his kind as surely as the other disappointments and heart-travail. He was realising something of which he had been warned by old hands – the utter inability of the white man in South Africa to appreciate or even understand the spirit animating the missioner, and the refusal to credit him with sincerity.

The next remark of Betts synchronised with this line of thought.

'Don't rely on the storekeepers in the district you are going to to help you. They don't love your class, and would rather sell you a bad brand than a good, any day.'

Mr Hyslop mentioned one or two names of European residents in the district and cautiously sought an expression of opinion as to the treatment likely to be received from them.

'As long as you don't cut their trade with the kafirs they won't hurt you, but it stands to reason as soon as you start trading they'll unite to down you.'

'Start trading? Missionaries are not traders,' Mr Hyslop exclaimed, aghast.

Mr Betts smiled knowingly. 'No, I know they don't take out licences for trade; that's what the storekeepers object to. If you'll be advised by me you'll make friends with them by giving them the option of buying anything sent out to you by the old women at home for the kafirs. Blankets is a good line, but tell your people the kafirs prefer them coloured – the more gaudy the better. You can get five shillings each from the storekeepers.'

The young man laid down his pipe and looked earnestly at his host.

'Mr Betts,' he said, 'I know I am young and very inexperienced, and probably I hold many views regarding work among the natives that I shall have to qualify. But surely you are joking at my expense when you tell me people say these things about missionaries?'

'People say? It isn't what people say, it's true. How do you think you are going to live up country on your pay? I know it's poor enough, like all pay in this infernal Colony. Look at mine – twelve pounds a month and whisky eight bob a bottle! I'm as much a Christian as you are – at least I hope so – but I wouldn't save black souls on the terms you people contract at unless I could make a bit extra on my own account.'

The missionary slowly filled his pipe. He abandoned the contest. It was hopeless to persuade this – Christian, that there was such a thing as self-sacrifice and earnestness of purpose regardless of material reward. But he recalled that he had heard Betts was a comparative newcomer in the land; he could not represent the feelings of the older residents. He earnestly prayed not.

He adroitly changed the subject to topography and climate. These proved matters of expert familiarity with Betts, at least that is what the missionary inferred, particularly climate. It was perfect, Betts said, especially in the region of Mr Hyslop's station, where the air was so exhilarating that it put life into a man within an hour of rising in the morning and made him capable of enjoying and enduring fifteen or sixteen hours' sleep a day.

'The one thing that makes me hang on to this awful job,' he confided, 'is the hope that I may be transferred to that section.'

He gave the missionary hints, which, if acted upon, would help towards the consummation of that great desire.

'As soon as you can, begin grousing about the bad roads. That will bring the farmers and storekeepers on your side. You missionaries are too fond of making the best of your grievances. I suppose you think it makes you look more of a hero if you have to rough it. You take my advice and grouse and grumble at the Government for neglecting the district. They won't pay any attention to you at first, because they are down on missionaries on principle; but if you show them that you are no Christian, but a snarly, bad-tempered beast that isn't going to be put off, they will respect you, and you'll get what you want. At heart they hate you, but all our Members of Parliament and the big bosses at the heads of the departments are great chapel-goers, and if you threaten to expose them as hypocrites and write to your head office at Exeter Hall about them, they'll buck up. They're afraid of Exeter Hall. You get the farmers and storekeepers with you and you'll win the rubber. Don't forget, Exeter Hall is your trump suit.'

Mr Hyslop mildly explained that Exeter Hall had nothing to do with him or his mission; that it was merely a place where many religious and philanthropic meetings were held.

Mr Betts was surprised. 'Anyhow, everybody out here thinks it's the London office of the Directors of Missionary Companies, and I wouldn't upset that notion if I were you; besides, I think you're wrong.'

For half an hour the missionary had to listen to a flow of slanders and accusations against Natal officialdom, which apparently consisted absolutely and entirely of descendants of all the worst characters of Dickens. The Pecksniff and Stiggins family seem to have been to Natal what the survivors of the flood were to the remainder of the earth.

It was futile for the young missionary to urge Lot's appeal for the existence of one just man in this modern Sodom and Gomorrah. Mr Betts listened impatiently to the plea, filled his glass, after insinuatingly suggesting that there was another bottle if Mr Hyslop liked to change his mind, then settled the matter under discussion once and for all.

'Look here, old man,' he said impressively, 'I'm a public servant myself. *Don't I know 'em*?'

Not being able to assert or deny, Mr Hyslop contented himself with an expression of regret that persons of such character should have the control of the country.

'It is the strongest argument that could be adduced in favour of work such as mine,' he said, making his first score in the discussion. 'I shall feel now a stronger incentive to place a higher ideal before the native, and strive hard in the work of Christian civilisation.'

Mr Betts smiled jubilantly. 'Hold on, old man, that's just where you're wrong again. Don't you see that the kafir's idea of being civilised is to become a Natalian and particularly a native policeman? Why is the native constabulary so popular with them? Answer me that. No, sir, your missionary civilisation means the production of a race of nigger Pecksniffs and Jeremy Diddlers. Haven't I had the brutes come to me and claim to be made herd boys and put to soft jobs because they love Jesus? Didn't I catch one blackguard here making a collection for a Missionary joss-house and spending the money on marmalade?'

The missionary parried the blow by continuing to urge that the presence of such bad white exemplars was a stronger reason for a better guiding influence. The apparent readiness of the native to work in the public service was a good omen for the success of his project for instructing him in useful trades.

'There you go again! Wrong, hopelessly wrong! Do you mean to say you consider yourself justified in teaching a raw kafir how he can compete against a white man? Is it fair when we have skilled workmen walking the streets to bring in skilled kafirs who can live on two shillings a day against the white man's ten?'

Mr Hyslop confessed that he had not looked at that aspect of the case. He did not think it would be quite right, nor was it his intention to fit the natives to compete with the white. He rather thought it was intended to teach them to do simple mechanical work – such as building their own houses, making their own furniture, and so on.

Betts laughed merrily and rudely.

'I suppose you'd include organ and piano building, and teaching the women how to make ball dresses? They're great on music and dancing, you know, and no civilised home is complete without a piano.'

'But they are luxuries,' Mr Hyslop answered in perfect seriousness.

'Look here, old man,' Mr Betts went on in a tone implying he was issuing his ultimatum, 'you take it from me, the kafir is quite satisfied to go on as he is. You couldn't build a house more suitable than the hut he puts up in a generation. Why the deuce do you Englishmen stick to the notion that every creature on God's earth must be unhappy unless he lives and talks and eats and dresses like an Englishman? That's what all your missionary nonsense comes to – make Englishmen of 'em, whether they live in the tropics or at the North Pole. You want a new sign for Christianity; the cross isn't comprehensive enough; it only suits Catholics and High Churchmen. I'll give you an idea and you might patent it in your own name as the universal trade mark of every branch of the religious business. It's a collection box and a pair of trousers. Man alive! before you have been on your station a week you'll be wanting to wear a moocha, and regret that Christians don't stick to the dress of Adam and Eve.'

The young man answered only with a feeble smile. This outpouring of iconoclasm following on a wearying journey depressed and saddened him. It was his first experience of sitting in the seat of the scornful. Since the day some four years ago when he left a soul-stirring missionary meeting aflame and radiant in the joy of a firm belief that he had been called to the mission field, he had lived in an atmosphere of applauding and sympathetic encouragement. He had been nourished on missionary reports and literature, and viewed the scene of his chosen labour through the amber mist of a romance no whit less mirage-like than the stories of weird adventure which have lured many a youth to Afric's golden strand.

By instinct and education young Hyslop was designed for the dreamy leisured ease of a University professorship – some soft, silent retreat, where the noise and turmoil, the greed and grossness of the strenuous life would be known to him only through the faint echo conveyed in a drowsily read paper by some ponderously prosy contributor to the somnolency of an annual conference. That there should exist in actual flesh such men as Gabriel Betts came as a shock; that he should be challenged to justify the need and utility of missions to the heathen against the arguments of a Christian Englishman staggered him. Had Betts called in question the right and duty of the clergy to denounce sin he would have felt no greater astonishment. True, he had received glimmering impressions in his student days that there were godless, selfish persons who took no interest in, and even passively resisted, the great and glorious work of regenerating the heathen; but he knew that, according to the missionary reports, these 'obstacles' invariably came to the missionary sooner or later, tearful and penitent, to testify to the change wrought in the native and themselves and to contribute prodigally to the fund for erecting church or mission house. He glanced furtively at Betts, but somehow could not picture him coming forward with tears in his eyes and gold in his hand to make atonement for the philistinism of that evening's discourse. And yet greater miracles were on record. The thought cheered him. He shook off his external signs of depression and asked for a fill from his host's tobacco pouch, offering his own in exchange in accordance with Colonial etiquette.

Betts noticed this and appreciated it. 'You're getting on,' he said encouragingly. 'But I wish it was your glass you passed to be filled. Whisky is the finest physic for fever in this country, and you're too good to die early. You'll be useful yet.'

The missionary blushed, not so much at the compliment as with the pleasure excited by its hopeful, cheering presage. The cumbersome appreciation sent a thrill of joy through him, for it expressed his own ardent desire, and atoned for much that had been uttered.

In the after time he frequently recalled the scene as pictured at that happy moment. The big, burly red-faced cleanshaven man in unbuttoned khaki jacket and riding breeches, squatting uncomfortably and low on an up-ended box, a big bowled pipe sticking upward from his mouth and the whisky bottle nursed upon his knee. The little green baize covered table crowded with papers, cheap novels and smoker's paraphernalia; the lamp-lighted interior of the small marquee tent, stuffy and hazy with tobacco smoke, and, beyond, through the wide open flap door the big bright disc of the moon low on the horizon, bisected through its centre by a thick black line of cloud, straight and even as if drawn across it with a brush.

The bisected moon became from that moment his emblem of hope.

But the missionary was to learn yet another lesson that evening.

The native personal attendant whom he had brought with him appeared at the tent door, and complained that he was being molested and insulted by 'the kafirs.' He was a Pondo, an educated mission boy, who had been assigned as interpreter and general assistant by the head of the missionary society's branch in Cape Colony where Mr Hyslop had gone through his brief probation.

Mr Betts looked up at the interrupter.

'My God, a makolwa! (Christianised native). I forgot you carried that sort of cattle. Of course my boys are down on him. Take off those clothes and get into a moocha. Chercher! Voetsak!'

This last was addressed to the native.

The missionary looked distressed.

'What does it mean?' he asked. 'He's quite a superior, educated young man. Why do your boys interfere with him?'

'Send him to the wagon and I'll tell you,' said Betts curtly.

The boy was sent off with instructions to come again when called.

'Look here, old man,' Betts began, 'I don't know where you fellows get your instructions and ideas from, but whoever advised you to bring that mongrel, dressed in white men's clothes, into a native district ought to be kicked. I know what's at the back of their brains, if they've got any. The idiots think that he will serve as a sort of sample of the goods you missionaries turn out, and I dare say he is. But what is he? Neither fish, flesh, nor good red herring. You see what my boys think of him. They won't stand him at any price. He's not one of them, and he thinks he's their superior. What's the result? The poor devil is a pariah, too good for his own class, not good enough for ours. What's going to be his end? Five years and twenty-five lashes for forging liquor passes at a shilling a time for kafirs. The jails are full of 'em. It's a wicked, selfish bit of ignorance – making a poor devil a martyr for life just to enable you to show him off as "another convert." Convert to what? A convert to all the vices of the whites and none of their virtues. I'll bet you my boys will keep a sharp eye on their belongings while he is in the camp, and for a month after you're gone every blessed thing that is missed will be put down to that makolwa. That's what the native thinks of Christianised kafirs. I'll bet you the row started through liquor. The boys always expect that a makolwa has either got some on him or can get it, and if he doesn't produce it there's trouble.'

'But there can be no progress without its martyrs,' the missionary observed.

'Exactly, I'm one myself. I'm being kept back in the public service because I'm always fighting that ignoramus of an inspector who has been put over a man like me because he has relations who have the ear of the big-wigs and I haven't. What I want to know is what right have you missionaries to take a boy from his own people when he's too young to understand anything, and make him an outcast against his knowledge and consent? Put the boot on the other foot and suppose you had been collared by Mormons or Turks when you were a kid and brought up in their religion. Would you be satisfied if they told you you were a blessed martyr to their cause? I dare say they would think themselves quite as much justified as you do.'

Mr Hyslop did not reply for a space. This was a type of opposition for which he was not prepared. He could understand people imputing mercenary and unworthy motives, but not this defiant challenging of the foundation of missionary policy. The attack on his boy James had pained him much. He had felt an especial pride and gratification in being able to show a living example of the polishing effects of Christian education, and now he heard that those very qualities told against the boy. He was certain if Betts knew how bright and clever the lad was he would alter his opinion.

He proceeded to defend his assistant, and catalogued his accomplishments for the benefit of his host.

Betts listened impatiently. 'I suppose he knows astronomy?' he asked with malicious sarcasm.

'Well, hardly so much as that, but he is quite clever at mathematics, and was for a time assistant to the surveyor who does the mission work. He is very fond of it, and can work almost any simple problem in land measurement,' Mr Hyslop answered, with genuine pride.

Mr Betts actually paused in the operation of pouring out 'just another little one,' and put the bottle down.

'Well I'm blest! He can do what I can't, eh? I, who am a superintendent of a road party under a fool who can't reckon the cubic contents of a bank of earth if it's an inch out of the straight. Now look here, as man to man, do you think it's honest and proper for you missionaries to teach an infernal nigger who lives on mealie pap how he can take the bread out of my mouth? I suppose if you had your way you would give me the sack and put him in my place? Yes or no, wouldn't you?'

Mr Betts was almost fierce. The application had come home very forcibly to him, particularly when he recalled the recent futile efforts of his chief and himself to perform a task that this nigger could easily accomplish. Mr Hyslop temporised.

'Of course we should not do that, but there is no limit to the acquisition of knowledge when one has a desire for it,' he said.

'Look here, old man, I'm full up. Don't let us talk any more. When I'm told that a nigger can beat me at my own job I'm done. I wish you'd change your mind and have a whisky. It's got to come, you know.'

Mr Hyslop was rather pleased at the proposed suspension of hostilities. He felt that he might have made a more effective defence of his position if he had put forward the spiritual side; but a materialist like Betts was hardly likely to be sympathetic with the aspirations of one who sincerely believed that his concern was less with the body than the soul of the despised heathen. He permitted his host to chuckle over his victory and encouraged him to dogmatise on other phases of South African experience.

The superintendent talked volubly but less fluently for an hour longer, growing more friendly and emotional as the whisky bottle grew lighter, and ended by forgetting that he had offered to give up his own bed to his guest and going off to sleep without making other arrangements.

The missionary slept in his wagon.

Betts was profuse in his apologies next morning, and by way of atonement acted as escort to his guest for a few miles.

On coming near what appeared to be a collection of kafir huts, of a more substantial type than those of a kraal, the missionary was surprised to see a white man peering at them from a door. A number of kafir children of that yellowish tint known to Colonials as 'snuff and butter,' were scattered about, and stared at the by-passers. The white man nodded and disappeared inside the hut.

'There's one of your Christian martyrs,' Betts remarked. 'He could tell you something about civilising savages.'

There was contempt and disgust in the tone. The missionary looked interrogatively at his companion.

'He was a decent white man ten years ago. Came to this country with ideas like yours, and was fool enough to act on them. He educated a kafir girl and married her. That's the result.'

Betts indicated the huts.

'Was it not – successful?'

'Oh yes, completely, she has converted him. He's a white kafir now, with plenty of time on his hands for educating his nigger family. Nobody except kafirs associate with him. Did you notice he hadn't the cheek to nod to me as he did to you?'

'But, surely, you don't boycott him?'

'My business is to boss kafirs, not to treat 'em as equals,' Betts answered decisively.

'But he is a fellow-Christian, a white man.'

'So are a good many low-minded brutes that I don't want to know.'

'Very sad' was the missionary's final comment. He was learning lessons hard to assimilate.

He was destined to receive one more shock before he parted with his mentor. Betts being uncertain of the route, hailed a party of natives travelling ahead, and failing to comprehend their answers to his questions, suggested that the missionary's boy James should act as interpreter.

The effect was surprising. The natives stared curiously at the boy, scanning his elaborate outfit of second-hand European clothes critically, and passed on laughing and chanting in mocking refrain the question put.

'I thought as much,' said Betts. 'Your interpreter is a Cape Colony boy. What can he know about the Zulu language? Not so much as I do. Listen to those brutes; they're mimicking his Zulu. I'll teach them to laugh.'

He galloped after the party, and catching up with a man, gave him three or four ferocious cuts with his sjambok across the head and shoulders. Betts did not intend to strike the kafir across the head, but the stupid creature turned to face his assailant just as the sjambok was descending, instead of running away, and received the blow across the eyes.

Betts took a cordial farewell of the missionary after impressing upon him the necessity of losing no time in making himself objectionable to the Government, and returned to camp.

When he was over the ridge and out of sight, the four natives who had fled from his corrective sjambok came to the wagon, leading the man who had received the thrashing. They asked for muti (medicine). The missionary gave an exclamation of horror and indignation. One eye of the kafir had been absolutely pulped and it required little surgical knowledge to show him that its use had gone for ever and that the wretched victim was suffering excruciating agony.

He applied such remedies as his slight medical training suggested and his medicine chest provided, and gave the kafir a lift in his wagon.

He had an interesting ethical problem to occupy the remainder of the journey. He had been the witness of a wanton and serious act of cruelty perpetrated upon an innocent native by a white man. Had the outrage been committed in England he knew that his duty would have been to lay an information, and appear as principal witness for the prosecution.

Was it not equally his duty to report the matter to the District Magistrate, and thus begin his career as a practical friend and protector of the native, coincidently with his work as a missionary?

But this would mean setting the white residents in opposition against him. Dare he risk that? Would it be conducive to the future welfare of his mission work?

The matter needed careful thought and guidance.

A week later Gabriel Betts received a letter from Mr Hyslop, informing him that the native had completely lost the sight of one eye, and that the other was seriously affected. He suggested that some monetary compensation should be made, as the native must for a long time be dependant upon his relations.

Mr Betts took up the sjambok that had caused the mischef – a tapering rod of rhinoceros hide, tough and flexible as the gutta percha it resembled. About a foot from the end it was broken and hung at an angle like a flail.

'That's the cause of it,' he soliloquised, viciously slashing the limp end. 'I must get another. I can't cut straight with a wobbly thing like this, but I reckon that kafir won't cheek a white man again in a hurry. Compensate him, eh? Encourage him to be impudent to his white masters! Certainly, Mr Hyslop. You are beginning well!'

CHAPTER IV

BULALIE UNDERTAKES A TRUST

Bulalie was very happy. Life with the road party gang was novel and full of pleasantnesses. His duties were light and easy, for he understood horses. The baas had two, a bay mare and a black gelding that had caused much trouble to the groom whom Bulalie had displaced, refusing to allow himself to be caught for saddling, and bringing much abuse and camp furniture at the head of the boy, for the baas never called for his horse until he was ready to mount, and the delay made him very angry. But Bulalie had the horse gift. He could almost talk their language, and after the gelding had once smelt him, he always let Bulalie do as he wished. So it came that the baas, whom the boys called 'Mafuta' because he was fat, said Bulalie was the best horse boy he ever had, and very rarely threw things at him, except when Bulalie laughed loudly at the funny words his baas used when he tried to talk Zulu in his anger. After a time Bulalie ceased to laugh because the blunders were so many and frequent.

But the great thing that caused most content to Bulalie was that he had made a friend of a Zulu named Bacheta, whom the baas always called 'Damthief' because he could not pronounce his proper name.

Bacheta's father had married a girl from Bulalie's own kraal, so that they were kinsmen, though they had never before met. He was about thirty years of age as the white men reckon, which meant that he was an umfaan of ten years when Bulalie was born; but he was a very, very old man in knowledge of the land and of the white man. He had been everywhere and done everything that a native could do, and words of wisdom came out every time he opened his mouth, so that Bulalie listened with as great care and pleasure as he had to the music of the concertina of Sebaas.

Before a week had gone Bulalie had learned more things than he had thought were in the world, for Bacheta liked much to talk and was clever in making plans to avoid working with pick and shovel, so that he might stay in camp and pretend to help the cook or the tent boy, but really to talk with Bulalie. He had ways by which he made the foreman so much afraid of him that he dared not complain to the baas when Bacheta refused to go out of camp. He knew how to be sick and lame when he would, so as to deceive even the white doctor who sometimes came to the camp, and was altogether a 'slim' kafir.

'Bulalie,' he would say when they sat together eating something which Bacheta had stolen from the tent of the baas, 'it is not wise to let the white baas or the inkozikas (mistress) know that you can do clever things, for then they will make you work the harder. I have been in the mines in Kimberley and Johannesburg, and know how to put in dynamite, and drill holes, but when Mafuta asked me if I knew I said, "What do you mean, baas? I am fresh from the kraal." You were wise to say you can take care of horses, because the work here is not great, and Mafuta being not a Colonial, does not know whether you understand them or not, but it is not always so.'

One day he took Bulalie a long way into the veld and dug out from an ant bear hole a bag in which were many wonderful things that Bacheta had collected in the many places he had been. He kept them hidden lest they might be stolen if he showed them in the camp.

There was one thing that was more wonderful than the white men's clothes, and the gold watch and the scissors, of which Bacheta had many, being fond of stealing them. Before he showed it to Bulalie he made him promise to kill the snake that held the spirit of his father's kraal if ever he spoke of it to anyone. Bulalie was fearful at making so awful a promise, but he was very curious to know what the wonderful thing was.

Bacheta took from his moocha a thick wooden peg that was a pin holding the moocha round his loins. With one of the scissors he scraped from a hole in the thick end of the peg the hard clay that had been burned into it, and brought out a bit of glass as big as the end of his little finger.

'This is a klippie, from Vaal River,' he said, 'what the white men call diamond, and it is worth more cattle than there is in the location.'

Bulalie looked at it and marvelled that so small a thing should be worth so much. He had heard of klippies, and had known natives who had been flogged with the cat and kept many years in jail for having them, but he had never before seen one.

'But why do you keep it if it is worth so many cattle?' he asked.

'Because I am waiting till I see my old baas from Vaal River, for whom I keep the klippie. He has gone across the blue water, but some day he will come back and will take it and give me so much money that I can buy more cattle than my chief.'

Then he told Bulalie why he had shown him the klippie.

'The police in Maritzburg are seeking me for sheep stealing. That is why I work with this road party instead of in the towns. They will find me soon, and before they take me I want you to take care of the klippie till I come back. You must speak no word to anyone, and never let your hands or your eyes stay on the peg or others will see that it is a strange thing and want to know what it is.'

Then a fearful thought came to Bulalie.

'Suppose the police should take me when I have your klippie?'

'You have committed no crime yet,' said Bacheta. 'They will not search you as they would me. You must always keep your moocha so dirty that the white men will not wish to touch it.'

Then Bacheta put the klippie back into the peg and packed in the clay tight and hard and they went back to camp.

That night Bulalie lay awake long, watching the stars through the rents in the tent and asking them whether he should tell Bacheta of what happened in his father's kraal.

For long the stars made no speech that was clear sounding till he looked at the very bright star in the East that showed where Maritzburg lay. Then it spoke plainly in the words of Bacheta – 'Never tell all that you know,' and Bulalie went to sleep.

A few days afterwards the thing that Bacheta feared came to pass.

Bulalie was grinding mealies for the horses when he heard the jingle that police horses make, and looking up, his heart turned to water for, coming over the veld were two police troopers, and standing at the door of his tent was the baas with nothing on but his shirt, holding a whisky bottle, pointing to it, and calling to the troopers, who laughed and rode up fast.

When Bulalie heard his own name called loudly by the baas he was very fearful, and for a little while thought that he would run away into the veld. But as quickly came the thought that he was wanted only to offsaddle and feed the troopers' horses.

So he went up quickly and bravely, taking care not to look at the troopers straight in the face. He led away their horses, and when he saw the troopers were in the tent, he ran quickly to find Bacheta and told him that the police had come.

Bacheta was very brave. He took the peg from his moocha and gave it to Bulalie, saying, 'Remember all I have told you. If I do not come back, all the things in the bag in the ant bear hole are yours. You know where to find me in two years.'

They had made a plan so that each should know where to find the other if trouble came and they were parted.

In half an hour the baas came out of the tent and blew his whistle as a sign for all the road party to come into camp. They came up slowly, for there were others beside Bacheta who were waiting for the police. They stood in a long line in front of the tent while the baas called out each name from his book. The boy so called stepped out that the police might look closely at him.

When it was the turn of Bacheta he walked out boldly, looking as if he marvelled what it should be for.

But quickly the oldest trooper took the handcuffs from his belt and Bulalie knew that Bacheta had been found.

They put another pair of handcuffs round a bar of the plough to make Bacheta safe till they departed.

Bulalie would have talked with him to comfort him, but Bacheta bade him go away.

'If they see that you are my brother they will ask questions about you, and perhaps take you also. Go away; you do not know me,' he said, and Bulalie went away very sorrowfully, for the camp would not be so pleasant now that his best friend was gone. But he thought of the klippie and the wonderful things in the bag, and when an hour later he saw the troopers ride off, and Bacheta running beside them with his handcuffed wrists tied by a leathern rein to the saddle, he hoped that he might not return, for then the bag would be his.

That night Bulalie slept with the klippie peg in his hand, and dreamed of cattle in such plenty that they made the veld red wherever he looked; and for many nights cattle filled his dreams till at last they went away, and he even ceased to think of the klippie.

When two moons had been born and died, and Bulalie had earned ten shillings and one sixpence that a white man who called at the camp gave him, there came news from Maritzburg which showed how good a prophet Bacheta was, and how well he knew the ways of the white men. He had been sent to prison for two years and was to receive twenty-five lashes, which was the thing that Bacheta had feared most, though he knew they must fall, for sheep stealing is the greatest of all wrongs that a native can do to a white man, and Bacheta was a great lover of sheep meat.

Several times the police came to the camp seeking boys who were wanted for stealing sheep long ago, and Bulalie began to lose fear at the sight of them and to feel glad that he had only killed his father instead of a sheep, for he knew that there would be but little fuss made when it was found that a bad and troublesome old kafir, such as Tambuza was, had died. The Magistrate would perhaps go himself to the kraal to ask questions, if it was a good and easy road from the magistracy, but more likely he would send the district surgeon with two young policemen who would ask many questions and write much in their books, and perhaps take away some of the young men of the kraal on suspicion, and keep them at the police jail for many days till there was no more work for them to do in the jailers' garden. But the young men of Bulalie's kraal were not so foolish as many, and knew that the jailer must not make them work until he had an order from the Magistrate. So they would refuse, and if they made a loud outcry and had money to pay a law agent to speak for them, they would escape the work, but only to be locked up all day in the dark cold cells, as had happened twice to Bulalie. Therefore it came that even those prisoners who knew that it was illegal to make them work before they had been convicted, preferred to do what they were told rather than be shut in the cell till they were blinded by the sunlight when they saw it again.

*   *   *   *   *

Bulalie had rightly predicated the position.

It was reported to the Magistrate forty miles away that his veritable *bête noire*, the sheep-stealing, faction-fight-provoking, drunken old representative of a once mighty line of warriors had been found in his hut dead.

He sent the Chief Clerk with the district surgeon and the usual escort of two police troopers to investigate.

The doctor being young was very much disposed to be fussy. He made a most elaborate examination of the injuries on the head of the dead chief, and decided that they had been caused by the heavy cast-iron cooking pot. The Chief Clerk having had a longer experience of the ways of his department, pointed out to the doctor that he would earn very little more in the shape of fees by making a fuss; that there was every prospect of a thunderstorm which would mean the flooding of the river and detaining them in a filthy foodless hut all night and probably all next day. It was so evident that the old man had met his death in a drunken row with his nephew Sebaas that it was waste of time to linger building up medical and detective theories that would bring neither profit nor glory, as no one would hear about them outside official circles.

Owing to the pig-headed obstinacy of the young doctor, who insisted on completing his investigation in accordance with his immatured notions of 'professional duty,' the Chief Clerk's warning was justified. The rainstorm burst while he was fiddling and messing about the dead body, and the flooding of the two rivers that lay between the kraal and the police camp rendered the return journey impossible for many hours.

The party took possession of the dead man's hut, putting the body outside. The youngsters of the kraal had to work hard to keep the pigs, dogs, and fowls from rendering it more unrecognisable than the scorching of the fire had made it.

The three widows made night hideous by their wailing and weeping in the adjacent hut, in defiance of the troopers' threats to cut pieces out of them with their sjamboks unless they desisted, and the youngest wife proved her ignorance and contempt of the rules and regulations of officialdom by molesting the body and adjusting the scattered limbs and clothing. This necessitated the troopers turning out in the darkness and rain to drag the stupid creature away, and, altogether, the young doctor's officiousness was well and thoroughly punished by as wretched a night as he had ever passed. Unfortunately, as is often the case, his blundering wrongheadedness entailed suffering upon the innocent, for the Chief Clerk and the troopers could not sleep.

The river went down by noon next day, and the troopers were enabled to proceed to the distant kraal where Sebaas was said to be engaged in arranging for his marriage.

That night he was safely lodged in the police jail on a charge of having murdered Tambuza.

When the Resident Magistrate heard from the Chief Clerk what had happened he was very indignant. 'Why the devil couldn't the young fool report death from natural causes? Here have I been cracked up by the press for the freedom from crime in my district, and this Johnny-come-lately must spoil it all by forcing a murder case on us. Damn him!'

'You are quite right sir,' said the Chief Clerk. 'But a few more nights like last will damp his official zeal.'

CHAPTER V

THE LIONS IN THE PATH

The Rev. David Hyslop sat on the step of the two-roomed mud-built structure that formed the mission house at Blue Krantz, and gazed meditatively at the sun-bathed landscape.

The horizon was broken by a square, wall-like mountain that, through the thin transparent air, seemed at most six or seven miles distant; but the gazer knew that nearly forty miles of plain and forest lay between.

'It is a land of deceptive distances,' he soliloquised. 'Like that mountain, my ideals seemed so near until I learned the trickery of the African atmosphere; now I begin to wonder whether they are not mirages.'

The young missionary had been six months at the station and was beginning to experience the spirit-breaking that is the invariable concomitant of the solitary life of the veld. It comes to the lonely digger and prospector, even when the reward that has lured them gleams actual and substantial in the ore in sight; how much more intensely must it grip the man who has toiled hard, to lay bare only barren rock?

The coming of the missionary was in a cloud of gloom and disappointment. Instead of finding at the station the fellow-worker whom he had come to succeed, he was appalled by the sight of a closed and deserted cottage and an envelope addressed to himself nailed to the door.

The missive told how the writer had waited for relief till signs of a sharp recurrence of the malady that was killing him impelled a hasty journey towards the coast.

'I can no longer conceal from my native servant,' he wrote, 'that I am spitting blood. This means that he will desert me, for fear that I should die, and he be arrested on suspicion.'

This passage had puzzled Mr Hyslop. He could not harmonise it with the pretty stories he had read and believed of native fidelity. He did not know that the ever-present dread of the solitary white dweller in the wilderness is an accident or severe and sudden illness. It is the signal for prompt desertion by his native servant. Tradition, that is, unfortunately supported by fact, has taught the native that his presence at the death of a white man may mean a long detention in the nearest jail while officialdom deliberately satisfies itself that he is in no way responsible. The rough crosses and heaps of stones that mark the resting place of many a victim of the solitary life might truthfully be inscribed, 'Died through desertion.'

Mr Alliston had averted this fate by expending his expiring energy in an attempt to reach the nearest town, but had collapsed and died in the tent of a gold prospector, who made a grave with his own hands, and was able to report with Christian fervour to Mr Hyslop – 'I did everything for him, down to stamping in the ground, and no black hands touched him from first to last.'

It was the crowning reward of fiteen years labour among the natives that none took part in the final scene.

The old prospector was satisfied that his act of toilsome self-denial atoned for many sins of omission, and gave him a claim to the assistance of the new man when he needed, as he frequently did, a temporary augmentation of his scanty food and cash reserve.

Old Boggis had been prospecting in the Colony for twenty years, and had never justified a prediction. He existed on hope and strict economy, tempered with outbursts of extravagance which took the form of a sudden raid on a remote farm or police camp, and borrowing a sovereign to purchase a new truss. That truss was a more productive gold reef than any he had struck with his pick. But Boggis was always cheerful, therefore a welcome guest at farm and camp, for the liver of the solitary life never shirks paying for pleasant company.

Already Mr Hyslop had begun to look forward to the week-end visits of the only white man within twenty miles of his station, and tolerated his coarseness and flippancy because of its humanity. Besides, the old man knew the native and liked him – with certain reservations.

The months that had dragged slowly since Mr Hyslop took possession of the station had produced a harvest of disillusionments. Everything was farther off than it had appeared at first sight. The languid inertness of his predecessor, dying of lung trouble, had resulted in the harvest of the mission existing only in the half-hearted hopes that were so frequently expressed in the written memoranda left for the guidance of the successor. The young man had studied the tabulated list of 'converts, actual and prospective' compiled by the dead and disappointed toiler, and the survey saddened and surprised him. Mr Alliston had been an industrious reporter; writing was the only form of physical effort of which he was capable towards the end, and the laboured, nervous strokes showed that even the pen was at times an unwieldy tool.

The list lay among a heap of other papers on the table at his elbow. The missionary took it up and scanned it again. It was a painfully human document viewed in the light of an inventory and record of five years' labour.

To the name of each member of the mission 'congregation' Mr Alliston had appended critical comments, and thus ran the inglorious roll:–

Magena.   Dubious; very hypocritical. Accept any assertion of change of nature with caution.

Mozulikase.   A confirmed cadger. Always shamming serious illness and wanting mealies or tobacco. Have hopes of him.

Titzani.   Owes a balance of £3 17s. on £5 lent him to pay a fine. A good shepherd and can get work but will not. Treat him firmly.

Kaluda.   Son of above. Has been a ricksha boy in Durban. Very intelligent and cute. Introduced various forms of gambling into his kraal. Has saved money but denies it. Owes still the £3 lent to him to go to Maritzburg to find work. Speaks a little English and understands it better. Hope to make him useful.

Lafuta.   Very intelligent. Is second in right to chieftainship, therefore should be cultivated. Suspect him of occasionally introducing liquor into the kraals. Has picked up many white vices.

The list catalogued twenty-three names, the comments growing less favourable, the minus qualities more numerous as it grew.

'If these be the pick of the basket what must the lower layers be like?' Mr Hyslop asked himself.

He had not long to wait for opportunity for sampling. Within a week he had listened to three or four demands for money alleged to be due to members of the flock for various services to the dead missionary and several pathetic appeals to be excused payment of rent, past and prospective, for land belonging to the mission.

Blue Krantz had an endowment of 15 000 acres of virgin land from the Government, which has always been liberal in this kind of support to missions irrespective of sect. Its generosity cost nothing to the Colony, for land was plentiful. Plots were let by the missionary to 'converts actual and prospective' at a pound per annum, which was exactly a sovereign a year more than the native would have had to pay had he chosen to erect his hut with his unregenerate brethren in the location. But occupation of mission land carried certain exemptions from the duties of residence in the native location which compensated for the irksomeness of owing rent to the missionary.

The income derivable to the mission from this source should have been about £50 per annum. Mr Alliston had twice brought it within £20 of this amount. The balance he offered to accept in the form of labour, but after witnessing three women thrashed by their conscientious lords for refusing to toil in the missionary's garden, he had paid cash for services rendered, and good-naturedly awaited the convenience of the defaulting tenants.

After several vain efforts to extract payment, his successor agreed to accept four attendances at service a month as equivalent to three months' rent. Mr Boggis generously volunteered to shepherd the defaulters; but as he stipulated for freedom to use his sjambok if argument failed, the missionary felt compelled to decline the kindly offer of lay assistance. He was rewarded by having three out of seven defaulters at his opening service, and gladly yielded to their demand for a handful of sugar as a 'bonsella' for having carried out an instalment of their compact.

The following Sunday over thirty natives turned up at the service, most of them bringing tin pots and calabashes as receptacles for the sugar.

When they found that there was to be no payment for attendance, most of them returned to their kraals; the remainder stayed to accompany the hymn-singing of the faithful by beating time on the cups and calabashes.

Unfortunately Mr Boggis was present with his sjambok. He had flourished it several times in a minatory manner, when it fell from his hand, and, being seized by a mischievous youth, was thrown from hand to hand till it alighted on the roof of the verandah. Half a dozen members of the congregation rushed to recover it with the result that the missionary had to spend the greater part of next day in repairing the damage.

'You're badly handicapped in having to follow a weakly chap like Alliston,' Mr Boggis remarked commiseratingly when the missionary had abandoned the service in despair. 'He began well by licking the gospel into their hides, but he hadn't the strength to keep it up. Consequently they ain't sensitive to saving grace. You can only reach their heathenish hearts by way of their backs or bellies. The back is the best. Old Schweitzer, the Lutheran missionary up Umvoti way, used to thrash 'em to chapel, and always had a good crowd. You made a mistake by sugaring the rascals. You've got to decide now whether you're going to fill 'em up with righteousness by way of the mouth or the skin. I'm afraid you'll be no good with a sjambok. You should have started as you meant to go on.'

Mr Boggis again offered to act as whipper-in on Sundays. He was getting old, he said, but he thought he could still handle a sjambok with the best.

'You mustn't have another fiasco like today's,' he added. 'You were weak in stopping me when I was going to get among them. A weak missionary is worse than useless.'

These last words had been haunting the subject of them ever since. They had depressed him the more because he felt they were true. He had taken up the work, prompted by an overmastering yearning to win souls by the strength of love. He had resolved to conquer by proving to black and white that he was a disciple and exemplar of the gospel of peace and gentleness. So far everything had tended to prove that the old prospector was right; that spiritual success must be wrested by the same assertion of masterful strength and forcefulness that brought victory to the mere seeker after material things.

He would have been influenced much less by the criticism had it been uttered by an avowed opponent of missionary effort like Betts, but old Boggis was distinctly sympathetic. He had declared his faith in missionaries, and had testified to good wrought; but he stipulated for conditions which the young missionary knew he could not fulfil. If he could not win converts by gentleness he could not and would not practise compulsion.

Then intruded the inevitable sequential question – was he a fit and proper person to undertake the task he had chosen? Had he not been carried away by emotion? Had he not assessed his fitness by a false standard of measurement?

He had come prepared for many disappointments and had found all and more than he visioned, but the greatest and most surprising of all was himself.

Every day brought evidence of his own limitations, and emphasised the lurking, growing fear that he had served too short a probation. Enthusiasm and whole-hearted faith in his cause did not atone for his inadequate equipment for his work. He had not the gift of tongues. The Zulu language, so charmingly alluring to the philologist when in print, proved a very different thing when approached as an oral actuality. It was comparatively easy and pleasant to trace the root of a Zulu verb to its suggested origin in a Phœnician synonym, in the quiet of the study, but not so easy to find and pronounce a phrase that would convey a concrete idea to a Zulu.

Theoretically Hyslop had a good grasp of the Zulu language; in practice he was almost entirely dependent upon the interpretership of his boy James – a Pondo – alien in race, language, and ideas to the Zulu; speaking their tongue with a strange mirth-provoking accent, and with a vocabulary limited to a degree that his master never realised. The missionary, attempting to preach through his mouth was in the position of a learned German savant who sought to impart his views on a recondite subject to an assembly of English scholars through the agency of an illiterate Northumberland or Cornish peasant.

Dula, the competent *fidus Achates* of the dead missionary, had protested and sulked when he found himself superseded. He took revenge in attending the services regularly, and from his seat on the verandah roof, leading the chorus of sarcastic 'ow's' that greeted the numerous verbal atrocities of the interpreter. It was some time before the missionary learned that James had but partially told the truth when he explained that these embarrassing interjections were expressions of approval.

The discovery of his own lingual inefficiency pained him, but he knew that hard study and practice would remedy the defect. He wished that this was the least of his drawbacks – that his studies of native characteristics and customs had been less academic and more practical. His preparatory reading had loaded his memory with a cumbersome stock of kafir folk-lore and history, vastly entertaining from the point of view of the antiquary and ethnologist, but utterly useless to a man who had to deal with the practical native of real life. It was doubtless extremely interesting to know what some erudite scholar thought to be the origin of the marriage gift of lobola, but it would have profited the young missionary much more to know the etiquette of approaching a chief when seeking a favour.

Already he had learned that he had viewed the mission field through a mist of romance; that most of his hopes and aspirations had been based on false premises. He had as yet seen among the natives no evidence of that hungering and thirsting after knowledge, and least of all, righteousness which he had been led to expect from the reports of earnest but optimistic labourers in the mission field. Instead, he had been astounded and disappointed at the stolid lack of curiosity in his own personality displayed by the natives. It was a fortnight before a passing kafir from the location took the trouble to look at the new preacher. Then he asked in the most casual way whether he had a pair of boots to sell for eggs. The boots he wanted immediately, the eggs would materialise when the hens decided to lay near the kraal instead of in the secret places of the veld.

The bona fide members of the flock, the occupants of mission land, were singularly shy. They kept away from the mission for weeks until it leaked out that the new preacher was not likely to dun them for arrears of rent. Then they took their courage in both hands and, *en passant*, several items of the missionary's kit, and began to borrow salt and sugar, and catalogue their ailments and grievances.

There was an epidemic of bronchial trouble in the kraals. At least, that is what Mr Hyslop inferred, for there came a surprisingly universal demand for a well known patent medicine in which laudanum is a prominent ingredient. He had given away his entire stock of the agreeable sedative before he discovered through the invaluable Boggis that the kafir took it as a preventative rather than a curative and that sleep is a popular prophylactic among natives. The mission kafirs were consequently very free from disease.

Among his minus qualities, of which Mr Hyslop was not aware, was an utter absence of the sense of humour. It was probably incompatible with a temperament so intensely earnest as his. He paid the price in much superfluous suffering. Had he been a member of some ascetic religious order he would have done penance with voluntary scourgings for having in his ignorance encouraged the pernicious drug habit in his flock. The perfidy and cunning hurt him sorely.

A little later he again fell a victim to native guile.

Mozulikase, whom Mr Alliston had labelled 'cadger' came to the house the first day that a milch cow was added to the establishment. He needed milk for the kraal, he said.

The missionary remembered the warning against Mozulikase's wiles and refused. The man drew himself up to his full height and dramatically impeached the humanity of the adamantine preacher. 'You know that the mother has no milk for her young kids, yet you say "let them die."'

James interpreted very freely.

Mr Hyslop relented. He was quite unaware that the mother had no milk for her babes, or that she had babes requiring milk. He felt sorrow for her and regretted his own remissness and ignorance of the affairs of his flock.

For a month the extra large calabash of the Mozulikase kraal was filled twice a day.

Then came the naive confession that the milkless babes were really two motherless kids.

Had the young man been dowered with the saving gift of a perception of the humorous he would have cherished and preserved that story to lighten the gloom of a missionary meeting at home. Instead, he made it the subject of his first didactic sermon and enlarged − with the aid of James − on the enormity of the crime of wilfully deceiving the innocent, localising the moral by comparing himself to a blind traveller directed along a path that ended in a bog.

The congregation were profoundly stirred − to admiration of Mozulikase, who was thus publicly certified by the missionary as a successful bluffer of the omniscient white man.

Next day the triumphant cadger claimed the cow on behalf of a relative from whom he alleged it had been stolen. Failing to get delivery, he gravely informed Mr Hyslop that it was his duty to assist the claimant in getting justice, which he could do by lending him three pounds to fee a law agent to issue a summons for unlawful detention of the animal.

Mr Boggis shook his head when he was told the story. 'There is only one way of saving your reputation,' he said. 'It's bad enough to make blunders in front of a kafir, but it's a hundred times worse to admit them. You must take one of those kids in payment for the milk and to get even on the swindler. Your reputation has been badly chipped. If you sit quiet they will consider you a poor weakling and there'll be no end to the games they'll play on you.'

Mr Hyslop did not like the suggested reprisal, but he saw the logic and wisdom of Boggis's advice. He could not employ a sjambok as the old man would, but he could assert himself in a dignified manner.

He personally seized one of the kids.

There was surprise in the kraal, the surprise that paralyses the bully when his victim hits out unexpectedly, straight and hard.

Mozulikase made a feeble protest, but it was evident that the missionary had scored; he felt the thrill of the victor and comported himself as master of the situation.

He tied a cord round the neck of the captured kid and dragged it from the hut where it had been hidden.

'I take this kid,' he said magisterially, speaking in creditable, because carefully rehearsed, Zulu, 'because it is mine by right; I do not need it, but I take it to punish the man who deceived me.'

The speech made its intended impression on the crowd.

And then came the anti-climax.

Instead of ordering one of the children of Mozulikase to take the kid to the mission house, the missionary took it himself!

Fatal blunder, discovered too late for amendment! The victorious general who would wrap in his handkerchief and carry home afoot the sword of honour publicly presented might extract kudos from the freak, but for a white man to act as his own herd boy in the presence of the assembled kraal; there was neither precedent nor palliation.

Next day he received from Robert Dando the storekeeper, a curt note requesting him to restore immediately 'the kid which you have wrongfully abstracted.'

He rode fifteen miles to the camp of old Boggis to seek his advice and explanation before acting. He had come to lean upon the old prospector in times of crisis.

'What does the man mean? What right has he to interfere?' he asked.

'I ought to have thought of this,' Boggis answered apologetically. 'It's all my fault. I forgot that Mozulikase is mortgaged body and soul to Bob Dando. I expect you'll have to give the creature up. It really belongs to Bob.'

When Boggis had finished his explication of the relationship of storekeepers to natives, the missionary was too astonished to speak for a time.

'Why, it's nothing but slavery!' he exclaimed when he had recovered from his surprise.

'It's a little bit like it, I must say, but I don't see how you are going to prevent it,' Boggis answered in his stolid unenthusiastic way. 'If a kafir wants things and hasn't got the money to pay for them, he's in the same position as a white man; he must go without or get credit. But the joke is that a kafir can get credit with a storekeeper when a white man couldn't. Bob couldn't order me to work for him if I owed more than I could pay him, but he can command the services of the kafir, to wipe out a debt. I should be surprised if there were half-a-dozen kafirs in this location who are not under Bob's thumb. He's not a bad chap, take him full and bye; he doesn't worry them with court summonses like some of the storekeepers, he gives 'em time, but he gets his pound of flesh. I hear he has ordered out about fifty of his worst debtors to go to work on the mines at Johannesburg. He gets ten shillings a head for them from the agent. It's not a bad way of arranging things since the Natal Government has stopped recruiting by agents for the mines. Bob can get as many boys as he wants and ship them into the Transvaal without any breach of the law. They go up as voluntary workers, but of course they have no choice. The Protector of Natives on the Rand sends down part of the boy's pay every month. It is supposed to be for the wives and children and the old people, but of course Bob gets hold of the ready cash and pays himself. Mind you, I don't say Bob don't play the game. I think he does. He practically keeps the kraal while the husband or son is away, and he expects his money when it has been earned. There are storekeepers who don't play straight, and make a fine thing of the business.'

'But I thought the chief was supreme, that he had the right to say whether a native should leave the kraal or not?' Mr Hyslop urged.

'Precisely; but suppose the chief owes Bob two or three years' store account? Some chiefs have expensive tastes and very little ready cash to gratify them with.'

'I have learned much, but every time I meet you I learn something more surprising,' Mr Hyslop remarked. 'And now what do you advise about this letter of Dando's?'

'You are in a cleft stick, preacher. If you give up the kid the kafirs will have the laugh over you, and your prestige, which isn't very high at present, will be simply wiped out. If you refuse, Dando will order Mozulikase to go to the magistrate for a summons against you and it's a hundred to one that you will lose. If you win, Dando will take up the quarrel and make your life a hell. You've got to go through the fire anyhow, and I blame myself for it.'

David Hyslop had reviewed these incidents while sitting on his stoep awaiting courage to finish a letter that had been growing on the instalment principle for a month, but was extremely small for its age.

He had let three mail days pass; the fourth was on the morrow.

Thus had he kept his promise to write to her regularly at every opportunity, reporting faithfully how the work progressed − be the record good or ill. The letter had been thrice postponed. He had feared to tell the truth.

This afternoon he had added another new experience to his rapidly growing stock. He knew why men lie to those whose good opinion they value most; he understood how pride goeth before a fall from self-respect. Pride, vanity, petty conceit had impelled him to break his promise, because keeping it meant telling the truth, and the truth was that every day of his life on the station brought proof of his failure − the failure of incompetence.

He did not attempt to deceive himself.

'My burden is greater than I can bear. I have not the strength I vainly believed,' he had written in his diary a few nights before, but he dared not transfer the confession to the letter. It would not be fair to her.

From the day they met on the voyage out when he had confided to the young English governess his artless enthusiasm, his dreams and imaginings, she had pictured him as a hero, and he knew it. No word of love had passed between them; theirs was only the deep friendship that has its source in sympathy. Hers was the self-sacrificing missionary spirit, born in the same roseate romanticism as his; little wonder that two such kindred souls should demand communion when apart; still less the marvel that he feared to confess that her hero had not merely feet of clay but heart and body of wax.

But, if he would be true to his professions and to himself he must tell her the truth; to write cheerfully and flippantly of his failures as he had several times intended by way of justifiable evasion of a painful duty, would be to lie by implication. He would be a coward no longer. He would write and confess his absolute failure.

There came a distraction.

A police trooper rode up, and after having made himself comfortable, and ascertained that he would be put up for the night, executed his commission.

He produced a summons to the Rev. David Hyslop to appear at the Court of the Resident Magistrate eight days hence to answer a charge of unlawfully seizing and detaining a young goat, the lawful property of Mozulikase; or alternatively to pay the sum of one pound as compensation.

The incident came as a blessing in disguise, for it jerked the young man out of the slough of despond into which he was sinking, and gave him a fresh interest in life.

He did not know that the paroxysm of mental anguish and depression through which he had been passing was one of the recognised South African plagues which few men escape. It usually attacks the victim after about a year's experience of the country, and the symptoms and effects vary with temperament. The steady young man who has come to secure a future generally arrives suddenly at the conclusion that it is not good for man to live alone, and decides on bringing 'her' out, regretting the step before the boat has touched Cape Town. The man possessing the fatal gift of epistolary fluency finds relief in penning to friends at home and perhaps an English newspaper, gloomy forebodings and warnings as to the future of the country. The common-place man who has not a literary last line of defence or domestic aspirations, opens a case of whisky and lays the first stone of an altar to Bacchus at which he most likely worships regularly for the rest of his brief days in the land.

The Rev. David Hyslop being prone to morbidity and introspection would probably have written a foolishly sincere letter of which he would have been heartily ashamed within twenty-four hours.

The receipt of a police court summons averted a calamity.

The evening he spent with the young police trooper he afterwards entered on the credit side of his 'account of the days of my life.'

CHAPTER VI

THE OFFICIAL VIEW

Mr Percy Perry, Resident Magistrate of the Blue Krantz District of Natal, was a success, officially, and, what was infinitely more important, socially.

That is another way of saying that his first consideration in the discharge of his duties was the public – the spoonful of farmers who made up the white population of his district. He was shrewd and experienced enough to know that so long as he gave satisfaction to them there would be no complaints to headquarters and, in consequence, no trouble there.

He had been R.M. of Blue Krantz nearly a year and, so far as he knew, there had been no application by a single resident for his removal, a circumstance so unprecedented that he was becoming notorious in official circles through never being heard of. The Attorney General, it was said, had been so impressed by the non-receipt of letters of complaint from Blue Krantz District that he had privately enquired of the Postmaster General whether there had been any reports of non-delivery of letters from that district. Being answered in the negative, he felt safe in filling up the vacancy he had, as a matter of customary precaution, left open as a place of retreat for the transferred R.M. of Blue Krantz.

Mr Percy Perry had succeeded Mr Grattan, who, after seven appeals to headquarters by the infuriated Blue Krantzers, had been transferred for the fourth time in six years to exacerbate another district.

Grattan was 'an old woman,' a 'disgrace to the Magisterial Bench,' an epitome of all the vices held in righteous abomination by justice-loving Colonials, and it was well understood that he would long ago have been retired on a pension were it not for his adroitness in bamboozling the Supreme Court into agreeing with his judgments when appealed against, as they generally were. How he had contrived to corrupt the judges was not clear, but that he had was sufficiently proved by the fact that they nearly always supported him.

It is extremely probable that many of the insinuations against Grattan were not justified, but it is a matter of record in the four courts from which he had been 'transferred' that he was the most aggravating stickler for finicking formality and the most impudent flouter of public opinion that had ever wasted the time of his subordinates under the pretence of thoroughly investigating a case.

More than once he had been known to discharge a kafir because the prosecutor could not make it convenient to appear in support of the charge, and he had not scrupled to insult the sergeant of police by refusing to accept his testimony as to what the absent prosecutor had said and thought when he gave the native into custody.

'If prosecutors will not take the trouble to come to court to prove their complaints, I am not going to punish a native on the strength of the secondhand hearsay evidence of a policeman,' was a frequent remark of his, and it naturally created intense bitterness, not merely because of the miscarriage of justice, but for the utter disregard of the convenience of the farmers whom he apparently expected to leave their comfortable stoeps and ride twenty miles to repeat what they had already told the police trooper who arrested the culprit.

The irritating perversity of the man had frequently been displayed by his rudeness to farmers who had taken the trouble to call on him and explain the points of their cases before they came into court. Even women were treated in the most discourteous manner. There was the well-known case of Mrs Barber, of Tigerspruit, who had had her native groom arrested for neglect of duty, after he had impudently taken out a summons against her for arrears of wages. Mrs Barber specially called on Grattan two days before the case came on in order to lay before him the actual facts, and particularly a record of the boy's past career, which she had obtained from friends, and showed him to be a lazy, thieving rascal. The magistrate not only refused to listen to her, but, taking advantage of her having no male friend with her, read her a lecture on attempting to interfere with the course of justice, and actually talked of dealing with her for contempt of court! When the case came on he gave judgment for the boy and dismissed the counter-charge.

This was too much for the district. A strong protest, signed by every white person in his jurisdiction, was sent to Maritzburg, and Mr Grattan learned that he could not insult a woman with impunity. He was 'transferred' within a month.

His successor was a man of the world. Mr Perry had, it is true, been born in the Colony and had spent the thirty-five years of his life there; but he had several times been to Cape Town and once spent a week in Johannesburg. He knew the kafir thoroughly, and was not likely to make the mistake of his predecessor in regarding native evidence as matter for serious consideration. He could grasp the facts of a case by a glance at the charge-sheet, and would get through his morning's work while poor painstaking Grattan was worrying over such details as whether the witness had answered 'Yes' or 'No' to a question.

'When in doubt give the white man the benefit of it,' was his axiom. Fortunately he never was in doubt when a white man was party to a case in which a native was concerned. When plaintiff and defendant were both natives they frequently got justice, for Mr Perry always favoured the native who made the greatest fuss and floundered deepest, for experience had satisfied him that it was difficult to tell the truth, while lies fell fluently.

Business at Mr Perry's court went very smoothly, and as he was resolved that there should be no cause for complaint on the part of the white residents as to his unduly favouring the natives, there was every prospect of his retaining his position.

When the Rev. David Hyslop arrived at the police court to answer the case of Mozulikase *versus* Hyslop, he was delighted and grateful for the cheery greeting he received from Mr Perry.

He had anticipated the meeting with some uneasiness, for he knew that officialdom did not yearn to take missionaries to its bosom. He accepted the magistrate's invitation to take a seat in his private office, and the cigar proffered by a jerk of the head in the direction of the cigar-box.

'You haven't been long in getting to close quarters with your blackguards,' Mr Perry remarked, without looking up from the heap of foolscap forms he was signing at stenographic speed.

'I see Mozulikase has been trying on his tricks. I know that gentleman, and I shan't be satisfied till I get him at the triangle. We suspect him of sheep stealing, but I won't let my troopers act till we are sure of a conviction. It damages us with the natives if we fail, and the new judge of the native court is getting so ridiculously particular in wanting a case proved to the hilt, that it makes us afraid to send natives for trial. I'll take it out of the brute's back the first chance I get. I wish you were the complainant instead of him. What are the facts?'

The guileless young missionary was absolutely charmed. True, he did not quite like the pronounced antipathy to the native manifest in the magistrate's tone; but there was no doubt Mozulikase was a very dishonest native and deserved censure. He told his story.

Mr Perry laughed heartily.

'You haven't a leg to stand on legally,' he said. 'You stole that kid right enough, but it wouldn't do to let the rascal know that. Unfortunately he is in the hands of Bob Dando. He owes him several pounds, and if Dando made himself objectionable I'm afraid he might annoy both of us. Does the kafir owe any rent to your mission?'

'Yes, four pounds.'

'That's capital. Issue a summons against him for the amount. I'll give you judgment on that, and adjourn the kid case. That will give him a chance to come to you to make terms. It will never do for you to let a kafir score over you in the court.'

Mr Hyslop felt very uncomfortable. If he was not entitled to retain the kid, he would much rather give it back, he urged.

The magistrate made a deprecatory gesture.

'Mr Hyslop, it is plain you do not know the kafir. As a white man you owe a duty to other white men, and if you are going to allow sentimental notions of justice to influence you you will be doing a wrong to yourself and your fellows. I have shown you how to avoid a serious blunder; if you are foolish enough not to avail yourself of it you must not be surprised if you have to pay a heavy penalty. You will make an enemy of every white man in the Colony.'

The missionary hesitated.

'Well, I won't press you. Take time to consider. I shall call the case, and you can ask for an adjournment to call another witness if you do not care to go at him for rent. A judgment is a good thing to have to hold over a troublesome kafir.'

The missionary was sorely troubled. He regretted having taken the advice of Boggis in the first instance. As a minister of the gospel he was not justified in seeking to avenge a trifling wrong. It was he who was the wrong-doer and his duty was clear. He would give up the kid and set an example of returning good for evil and acknowledging an error.

He came to this conclusion as he walked outside the court house, watching the medley of black humanity that squatted in the roadway and crowded the spacious verandah. He caught sight of Mozulikase looking very perky. He was in consultation with his lawyer. The impecunious cadger of milk for a starving family of kids had managed to find a sovereign to retain the services of a European law agent to press his claim to a kid worth at the most three or four shillings.

'Poor fellow! how keenly he must have felt the wrong I have done him, to make this sacrifice,' the missionary soliloquised.

He spoke to the law agent and intimated his desire to act justly by surrendering the kid.

The law agent looked at the missionary with a contemptuous scrutiny.

'I can't discuss the case,' he answered brusquely. 'It must come on in the ordinary course so that I can get an order for my costs.'

The case was not called for a couple of hours. This gave Mr Hyslop an opportunity to observe the procedure of a native magistrate's court.

A native constable in neat black tunic, a knobkierie in his hand and a pair of handcuffs at his belt stood just outside the door. He called a name, and a kafir responded. The Zulu constable seized him roughly by the collar and projected him into the court. He was only the complainant; the defendant was sitting with his back to the Courthouse wall taking snuff. He had not noticed that his case had been called. His first intimation that he was wanted came with the constable's bare foot. The flat sole struck his chest and scattered snuff and snuff spoon. Then the official hand grasped his collar and assisted him to rise while a smart cut on the flank with the knobkierie steered him to the door.

It was a civil action arising out of a dispute as to the ownership of some fencing poles. There were about a dozen witnesses on each side waiting to be called. They stood on the verandah and discussed the case clamorously. The magistrate sent a messenger to order the noise to be stopped. The Zulu constable rushed into the crowd, repeating the order in a voice that drowned the interrupters.

A young white clerk emerged from a room, a pen in his mouth and the wrath of the noise-distracted in his eye. He rushed at the constable and gave him a sounding slap in the face, with the information that he was a noisy brute.

The crowd of kafirs grinned their satisfaction, for the native constable is always a tyrant. But it is not wise to laugh at officialdom; it has too many chances of getting even, as those indiscreet smilers found when it was their turn to pass into court. It was only their condition of rigid preparedness that prevented their approaching the witness-box head-first. As it was, they each advanced with one hand raised in salute to the magistrate, the other rubbing away the bruise made by the constable's knobkierie *en passant*.

The case of Mozulikase *versus* Hyslop did not occupy long.

The law agent informed his worship that he believed the defendant was prepared to allow judgment to be signed against him.

Mr Hyslop bowed acquiescence.

The magistrate formally asked if the defendant consented to judgment, and received his reply with a grimace of obvious annoyance.

'This carries full costs, Mr Hyslop,' he said, going on with his writing.

'I am prepared for that,' the defendant answered cheerily.

He was not so prepared as he believed. It was his first experience of civil process in the Colony, and the price he paid for it was seven pounds ten.

The magistrate met the missionary that evening at the little store and hotel at which he put up for the night.

'You have done a very foolish thing, Mr Hyslop,' he said. 'I did my best to smooth things for you, but you would not be advised.'

The missionary was piqued. He felt he could now deal with the magistrate on level ground, and told him, quite plainly, that while he appreciated the effort to secure victory for him, he could not, as a professor of Christianity, be a party to an act of injustice, as he now recognised it to be.

'Justice is justice, whether in Africa or England,' he remarked rhetorically.

The magistrate smiled. 'Let me tell you a story, Mr Hyslop. You may not see the point now, but you will when you know kafir nature better. The other day my three young sons saw an ox belonging to a neighbour floundering in a marsh. They took some trouble to get assistance and the ox was saved. The owner gave each of the lads half-a-crown. I let the two elder keep the money, but took it from the younger. Now I suppose you would call that an act of injustice, as they had all worked equally hard at saving the ox. But why did I take it from the youngest? Because he is very youthful and not in the habit of having money. Consequently when he does get a coin he generally gives it to a kafir or spends it foolishly. The kafir is like my youngster. He must be treated as a child; justice that might be appreciated by a white would be misunderstood or abused by a black. I know you won't agree to this, but just think over it.'

Mr Hyslop agreed that the raw kafir might not at present be in a condition to appreciate the higher morality, but that was no excuse for a white man not practising it.

The magistrate was not in the humour to argue; it was foreign to his environment. He was more at home as a dogmatist.

'I know I am wasting time in attempting to advise you,' he answered, 'but I can't forget that you have done a thing today that will result in more mischief than you imagine. You have shown the kafirs that they can take any liberty with you, and they will do it. I don't care much about you, but I do care about other people in the district, and myself. I am bound to have a lot of trouble from your natives, and I warn you that I shall stand no nonsense. I shall lay it on as thick as the law allows, and you will find that I shall have the support of every white man in the district.'

Mr Perry's tone was that of a very much aggrieved man. The missionary mildly intimated that he did not see any reason for it.

'But it is a personal matter; it affects me considerably. I can't afford to get a reputation as a magistrate who gives judgments in favour of kafirs against white men, even if they are missionaries. I've all my work cut out to keep on good terms with the public and the authorities. We have one or two fussy meddlers in the Government just now, who have allowed themselves to be influenced by nonsensical Exeter Hall notions about justice to natives, and a magistrate has to walk very circumspectly, as the Bible puts it. I had a murder case the other day – you may have seen the report. A native named Sebaas killed a petty chief named Tambuza. The case was as clear as any I have ever had. I sent him for trial, and now the Law department is worrying me with enquiries and implying that I hurried the hearing. This means that the Government, or one or two officials, are suspecting me of undue severity to natives. When your case gets known others will accuse me of pandering to them. In any case I'm between two fires. Can you wonder that I'm annoyed at the way you have put me in the mud?'

Mr Hyslop assured the ruffled official that if any hostile criticism resulted he would at once publicly declare that the decision was perfectly just.

Mr Perry interposed impatiently. 'That remark shows that you do not understand the position. It isn't a question of justice. What the public will look at is the fact that I have given judgment in favour of a kafir against a white man. They are not concerned with the rights or wrongs of your quarrel. All they will see is that the kafir has got the laugh of his master, and we can't afford to let kafirs laugh at us. You have forced me into a very disagreeable position, and I don't thank you for it.'

And the magistrate went to the billiard room to have a hundred up with the jailer.

There were ten or a dozen people in and about the little hotel – farmers passing through to or from the railway thirty miles distant, and officials resident in the 'camp', as the magistracy of Blue Krantz was called locally.

It was a typical Natal seat of native government. Mr Perry as R.M. was the chief, and in the half-dozen comfortable bungalows that spread over the square mile occupied by the village lived the District Surgeon, the Sheriff or Court Messenger, the District Road Inspector, the Chief Clerk, who also acted as Assistant Magistrate, and a clerk or two. At the police barracks six troopers under a sergeant passed part of the day in devising methods for killing the rest of it or in calculating the hours to the end of the month when pay day would enable them to obtain a fresh supply of whisky from grumpy mistrusted old Burgess who 'ran' the straggling brick and iron structure that did service as the hotel.

Mr Hyslop sat on the verandah awaiting the evening meal. The Burgess family were in occupation of the hotel dining room and showed no disposition to hasten the turn of the guests. Colonial hotels are 'family' hotels in the full sense of the term, for the proprietor's family monopolise the public room and are invariably served first, whether they sit down before or with the visitors.

It might have been hypersensitiveness on the part of the young missionary, strange to Colonial ways, but he had an uncomfortable feeling that he was being boycotted. No one except the magistrate had taken any notice of him, although people were passing and repassing every minute from bar to billiard room. He was not surprised at being ignored by the proprietor, for although only a very short time in the country, he knew that Colonial hotel proprietors are not supposed to take any interest in their visitors, unless they are personal friends or acquaintances. The kafir who answered to the English equivalent of chambermaid had shown him the room he was to occupy with a stranger, and the duties of hostship had been fulfilled. Besides, the missionary in his simplicity did not know that visitors were supposed to spend their time and money at the bar. Not doing this, he was not wanted. Colonial hotel-keepers do not grow rich on supplying bed and board.

Mr Hyslop had exhausted all the available means of outdoor distraction. He had visited his horse in the paddock, walked round the bright brick-walled jail, and noted with surprise that the gates stood wide open and the native prisoners walked in and out at their work and even far up the 'street' supervised by one Zulu guard who lounged against a garden fence opposite the jail entrance.

The heat was intense, although sunset was only an hour distant, and the missionary returned to the shelter of the hotel stoep determined at all risks to speak with some white human being. It had occurred to him during his short perambulation that the standoffishness of the party at the hotel might be the natural reticence of the average Britisher to treat a parson as an equal. He knew that he had been accused of undue shyness and reserve, and he had often wished he could affect some of that freedom and unrestraint in the presence of strangers which is a characteristic of the Colonial.

He walked boldly into the billiard room and sat down. The magistrate had gone, and the jailer, the local billiard champion, was showing fancy strokes for the benefit of four or five spectators. A hum of talk was going on. It ceased as he sat down and took out his pipe and tobacco.

An elderly farmer whose shrill falsetto voice and uncouth Yorkshire accent had been loud in the din occupied the other end of the bench. He turned sharply, looked hard at the missionary for a moment, then handed him his tobacco pouch. 'Try this,' he piped. 'I've been taking your part', he added nonsequentially.

'I'm very much obliged,' Mr Hyslop answered, and he meant it. He was thankful for the implied friendliness, but before he could enquire the nature of the attack and defence the old man demanded:

'Do you or do you not tell the kafirs they are as good as white men?'

'I don't think I quite understand your question,' was the mild answer.

'That's evading the issue,' the Court Messenger interposed. He was a patriotic young Irishman who had never seen Ireland, and was famous for his copious use of legal phraseology interlarded with malformed misquotations in Latin.

'An evasion is a *suppressio vero* and *suggestio falso*,' he added, looking round at the company, and nodding his head by way of italicising the assertion.

The missionary smiled. He had an idea that this comedian-like young man was trying to be funny, not knowing him.

'Give the man a chance,' someone remarked.

The Court Messenger left his seat on the corner of the billiard table and stood before the missionary.

'The point at issue, sir,' he said, 'is simply this. The allegation by me is that you missionaries, *enn block*, promulgate as a matter of policy, that is doctrine, for I have reason to know that you – that is all of you, *enn mass* – receive memoranda of instructions from your Chief of Department, which memoranda sets out what might be termed course of procedure. What I ask is, is that so or is it not – a plain answer to a plain question?'

He looked round the room and nodded again, a defiant nod that said, 'I've cornered him.'

The missionary could not resist laughing.

'Really, sir,' he said, 'I'm afraid I must repeat what I said just now – I don't think I have quite caught your question, but if you mean, do we missionaries act on instructions from those who direct us, my answer is, yes, certainly.'

The Court Messenger nodded three times and resumed his seat on the billiard table.

'That is quite sufficient, I am satisfied; that was my contention. Now, Mr Flemming, what have you to say to that damaging admission by your own witness? You are absolutely *ultra viries*.'

Mr Flemming, the gentleman with the high alto voice, was annoyed.

He left his seat and walked on to the verandah, then put his head in at the door and glared savagely at the Court Messenger.

'You gibbering baboon! What do you know about Christianity or any of you public officials? You spend your lives among criminals and think every man you meet is one, whether he is a missionary or anything else. You are more in need of missionaries than the kafirs. Go to the devil, all of you.'

Mr Hyslop could not help wondering what the company had been saying about him. He learned later, for Mr Flemming occupied the other bed in the small apartment.

As he lay half undressed outside the coverlet smoking and swearing at the mosquitos, he explained that he had tackled the Court Messenger for asserting that missionaries were all bent on stirring up the kafir to dispute the authority of the white and that they taught the doctrine of equality – a thing no man who was a man would think of doing.

'I'm a religious man myself,' Mr Flemming went on, 'and always brought my children up in the way they should go. I've nothing to reproach myself for on that score I can tell you. Prayers night and morning, and no shirkin'! I give 'em to understand they had a Christian home, and if they didn't take to religion kindly I'd sjambok it into 'em, as my father did to me, and I tell you I had some trouble. My eldest boy Tom – what's married and farmin' out Umvoti way, used to kick, but I knocked the fear o' God into him as he'll tell you. Now he's death on missionaries. There's a Trappist place near his, and he's always rowin' with them fathers. He won't let them take a short cut across his farm, but makes them go over the mountain three or four miles out of the way. I wouldn't do that. It's rough on the oxen, for it's an awful pull up that road, and the oxen can't help belongin' to a mission.'

Mr Flemming paused to indulge in an expression of his feelings on the subject of mosquitos. When he had apologised for his language he resumed his discourse.

'Tom is like most Colonials – he can't stand a Christian kafir, not at no price. I had one once, and I didn't find him no wuss than a raw kafir, but I'll tell you what, mister, you missionaries ought to rub it into them that they must work for less. They can't expect the Government to give valuable land to missions and then have the kafirs brought up on 'em askin' better pay than a raw boy fresh from the kraal, where his bringin' up ain't cost the Government nothin'.'

Mr Hyslop suggested that a mission kafir having been taught to work more intelligently was surely worth more than a raw kafir.

'That ain't the pint. We farmers don't want kafirs with big notions of cleverness. What we want is for 'em to work as well as the raw kafirs and be as obedient. We can learn 'em all we want 'em to know. What you missionaries have got to do is fill 'em up with good religious notions, so that they won't steal our sheep or shirk work, but do it for the same price as a raw kafir. There was a parson chap out from home preachin' at Maritzburg once, and he give us to understand that the missionaries were ordered to rub it into the kafirs that they must work for the white man. The dignity of labour he called it. You preach on them lines, and you'll have all the farmers agreein' with you. Work at cheap rates is what is wanted, and if religion will bring it, you may count on me for one not to oppose you. You don't know how difficult it is to get boys to work at our price. Rub the Catechism into 'em, about bein' meek and lowly to all their betters, and bein' content in the state o' life to which it has pleased God to call 'em. Teach 'em what the Bible says about their bein' the children of 'Am and bein' under a cuss, and don't forget the dignity o' labour. The lazy brutes hate work, and I tell you I quite expect to live to see the day when we farmers and our sons will have to work. It's comin' to it. That's why I say "rub in religion."'

CHAPTER VII

FOLLOWING THE STAR

For some time Bulalie had been conscious of a slow but sure growing suspicion that he was destined to stay with the road party a very long time if he waited till he had saved out of his monthly pay of five shillings, sufficient to justify his return to the kraal, and a life of moneyed independence.

He had practised strict economy and much self-denial, even refusing to accompany the others to the store on the Saturday following pay day, lest he should be tempted to break into his hoard. He had ten shillings hidden in Bacheta's sack in the ant-bear hole, and three shillings and two sixpences tied in various parts of his blanket. The rest he had squandered on jam and a second-hand mouth-organ, with most of its music dead.

At night the star that hung over Maritzburg kept him long awake, calling him to go to it. Many natives, who had worked in the town, had come to the road party, and they all talked much of the wonders of Umgungundhlovu (Maritzburg), but, most of all, of the money they earned there, and the kafir beer and white man's rum that could be had so easily by those who knew how to find the places where it was sold, and keep their eyes open for the police traps – the native constables without their uniform, who pretended to be friendly kafirs fresh from their kraals, but were really false friends sent to lead others into temptation and capture.

But Bulalie had learned much of the ways of the towns by listening to those who had been in them, and he was sure that he had cunning as great as those who had escaped the traps and the imprisonment and lashings that followed, and he hungered to get among the houses that were made of hard bricks and stone and walk on roads that were smooth as the walls.

One day two things happened that helped him to resolve firmly that he would no longer lie awake and hunger for Maritzburg and money when he should be sleeping.

Baas Mafuta had been angry and kicked him, and put a new boy, just come to work with the road party, to clean the stirrup leathers which Bulalie had done

badly. That night when he was complaining in the tent of being put away for a
new boy, Sekoos, a Basuto whose time to leave the party would come next
Saturday, told that he was going to Maritzburg to work in an hotel where he had
been kitchen boy for six months and had plenty of white men's food and thirty
shillings a month. If Bulalie would go with him, he could work in the stables,
where there were many horses, and perhaps get two pounds every month.

Bulalie's heart took fire like the long grass in winter, and he could not sleep.
He lay all night thinking plans by which he might make the baas pleased and
good-tempered, so that he would not kick him and refuse to pay the money due,
which was his way when kafirs wished to leave whom he wanted to stay. If the
baas said nay on the last day of the month, Bulalie would have to wait another
long month before he dared ask again, or else go away secretly at night, leaving
the wages that were owing to him.

Sunrise came and time to work, but he had not yet hit on a plan, as he must, if
he would go away with Sekoos, because it was now Friday, and Mafuta was
going away to play tennis till Monday, as he often did when he knew the District
Inspector was not likely to come for many days.

When the baas had finished his breakfast, Bulalie filled his heart full of
courage and went to him.

'Baas, I must go away; there is sickness in my kraal,' he said.

He was careful to stand well outside the tent so that if the baas threw things
they might miss him, for he could not throw straight very far.

'Go fetch the horse and saddle her,' was all the answer the Baas made.

'Then will you give me my money and my pass and let me go?' Bulalie
asked, very meekly, and in plain, easy Zulu, so that Mafuta might understand.

'I'll give you a pass to the hospital if you don't do as I tell you,' he said,
angrily; and Bulalie went sorrowfully to catch and saddle the horse.

Gabriel Betts was much perturbed by the request of his horse-boy. He did not
object to his going; as a matter of fact he had decided to get rid of him on the
score of economy. It was a piece of impulsive foolishness that had induced him
to engage and pay for a servant when he could have one from the gang for
nothing. But he often did equally illogical things to gratify a momentary whim.
What bothered him now was that he owed the boy seven-and-sixpence – five
shillings legitimately, and half-a-crown which in a fit of drunken generosity he
had promised the boy as a reward for finding and extricating him from a deep,
wet sluit, into which he had fallen one night when extra full of whisky. All the
cash he possessed was eighteen shillings, and it was at least a fortnight to pay
day, with two week-end excursions intervening.

He decided that the boy must wait till funds arrived. If he bolted in the interval, seven-and-sixpence would be saved.

He momentarily wished he could do as some employers of kafirs did — make sure of the boy running away by giving him a good sjamboking and threatening another for next day. He knew men who saved pounds a year on their labour bill by the simple expedient of paying with the sjambok. He had never tried it yet, nor was he satisfied that Bulalie would run, after one thrashing. Experts at the business did it systematically, beginning about a fortnight before wages were due, and finding a pretext every day for making the boy wish he were dead. Betts could not be deliberately cruel. His brutality was only the result of loss of temper; he could not keep up a show of anger he did not feel; besides, sjamboking was an exhausting operation to a big, fat, lazy man. He would get out of the difficulty more easily. He would tell Bulalie that horse boys were required by law to give a month's notice.

He carried out his resolve when he was mounted and ready for the journey.

Bulalie received the statement in silence for a moment, then when he knew that he must wait another month he cried out:

'No, no, baas, give me half my money and let me go now.'

Betts rode off at a fast canter; he could not bear to hear the pleading of the boy, for he had a considerable amount of softness in his nature.

Bulalie discussed the matter with Sekoos.

'You cannot travel to Maritzburg for four days without money, for what you have will not be enough to buy clothes and pay for passes,' the older man said.

Then Bulalie joyfully bethought him of the sack in the ant-bear hole, and they went out together and dug it up. There might be something there, Sekoos said, that they could sell to provide food for the four days' journey to Maritzburg. Bulalie had often gone out to the hole and feasted his eyes on the contents of the sack; but most of the articles were new and strange to him, and he did not know either their use or value. That is why he allowed Sekoos to share his secret; his wondrous knowledge of the world would enable him to tell the worth of the treasure.

He turned it out carefully into his outspread blanket, and Sekoos examined each article with the critical eye of an experienced purchaser.

First came a white man's coat, a dress coat in good condition, then a white waistcoat and two or three pairs of socks — all quite good and fresh. Bacheta had evidently got possession of the outfit of a white man going to or from a dance or dinner. It was complete, even to shirt, white tie, gloves and studs, but there were no trousers.

Sekoos pointed out the serious nature of the omission. Bulalie could wear the shirt and coat, but he must have trousers, for no native was allowed in the town without them.

The gloves sent a thrill of reminiscent horror through Bulalie. Many years ago he had accompanied his father to the magistracy, and saw the white ladies hitting a ball with funny things like small shields covered with network. While he looked on another lady rode up and joined the players, and he saw that while her face was quite white her hands were black like his own, only more so. He marvelled much at this, and thought it strange that her face should not be the same colour. As he looked and wondered a horrible thing happened. The lady skinned her hand. The black skin peeled off, leaving the inside white like a chicken when the feathers are boiled off.

Bulalie put his hand to his mouth screaming 'Ow!' and ran away. He heard the ladies laughing loudly, and this made him more fearful for he knew there must be witchcraft, for white people always laughed at it.

Long afterwards, when he had ceased to be an umfaan, a girl of his kraal who had been a servant to a white inkozikas showed him a glove and told him there was no witchcraft in it, but he had never forgotten, and wished that the gloves were not in the bag, for witchcraft is bad at the beginning of new enterprises.

Then came many small packages wrapped in handkerchiefs or paper, and Sekoos exclaimed 'Wu!' when Bulalie untied them. They were rings of gold, bracelets, watches and many little things that neither of them knew the use of, though Sekoos was sure they were worth much money, if only they dared to sell them. Of the knives, spoons, scissors, thimbles and other things that white women use, Sekoos thought little, and let Bulalie keep, but the gold things he made into a small bundle and tied into a corner of his blanket.

On Saturday at noon Bulalie packed up his few belongings in the tent, before the work party came off the road, and went to the ant-bear hole and waited for Sekoos. Then the two began the long walk to Maritzburg.

Bulalie had never before been so far towards the sea, but he did not feel that he was in a strange land, for he had listened with wide ears when kafirs who had often made the journey told of the way. When they came to the spruit where the snake lived that carried a flame in its head, he recognised it, though he had never before seen it, for he had the great memory, so that he never forgot when he had heard once the way described – the trees, the spruits and the paths across the mountains.

They slept that night at a kraal where Sekoos was known. Bulalie had a great fright, for in the kraal was one Malini who had been in prison in Maritzburg where he had seen Sebaas awaiting trial, and he told of the murder of old

Tambuza, not knowing that he spoke to one of the dead chief's kraal, for Bulalie had told them, when asked, that his kraal was in another place, very far away.

When next day they saw a small town, Bulalie was sorry that Sekoos would not go through it for fear of meeting some trouble that would bring to light the gold things that he carried.

'When we get to Maritzburg,' said Sekoos, 'I know where I can turn these things into money, but until then we will keep away from white men.' And Bulalie thought of the klippie he carried in the peg in his moocha, and saw that Sekoos was very wise.

There were two things that caused Sekoos much thought. First that Bulalie had no trousers and would have to buy some before he could walk in the town. Bulalie had not said that he had ten shillings in the sack, having shown only the four that he carried in his blanket, which would not suffice for trousers, and pass money, to say nothing of food. Sekoos had his month's pay amounting to thirty-one tenpences, but having learned in the towns how valuable money was, and how wretched a creature was a kafir who had none, he did not wish to have to pay anything for his friend as he would have had he not learned to be selfish. It was true that he had the gold things belonging to Bulalie, but a kafir dared not show them to any but those he could trust, and it might be many days before he found such.

The second matter was even more serious. Bulalie had no pass to go through the country, so that he might be arrested and flogged if the police found this out. Sekoos knew a makolwa (Christian) kafir at a store, who would write a pass for two shillings if he had one to copy from, but if he had none, the task was more hard and dangerous, and he was obliged to charge more, often as high as five shillings. The store lay three hours' journey off their road, but they must go, for it would be more dangerous to travel without a pass than to risk buying a forgery.

He explained the difficulty to his companion, who, of course, replied that what Sekoos said should be done he would do; so they altered their way and set out for the store.

There was a great grief for them when they reached the store. The makolwa was away with the wagon, and would not be back for two days. The storekeeper was a white man who had been there many years and understood kafirs. He had not spoken long to Bulalie before he saw that he was raw and had no pass. He also knew why he had come to the store, but he made no sign that he knew, telling them that the makolwa would be back at sundown, for he wished them to stay and spend money, and did not know that Sekoos had first spoken to other kafirs and knew the truth.

Sekoos bought some bread, being careful to show only the sixpence he paid for it.

They went and lay by the wall of the cattle kraal, and ate the bread, talking the while of what they should do, for they feared to wait so long for the makolwa, lest they should have to spend more money, for if they lingered about the store without buying things they did not want, the storekeeper would drive them away, and perhaps make Bulalie stay and work for him, knowing that he had no pass.

They waited till they saw the storekeeper go into the house to sleep away the hot afternoon, then they walked off.

'If any policeman asks you for your pass, you must say you lost it,' Sekoos said. 'I have mine to show that I worked with the road party, and perhaps when I show that, and say that you worked with me, they will ask no more questions.'

On the fourth day they came in sight of Maritzburg, having had only a very little trouble on the way, for when they saw white men riding towards them on the road Bulalie would lie down in a donga or the long grass, while Sekoos walked boldly on.

On the last day Bulalie got his first whipping from a white man.

They had turned a sharp corner of a hill where the path was narrow. A man was riding towards them. Bulalie quickly threw up his arm to give the salute 'Inkoos!' when the sack fell over his head and frightened the horse, making him run down the steep sides of the path. The man rode at Bulalie, and struck him many times with his sjambok, and would have flogged Sekoos also, but he, being cunning, climbed up the steepest part of the bank and escaped.

Bulalie was not much hurt. The sjambok had made a deep cut on his shoulder, which bled after a time. Sekoos filled it up with wet mud and the pain nearly went away.

As they would soon be in the town, Sekoos took Bulalie into a donga to show him how to put on the clothes. Bulalie had never yet worn the clothes of white men, and would have trouble with the buttons if he were not shown how to pull them through the holes.

Sekoos having worked at an hotel, knew that the coat was of the kind only worn by the waiters and the white baases at night, but he would not tell Bulalie this, but pointed out what was quite true, that it was new. But when it was on it did not look quite as a coat should, for Bulalie was tall and the coat had been made for a little man, so that the tails stuck out behind, making Bulalie look like a tick bird, especially as his legs were long, and the white shirt made him look still more like the white-breasted tick birds.

They went to a wayside store kept by an Indian coolie where Sekoos knew they could buy trousers. After looking at many which would cost more than Bulalie could afford, the coolie showed them a soldier's red coat and a pair of trousers that had once been white linen, and offered to take four shillings and the coat and waistcoat Bulalie had on. They tried hard for long to persuade him to sell the trousers alone for two shillings, but he would not, so that Bulalie had to agree to the hard terms, thus learning what he had often heard, that the coolie is no friend to the kafir, but robs him always.

That afternoon Bulalie saw Maritzburg and found it almost as wonderful as he had dreamed, but Sekoos would not let him stay as he wished, and look at the shops; neither would the police, for forgetting the warning of his friend that natives were not allowed to stand on the pavements, he boldly walked up to a window where some very tiny white babies with pink faces were crowded together or hung up by strings, and was hit over the knees with a knobkierie by a Zulu constable and pushed roughly off. Sekoos took him by the arm and led him away to a place where a large number of kafirs were standing about. It was the Pass Office, a place he learned to know very well before long.

They waited an hour till their turn came, when they went into a room and were questioned by a white man who spoke Zulu well. There was at first some trouble about Bulalie having no pass, but the white man was not like many who made difficulties. He asked many questions about Bulalie's kraal, his chief, and where he had worked, but Sekoos did all the answering, and after being very much frightened lest the truth might come out that he was escaping from his kraal, Bulalie had a pass given him, for which Sekoos paid, and he was free to go where he wished till the bell rang at nine o'clock, when all kafirs must be in their sleeping places.

CHAPTER VIII

'THE MISSIS'

Bulalie was not wanted at the Hotel where Sekoos resumed his position as kitchen boy, but he had no difficulty in securing an engagement at a pound a month as a kitchen boy and general factotum at the boarding establishment of Mrs Hopgood. There is never a glut of kafir labour in the Colony, thanks to the short terms of service which satisfy the yearnings of most natives. To the average native, unlike his white brother, labour is only an incident that occurs once or twice in his life. He gives his services for such a period as will bring him the amount of cash that he has decided will suffice to establish him as a happy married man in his kraal, or pay the few pounds owing to the storekeeper or to the chief who has advanced the money due for a fine inflicted by a magistrate, or for payment of hut tax. The date when he can give notice to quit, or leave without that tiresome formality, can be easily calculated, if he is careful to abstain from expensive luxuries in the shape of puza (liquor), white men's clothes and magisterial fines.

Bulalie, after using up his stock of arithmetic, had figured it out that in three years he would have earned sufficient in money and experience of the objectionable side of the white man to justify a return to the kraal and happiness.

Fortune had stood by Bulalie all through, and particularly in finding him a Missis in Mrs Hopgood, for he would have been a very dull kafir had he been unable to learn much through her instrumentality. She was a Colonial woman, and boasted that she understood natives. Certainly few mistresses had better or fuller opportunity for studying the various brands of native servant. Her establishment had become famous in native circles as a sort of probationary purgatory. On an average eight cooks and sixteen kitchen boys engaged and deserted every year, which was rather above the average in houses where the mistress did not understand the kafir quite so thoroughly as Mrs Hopgood. But her explanation was logical. She was too indulgent, and reaped the reward in persistent ingratitude.

Every Colonial holds the theory that gratitude is an unknown attribute of kafir character, and some who have taken the trouble to look at a dictionary of the Zulu language are aware that it contains no word equivalent. But Mrs Hopgood spurned theories. She had hard facts to deal with, consequently she was never at a loss for a subject for conversation with other mistresses. In fact, Mrs Hopgood and the native servant problem were synonymous terms in her set.

It must not be inferred that she was a female Legree, or that floggings and tortures formed a regular feature of the Hopgood regime. As a matter of fact she rarely resorted to violence, whatever the provocation, for, as she put it, that was a man's job, or the magistrate's, and she would scorn to soil her hands on the dirty brutes. If the notion got abroad, as it did, that Mrs Hopgood used the sjambok and broomstick as freely as her tongue, she had only herself to blame. Threats of 'the finest hiding you ever had' were so frequent that they would have carried no weight if the threatened had only stayed long enough; but they never did, and it is quite possible that the good lady suffered as the result of the imaginative after reports of her ex-servitors.

As a Colonial used to kafir servants from infancy, she well knew that they have a greater horror of a nagging tongue than of the sjambok. The lash is bad while it lasts, but the duration is brief. There was, however, no cessation of the torture of the tongue.

Scoldings, revilings, abusing, threatenings, complainings – from early morn till dark, and sometimes longer, poured from the fluent tongue of the Missis, in Zulu, English, Dutch and scraps of Hindustani, and the provoking cause always the same – the obstinate ignorance of the kafir.

Mrs Hopgood was only a little worse than the average Colonial woman, because, like Martha, she was troubled about many things, and, as she expressed it, 'enjoyed very bad health.' She likewise was afflicted with that very common form of mental myopia which prevented her from seeing the absurdity of treating and regarding the kafir as merely a superior type of ape, but expecting him to have the intelligence and reasoning power of a civilised creature. Fluent though she was, her Zulu vocabulary was of the smallest, yet her choicest epithets were reserved for the 'idiotic fool' who failed to understand her. The kafir has many provoking shortcomings, but none which irritate so much as his density in grasping the meaning of an order in English, however loudly shouted. This stupidity is responsible for thousands of kicks and blows that might be reserved for other offences, though it must be confessed that it is galling to a patriotic Englishman to find a conquered and subject race so ignorant of the language of its masters.

There was another reason for the absence of harmony in the Hopgood kitchen. His name was Dick, and he was a slave, though he did not know it and his owner would have boiled with indignation had anyone repeated publicly what some of her young men lodgers sometimes said privately on the subject.

Dick was a kafir of indeterminate origin, but presumably Zulu. Eight years before, when Dick was about ten years old, he came as nurse-boy with a young Englishwoman who had lodged with Mrs Hopgood a few months, then departed for the Transvaal, arranging to send for Dick later. This she had forgotten to do, and the lad had remained ever since, a not unwilling slave to his Missis, quite content and blissfully indifferent as to his future.

The arrangement suited Mrs Hopgood. She had a well-trained servant for nothing, except a calico suit twice a year and his food, and, above all, that treasure of all treasures, a servant that was not likely to leave at the end of the month.

It is but just to Mrs Hopgood to emphasise the fact that Dick was a spoiled, too-well-treated helot, and his lot as an unconscious slave fifty times happier than that of the 'free' natives. Mr Benson, a Civil servant who had boarded with Mrs Hopgood for several years, used to cite the case of Dick as a triumphant vindication of slavery over the free system, to the horror and partial conversion of English newcomers.

Dick, he would point out, being a valuable chattel which had cost his mistress many pounds for food and clothing, she was not likely to damage its utility by bad usage, which was proved by the care and attention the young reprobate received at the first symptoms of indisposition. He was physicked copiously, had first pick of the leavings from the table, and the only stretcher bed in the tin shed at the bottom of the back yard that formed the sleeping quarters of the servants. He was always decently clad, because Mrs Hopgood had a degree of pride in her pet servant, and was sensitive to the criticism of neighbours. Dick's moral welfare was to a very great extent guarded by his mistress refusing to allow him to frequent the company of the free natives. By withholding the necessary after-hour pass she could always ensure his being at home at night. If, as occasionally happened, a white person administered a deserved corrective thrashing to the impudent youth, he could generally rely on the championship of his Missis, for while she denounced him in the kitchen as the worst kafir in the town, and occasionally tied him up to the stable manger and marked him liberally with a riding switch, she took care that no one else abused him either with tongue or lash.

'What happens,' asked Mr Benson, 'if one of the free boys gets ill? He is bundled out neck and crop to die or recover somewhere else. If he complains that the food supplied is insufficient, as it generally is, he is threatened with a thrashing and probably put on a still shorter allowance. If he gets thrashed by a neighbour, Mrs Hopgood will probably convey her thanks for having the job taken out of her hands, and if the clothes of the boy are too ragged for decency, she gives him the alternative of getting a new fit out at his own expense or leaving. In short, it's the case of the man without a conscience who borrows your horse. He takes all he can out of it, and returns it finished up while his own is well looked after in the stable. No, sir,' Mr Benson would add, 'slavery appeals to the universal instinct of possession. No man in his senses will neglect and injure a horse that cost him money, but he isn't going to worry himself over the crock he can hire for a few shillings at owner's risk. Mrs Hopgood has the chance of hiring half-a-million kafirs at thirty shillings a month, but Dicks at nothing a month are scarce and worth taking care of.'

A smart young journalist was so much impressed by Mr Benson's ironic sophistry that he wrote a clever plea for the re-institution of slavery, which was openly deprecated by some but secretly approved by every Colonial in Natal.

Dick was the tyrant of the kitchen, and responsible for more than half the trouble there; but with feminine obstinacy his mistress refused to recognise the fact that her pet was a devastating influence for evil, and fondly and honestly believed him to be, despite what she might aver in anger, a model native. To the newcomer in the Colony Dick was presented as a type of what the raw kafir might become under civilising influence, and more than one simple Englishman or woman had enthused over and petted this 'very interesting native,' utterly ignorant of the fact that Dick was a hopeless embodiment of all the vices, and few, if any, of the virtues of civilisation.

It would have been surprising had he been otherwise, for the atmosphere of the Hopgood Boarding House was at best negatively moral. As a good-looking ten-year-old umfaan, full of animal spirits and quaint and monkeyish tricks, he had contributed to the amusement of the lodgers, who encouraged the very impertinences and liberties they resented when the lad grew older. He was taught, parrot-like, a number of English slang phrases that sounded very funny in the mouth of a ten-year-old kafir, but were intolerable in a youth of seventeen or more, and secured for the unfortunate victim of white men's thoughtlessness many a blow from the unappreciative. As to the 'moral influence' which Mrs Hopgood honestly believed she had exerted, it consisted in creating in the mind of the youth a confused notion that certain acts produced blows and abuse, but under other conditions, approval, silent or expressed.

Dick knew, for instance, that it was wrong to make a noise in the house when the Missis or the lodgers were taking their afternoon siesta, but there were other rules as full of puzzling exceptions as the German or English grammar. When he forgot to post a letter given him by Mr Jones, the elderly and unpopular, because 'particular', lodger, he was let off with a threat of a thrashing which was softened by the overheard remark of the Missis that 'old Jones was always fussing about some trifle.' When Dick postponed for a day or two the delivery of a note given him by Mrs Hopgood she seized the occasion to give him at one tying up all the thrashings she had promised for a month past. More than once she and the lodgers had laughed heartily at the narration of how Dick contrived to evade the police who would have 'run him in' for being out at night without a pass; but when the lad was caught, and the Missis had to pay the fine of ten shillings, she failed to see the humorous side of the freak, and made Dick's back resemble a braised beef steak.

Much the same perplexing uncertainty was associated with the simple act of annexing stray coins. When Mr Jones discovered and bitterly complained that Dick had been systematically purchasing a cheap brand of tobacco when sent out shopping by the old gentleman, and charging him for the best, Missis and lodgers laughed uproariously, and agreed that Jones's meanness deserved punishment; but when, encouraged by the applause, the boy tried the same trick on young Wilson, Mrs Hopgood's tame lodger, she gave the young man full authority to make the 'wicked thief' remember it, which he did.

Had Dick been capable of expressing his thoughts and experiences epigrammatically he would have defined wickedness as doing something which made the Missis lose her temper, and righteousness and virtue as any act which made her and the lodgers smile.

There were, however, many acts which had not been classified, for the simple reason that Dick had a vague idea that they would not interest either the Missis or the lodgers. He never told her, for example, that he turned many an honest sixpence by buying liquor for kafirs in defiance of the strict law which punishes selling to natives with stripes and imprisonment. Dick had early in his career realised the magic potency of those little scraps of paper signed by the Missis or any white person, authorising whoever it might concern to 'pass my boy Dick till – o'clock' or to 'please supply my boy Dick with – bottle of Black label.'

Dick had forethought marvellously developed for a kafir, who as a rule knows no tomorrow. He had a supply of these convenient documents in a tobacco tin under his mattrass. Truth impels the shameful admission that they were written for him *en bloc* by an ex-lodger who was drinking himself to death as fast as his straitened means and opportunity would permit, and the price of his infamy was a stray bottle, or flask secured by Dick as part of his commission from the kafir client.

Dick further refrained from distressing his indulgent mistress by informing her that many a night when she believed him to be fast asleep in the well ventilated tin hut at the bottom of the yard, he was enjoying himself in the company of a party of kafirs in one of the secret drinking shebeens that the police are always unearthing; neither was she aware that Dick was an expert at sundry amusing games of the thimble and pea genus, and contrived to pick up thereby much stray silver from his less gifted brethren.

In fine, Dick was a very fair specimen of the type of 'slim' kafir whom Colonials, not without reason, cite as a shocking example of the effects of educating the native. The mistake they make is in suggesting that Dick had been educated. He had only assimilated knowledge from such sources as were available by his own observation.

Bulalie, kafir-like, recognised and acknowledged Dick's stupendously superior wisdom with reverent admiration. It is not consonant with native usage for the elder to look up to the younger, but Bulalie could not resist giving expression to the admiration he felt, and gladly permitted Dick to assume the mentorship.

In one way this was advantageous, since the friendship of the tyrant of the kitchen meant exemption from much abuse from the Missis. Dick understood the art of asserting and using his mastership. He could make the lot of a fellow servant a veritable hell by tricking him into breaches of the Hopgood code. An assertion against the industry or integrity of a servant by Dick, carried more weight with the Missis than the clearest evidence of innocence.

'The boy is devoted to me, and won't allow me to be imposed upon' she would often declare, and Dick was clever enough to live up to his reputation by a show of devotion that was often embarrassing, since it brought about so many vacancies in the kitchen.

Bulalie saw a great deal of town life under the aegis of Dick, and two or three times had a narrow escape from falling into the hands of the police when returning from unholy excursions to the shrine of Bacchus or Venus; but Dick's astuteness pulled him through, though the fright kept him indoors for many nights.

This was the beginning of the undoing of Bulalie, for, chafing at the monotony of his self-imposed imprisonment, he yielded easily to the promptings of his evil genius and gave him four shillings to obtain a bottle of rum for strict consumption on the premises.

It was Bulalie's first experience of the delights of drinking without let or hindrance. So far he had not drunk more than one tot at a sitting. This night he made free of the bottle, and within an hour was affectionately drunk. He gave a pass to his tongue, telling Dick many things that had hitherto been close sealed in his bosom, and of course he showed Dick and the cook, who was the guest of the evening, the klippie that had been embedded in the hollow peg since it was put there by Bacheta.

Dick had never been to Kimberley, but he knew many kafirs who had; therefore he fully realised that Bulalie not only carried with him something of great value, but that its possession was a serious offence for which Bulalie might be called to account. He had also learned enough from the drunken maunderings of the boy to know that he had reason for not desiring to get into the hands of the police.

There is no word in the Zulu tongue that precisely expresses the idea of blackmail; the plan that rapidly shaped itself in the brain of Dick proved that if it had existed there would have been a use for it. He decided to possess that stone.

He was too sensible to take it by force; he even affected indifference on the matter and helped Bulalie to restore the klippie to its hiding place. He knew that in his present boisterous, excitable condition Bulalie would resent any attempt at forcible possession, and probably make a noise that would arouse the sleeping cook and even the lodgers. He contented himself with warning Bulalie against the cook, helped him to curl up in his blanket and lay down himself to make plans.

During the next few days Dick made many attempts to induce Bulalie to part with the stone. His principal argument was the danger of its being discovered by the police, when, as was more than probable, Bulalie fell in their hands for breach of some one of the hundred rules and regulations that beset the town kafir; but the boy had recovered his senses with memory of the overnight indiscretion and had carefully hidden the stone in an accessible but inconspicuous spot, continuing to wear the peg in his moocha.

Dick cajoled, and even threatened till Bulalie refused with a vehemence that warned the tempter off. He extracted the peg during the night and finding it empty resolved to hand over the quest to another.

He confided to his mistress that Bulalie had brought from Kimberley, where he had worked, a diamond, and gave a description of its size and appearance that set the heart of Mrs Hopgood palpitating. As a Colonial woman she was sufficiently well acquainted with the records of the diamond fields to know there was nothing unlikely in the story of a kafir carrying a valuable gem concealed about him. She had a vivid recollection of an incident of her girlhood. A kafir servant died on the farm of a relative. The knowledge that he had worked on the diamond fields and had a peculiar lump on the calf of his leg induced the employer to conduct a private post-mortem examination. He opened the lump and was rewarded by finding a fifty-carat stone which had been concealed in a cut made in the flesh for the purpose.

A stone such as Dick described would tempt any kafir to incur risks.

Mrs Hopgood resolved to transfer those risks to herself.

Had Bulalie been more experienced in the ways of white mistresses, he would have noticed a very great and sudden change in the treatment he received at the hands of Mrs Hopgood. Being quite raw, nothing new surprised him, and the little acts of kindness and consideration which the Missis all at once bestowed upon him were noticed only because they had the effect of robbing his work of much of its irksomeness. That she should now and then talk to him about his kraal, his hopes and desires did not astonish him, because, never having had a Missis, he had no means of comparing or contrasting her with others. All he knew was that somehow she had ceased to hurl abuse at him and did not mention the sjambok.

Mrs Hopgood knew much better than the subject how successfully her scheme was developing. Within a week Bulalie had overcome his conversational shyness, and talked freely to his mistress.

She had noticed that he was reticent on one subject – the circumstances of his leaving his kraal, and connected it with the diamond. One day she made a bold shot at a venture.

'Have the police ever tried to find out where you have hidden your brother's klippie?' she asked with fine indifference.

Bulalie was completely thrown off his guard.

'Do they know I have it?' he asked in alarm.

'Of course they do. White men are very clever; they can find out anything they wish to know.'

Bulalie's heart began to beat hard.

The Missis saw that her shot had got home.

'They are coming to look for the klippie,' she went on. 'If they find it they will not give it to you again, but will take you to prison and flog you till the bones show.'

Bulalie was getting horribly scared. The Missis continued, 'I should not like them to do that. You are a good boy, and I am going to give you two pounds a month when you have learned a little more.'

She waited for this item to sink in. Bulalie was obviously gratified, but not demonstrative. He had asked two pounds when he was engaged, and quite expected it.

'If the police take you you will be away a long time, and I shall have to get another boy. You had better let me keep the klippie for you, then the police will not find it or take you.'

Bulalie had partially got over the scare caused by the blunt announcement; the quiet disinterested manner of the Missis reassured him.

'They will not find it,' he said confidently.

'Yes they will. You have hidden it in this yard, and the police will pull every stick and stone apart. If you won't let me keep it for you, you must take it away. I won't have the police hurt my property for the sake of a worthless bit of stone that may not even be a Kimberley.'

'But it is,' Bulalie protested.

'Bring it to me tonight after dinner and I will tell you. It is right that I should know what is hidden in my place.'

Then Mrs Hopgood, knowing she had sown her seed on the right ground, curtly dismissed the boy to his duties.

Bulalie made Dick his confidant and asked his advice. The wily youth was prepared for this. He assured his friend that he had known for some time that the police had been seeking him, but did not know the reason till he had seen the diamond. He had, he said, been interrogated by a policeman on the subject, and though he was sworn to secrecy, he felt bound to tell Bulalie that the police were coming to search the place, probably that very night. He strongly advised handing the stone for safety to the Missis.

Bulalie surrendered after holding out an hour or two longer. He removed the klippie from the hole in a fence-post and handed it to his Missis.

Mrs Hopgood gave a gasp of astonishment when she examined the stone in the privacy of her bedroom. It was a diamond of 150 carats at least, perfect in colour, worth – she felt giddy when she made a mental effort to assess its value. It was the largest stone she had seen, so large and perfect that the difficulty of turning it into money would be fifty times greater than if it had been half the size. But whatever its value she knew she was now a rich woman, and that her life as the slave of an exacting crowd of boarders was over.

Her elation was noticed at the dinner table that evening. Insolently strong in her sense of coming freedom, she indulged in a luxury for which she had often yearned – courage to resent the cavilling complaints of old Mr Jones and tell him what she thought of him. When he mildly suggested that he was entitled to receive what he paid for, and that even if she was the lady she claimed to be she was none the less in the position of one who had engaged to give certain service in return for certain payments, she haughtily expressed the satisfaction she felt in being able to inform Mr Jones that she would shortly be quite independent of him.

That speech was destined to rise up in judgment against her in the not remote aftertime.

Continuing the foolish policy of abusing the bridge that had carried her over, Mrs Hopgood dropped Bulalie as suddenly as she had taken him up. The first time he opened up a conversation, he was brusquely admonished to talk less and work more, and within a week had been abused and threatened as often as before the transference of the diamond. He was puzzled, and began to think uncomfortable thoughts, especially when the Missis twice pointedly intimated that if certain trifling errors were repeated he would be sent away.

But the thing that weighed most with Bulalie was the non-appearance of the police. He had come to expect and look for them, with the faith of a child in the fulfilment of a pleasant promise. He had thought over what he should say and how he would comport himself when questioned; but no opportunity came for testing his conduct in the hour of trial.

One day he was sent to the police-station by his Missis with a note. He went with the calm resignation of a martyr.

A marvellous thing happened. Although he was kept waiting for half an hour, while constables, white and black, passed in and out, although he was asked his name, not a word or sign was made to show that he was wanted at the station.

He did not know that he was merely the bearer of a complaint by his Missis against the nuisance caused by noisy kafirs in the adjacent yard. It was sufficient for him to know that he had run the gauntlet of the police. He no longer feared them, neither did he now believe the alarming stories of Dick and the Missis.

He waited till the midday meal was over, and the Missis preparing for her afternoon sleep, then boldly entered the house and whispered:–

'Please, Missis, give me my klippie. I want it.'

Mrs Hopgood, big and muscular though she was, felt her heart beat, and Bulalie noticed that she turned pale. A foreboding of evil possessed him.

'I must have it, Missis,' he pleaded.

She was at the door of her bedroom, and entering, was about to shut out the impertinent importunate. He followed her, and had one foot inside the room, one hand on the door.

'Go away, you brute,' she said, slightly raising her voice.

'Give me my klippie. It is there.'

He pointed to a little leather bag attached to a chatelaine chain in which she had placed the stone when he handed it to her.

'Go away. I have no klippie,' she said.

Bulalie uttered a cry of alarm and snatched at the bag. As he advanced he pushed the half-closed door against her, and she stumbled backwards, uttering a piercing shriek, which developed into hysterical cries of 'O, you blackguard! How dare you! Dick! Mr Jones!'

There was a scurry in the passage. Several persons crowded round the door. Bulalie was struck violently on the neck and fell against a washstand, which cracked and scattered. Mrs Hopgood continued to shriek. More people came in from the street, and all struck at Bulalie with some extemporised weapon till he was dazed and bleeding.

The contents bill of the evening paper had extra big lines that afternoon:—

KAFIR OUTRAGE ON WHITE WOMAN!
MISCREANT CAPTURED!

CHAPTER IX

FOR THE DEFENCE

The newspapers almost doubled their circulation next day. The latest kafir outrage came as an agreeable variant on the perpetual theme that keeps the Natal press full – the greed and aggression of the Cape and the Orange River Colonies. A mass of railway statistics tending to show that Natal was getting only nineteen twentieths of the carrying trade to the Transvaal was sacrificed to make room for the latest exemplification of the native peril. The leading journal told the story with its customary judicial impartiality.

'Another of those startling outrages which too frequently provoke husbands and brothers to yearn for an introduction of the drastic methods of American lynchers has to be reported.

'Yesterday afternoon, Mrs Hopgood, the well-known proprietress of the boarding establishment in King Street, had just retired to her bedroom after luncheon, when she was induced to open the door by hearing herself called in a whisper by her kitchen boy, a big truculent-looking Zulu named Bulalie. The boy asked for a shilling, and Mrs Hopgood was in the act of taking the coin from a bag she carries at her waist, when the scoundrel made a sudden rush into the room, seized her with one hand and with the other attempted to close the door. A severe struggle ensued, in the course of which Mrs Hopgood was thrown savagely to the floor. She defended herself courageously and her calls for help brought prompt assistance and doubtless prevented the perpetration of as infamous a crime as ever horrified the Colony. The miscreant was secured and handed over to the police and will be brought before the magistrate this morning.

'Great credit is due to the tact and promptitude of Sergeant Jones, who was ably assisted by Constables Roberts, Webb and Watson. Messrs. A. Bates, R. Wiltshire and Samuels, of Samuels & Co., harness makers, also lent timely aid in capturing the kafir, who made no resistance.

'Enquiries late last night showed that the victim of the outrage was recovering from the shock, and will probably be able to appear against her brutal assailant this morning.'

Mrs Hopgood was able to appear at the police court, where, having been accommodated with a seat and a glass of water, she told the story much as reported in the paper, speaking in a subdued tone, and comporting herself with a quiet dignity that did much to augment the large sympathy of the spectators.

In reply to the questions of the polite Chief Constable who prosecuted, she said that Bulalie had no grievance that she was aware of, he having always been treated with the kindness and consideration her native servants received, though she had on one or two occasions found it necessary to repress certain attempts at freedom on the part of the boy.

At the conclusion of her evidence Bulalie was formally asked if he had any question to put to the witness and promptly demanded to know why she refused to give him back his klippie.

Mrs Hopgood smiled and shook her head when the question was interpreted. She hadn't the slightest notion what he meant, she said.

Bulalie began a statement but was at once ordered to be quiet. If he had no further questions to put he must reserve his statement for another time, the magistrate explained.

Bulalie subsided.

The evidence of the lodgers who had assisted in the capture of the prisoner was taken, and the hearing adjourned for a week to afford some enterprising law agent an opportunity of taking up the case if the accused had money to pay him. Bulalie having been securely handcuffed was marched with twenty other unfortunates through the streets to the jail.

He was duly interviewed by Mr Darter, the tout and manager of the very extensive business of Welcome and Barber, who made a speciality of taking up native and Indian cases, and were in consequence looked down on and envied by the more dignified section of the profession; for they were making money by the hatful.

Mr Darter was Colonial born, and knew both kafir and Indian thoroughly. He had made money out of them as storekeeper, labour agent for the mines, boss of a sugar planation and caterer for the supply of food for Indian coolies, and had turned his peculiar knowledge to good account by financing the youthful and struggling firm of Welcome and Barber in which he was nominally managing clerk of the native department, which meant everything, for very few white clients were on the books.

Mr Darter was a young man who would have succeeded as a commercial traveller for an unpopular firm. He was strangely un-Colonial in his push, tact and resourcefulness, and as he was never likely to be struck off the rolls for malpractice, not being on them, he was recognised as the man who will some day redress the wrong under which Natal writhes – the gradual absorption of its land by the successful Indian. In the fulness of time there will not be many kafirs in the Colony whose cattle and possessions are not mortgaged to Richard Darter, alias Welcome and Barber, as security for law costs.

He spoke kindly and depressingly to Bulalie, told him he was very foolish to assult his missis, and that years of imprisonment and countless lashes were his certain fate unless he was properly represented at the trial by a man who knew how to soften the heart of the judge. How much money had Bulalie.

Eight shillings and such of the month's wage of a pound as might be due to him was all that the frightened boy could promise.

Mr Darter was in no wise discouraged. He had many a time taken five shillings on account from a native client and ended by getting possession of a hundred pounds worth of oxen and a lien on the produce of the remainder for five years to come. He questioned Bulalie as to his kraal, his people, his prospects as heir to the paternal estate.

Bulalie did not wish to involve his people, so gave evasive replies, but Mr Darter's business largely consisted in interesting friends and relations in the misfortunes of their kinsmen. If he depended for fees on what he got out of the actual parties to an action or prosecution he would not make £5 000 a year and 'possibles.' He had sold up many a kraal and ruined scores of fathers, uncles and brothers through appealing to the clannishness of the native and persuading them that it was their duty to assist a relation in distress by guaranteeing the costs of the defence.

The case which had established his reputation as the smartest man in the business had at first been much less promising than this of Bulalie.

The ten-year-old son of a petty chief seriously hurt a white boy while playing with him, and was promptly given into custody. Within a few hours of hearing of the case Mr Darter was interviewing the little kafir's father in his kraal, pointing out that the death of the victim and hanging of the murderer were inevitable in the absence of proper defence.

He returned to Maritzburg with three pounds in cash – all the old kafir could raise – and a properly drawn authority to sell as many of the father's oxen as were necessary to discharge future liabilities.

He had omitted to mention that the chief of police had refused to take the charge, the proof that the injury was a pure accident being conclusive.

A few days later he again visited the father, explained how by the expenditure of money, skill and eloquence he had secured the acquittal of the youth, and proceeded to collect his bill. Ten oxen worth at current prices eight pounds apiece were driven into town and put up for sale at an inconvenient time, and in the absence of purchasers bought in by an agent of the astute Mr Darter for three pounds apiece, which left the kafir still twenty pounds in debt. Other cattle were seized under the terms of the agreement, but somehow failed to fetch anything like half their value when put up to auction.

When nearly two hundred pounds worth of cattle had been seized and sold, and the debt, expanded by 'interest and costs of collection', continued to remain in the neighbourhood of twenty pounds, a mischief-making farmer got hold of the story, and incited the kafir to lay the case before the local magistrate who privately reprimanded Mr Darter.

That resourceful gentleman promptly commenced an action for slander against the farmer, who frankly withdrew his calumnies and paid £25 to avert litigation. The farmer had no alternative but pay and look to the kafir for reimbursement. He put in a claim for £30 against the native, retained Mr Darter's services and the case took its place in the books of Welcome and Barber as a permanent asset of the firm.

Thus it came about that the firm of Welcome and Barber got their reputation for making money by never going into court.

Mr Darter pressed Bulalie on the subject of his relations, but could get nothing. His quick perception enabled him to guess that there was a reason for his reticence. He resolved to look up his client's domestic record – a process comparatively easy. When however Bulalie told with certain reservations the story of the handing over of the diamond to Mrs Hopgood, Mr Darter grew keenly interested, and succeeded in extracting much more information than his simple client guessed he had imparted. He further learned that Sekoos was the bailie of certain valuables, and after cautioning Bulalie to preserve silence he departed.

Mr Darter was a hard, whole-hearted worker. Had Bulalie paid as lavishly as an Indian coolie, his case could not have received more attention from his legal adviser. The charge and its consequences did not worry the manager. He knew that there could be no defence, since it was only a matter of the assertion of a white woman against the denial of a kafir. The business of Mr Darter consisted in making sure that he would be well paid for undertaking the unpopular task of identifying his firm with a case which no lawyer who cared for public opinion dare appear in.

Secretly, Mr Darter fully believed Bulalie's version, but the private opinions of a legal adviser could not be allowed to influence business.

He interviewed Sekoos at the hotel, and half an hour later locked up in his private safe about fifty pounds worth of jewellery, which showed that it is foolishness to accept the statement of a kafir when he pleads poverty, and more than foolish to decline to take up a case because the client appears to be poor.

The investigation of the affair of the diamond would have to be conducted very carefully. Mrs Hopgood was not a kafir and not so easily intimidated.

Bulalie did not feel very unhappy the first day or two. There was so much that was novel to distract him. It was like being with the road party again, not alone because of the number of kafirs, but because there were so many there that he knew, either working out their punishment, or, like himself, waiting to receive it.

He was only passing through a stage of the civilising process that is undergone sooner or later by every native who leaves his native kraal. Natalians are sensitive on the subject of native punitive statistics, therefore even had Bulalie wished to know, he would have experienced some difficulty in learning from official sources the chances he or any other kafir had of keeping out of jail.

He met six of the boys who had been with the road party during his own brief connection with it, and probably a score of kafirs whose acquaintance he had made in Maritzburg, so that he could not well feel lonely. The nature of the charge against him was known to every kafir in the jail before he had been there an hour, for news travels fast in kafirdom.

He received much sympathy, from which he gathered that his conviction and flogging were foregone conclusions. He had a grave suspicion to that effect himself, for he had learned much from Dick at night in the sleeping hut.

One old Basuto who took no pains to conceal the fact that he had several times been tied up to the triangle, was very depressing. He told Bulalie he was a great fool to do what he had, but, he added, 'It is well for a young man to get his lashes early, for he can bear them better, and it helps to make him learn to fear them, so that he may not have the pain and shame of them when he is older.'

Nobody spoke of the case except to show that they knew Bulalie to be doomed, so he refrained from telling his version or discussing his trouble, partly because Mr Darter had enjoined silence, partly because the subject was not pleasant and his comforters had no plan for helping him.

One thing gave him a little satisfaction. He had heard that Bacheta was in the jail, and feared very much having to confess to him the folly that had brought this trouble and lost the klippie. He learned that his friend had been sent off some weeks ago to work at another jail, and he rejoiced, though, but for the wrong he had done him, he would have been glad to have his comradeship in the jail. Bacheta was not so wise as Dick but Bulalie could not forget his first instructor.

Life in the prison was not nearly so bad as Bulalie had feared. Natal officialism is severe and strict, often inconsiderate in its treatment of the native who comes under its penal provisions, but in the concrete it is not brutal. It is not a mere figure of speech the Colonial employs when he declares in his wrath that imprisonment is no deterrent to the kafir. Short terms of detention certainly are not; long periods reduce him to apathetic animalism. His one real terror is the lash, yet it whistles daily, and the average number of lashes laid on yearly keeps proportionate pace with the increase in the kafir population and justifies those irritating and abnormal curiosities of Colonial life, negrophilists who argue from the increasing figures that the lash is no deterrent.

The silent system is mercifully unenforced on natives in Colonial prisons. The warder in charge of a working party restrains their garrulity because it might interfere with their work, but inside the jail, and particularly in their cells, where they are crowded in batches, they chatter incessantly. The old hand boasts of his undetected crimes, the tyro, of those he would commit if he had the opportunity, and learns more infamy while expiating one trifling offence than could be atoned for by a life sentence.

Bulalie found it highly diverting, and within four days the only anticipatory terror his coming conviction had for him was the lashes.

They haunted him sleeping and waking. He found himself looking at every back that was bared in his presence, for those ugly furrows that were the most ineradicable childhood's impression of this dead father. He had often when bathing in the water hole looked at the reflection of his own smooth, shapely shoulders and wondered if they would ever become disfigured like his father's. He nurtured a fervent hope that he would escape. It was not impossible. He had known several young men who had been years among the white men come back to the kraals with no sign of the lash upon them. Now that hope was dead; it had given place to another – the hope that the lashes would be laid on by a white warder and not by a kafir. It is the earnest prayer of every victim before he is made fast to the triangle and a subject of anxious speculation.

Mr Darter came twice to see Bulalie. He was more desirous of learning all he could about the diamond than of discussing his client's version of the outrage. He had apparently satisfied himself that no financial assistance was to be obtained from Bulalie's kraal, for he did not mention his relations. Neither did he tell how Sekoos had called on him with a sovereign and a promise to bring another towards the defence of his friend, when he received his next pay. He got a very full description of the diamond, and took the peg that had been its hiding place. Bulalie described how the klippie had filled the entire hole, and Mr Darter's greedy eyes dilated with astonishment.

By way of an after thought, just as he was leaving, he told his client that he would go before the magistrate on the morrow, that he was to say nothing, but wait till the great trial came.

Bulalie's heart gave a little jump of sadness, for he had, during the long nights, thought several times that, after all, the missis might be content to keep the klippie and tell the jailer to let him go, because she must know that he had been much more hurt than she was. His face and arms were still sore with the hard blows that the men gave him when they dragged him away.

He put his thoughts into words, and asked Mr Darter to tell the missis that she might keep the klippie if she would say he might leave the jail.

Mr Darter looked very angry. 'Why should I do that, when I am going to make her give the klippie back and tell the magistrate to let you out of jail?'

Bulalie was filled with sudden joy. He clapped his hand to his mouth and shouted 'Au!' and paid no attention to Mr Darter's repeated warning against mentioning the klippie in court or jail.

'I am going out soon,' he said to the prisoners in his cell.

The old Basuto looked at him pityingly; the younger men laughed.

Bulalie did go out next morning. He went to the police court and listened while the lodgers and the policemen told how they had dragged him away from the prostrate body of his mistress. They told of many things that were new to Bulalie, but he was not angry. What mattered it what they said now? He had reckoned up the days to the big trial. They were forty-two. Yesterday when he believed that the lashes were coming he was glad that the days were so many, now he was sorry, but perhaps they would go quicker seeing that he was happy.

The interpreter asked him if he had anything to say before the magistrate spoke.

Bulalie remembered the instructions of Mr Darter and answered 'No', loudly and cheerfully, and smiled when he saw that the people in court seemed surprised at his boldness and loudness of speech.

The reporter also remarked it. 'The prisoner on being asked if he had anything to say shouted "Ikona!" in defiant tones, and laughed as he was removed. On the way to the jail he skipped and sang as though he regarded his crime as a huge joke.'

Thus the paper next morning.

CHAPTER X

MERCY AND JUSTICE

Dreary, long and anxious were the days to Bulalie. There was nothing to do but eat and sleep and talk of the cases of the kafirs, who were coming in every day. Of his own troubles he had ceased to speak, because all that was to be said had been said so often. He waited and watched with hungry eyes and ears for Mr Darter, who now and then came in to consult with fresh clients, but he always passed out so quickly that there was no chance of speaking with him. Once Bulalie ventured to call his name as he passed. Mr Darter looked round and nodded but did not speak. On another day Bulalie went up to him while he was speaking with a kafir client, and asked in a whisper, 'Has the missis given up the klippie yet?'

Mr Darter became very angry. 'Never speak to me again till I speak to you,' he said. 'If you do I will have nothing to do with your case.'

Bulalie went away very sad, for he had foolishly told his friends in his cell that he was going to hear good news the next time his lawyer came.

And so the days went very slowly. Sometimes Bulalie was happy with hope, but mostly quiet and sad with fear, for he heard no news, only things that made him dread the day of the great trial.

There were many floggings in the jail, and the knowledge of them made Bulalie feel very sick. He did not see them, for they took place in a small yard hidden by a high wall, but he always knew when they were going on, because the doctor only went to that part of the jail when there were kafirs to be lashed. He used to see the flogged natives afterwards, and often wished to ask them something about it, but they all kept their lips shut tightly for days, and Bulalie learned that they did this because if they opened their mouths they could not help screaming with the pain which would make them appear like women, or coolies, or Shangaans, who always scream at the triangle and long after they are untied.

All day Bulalie had nothing to do but sit in the cell with the rest of the prisoners waiting like himself for the great trial, or outside in the sun, when the white baas who looked after the untried prisoners was in a good temper. But most of the time he was shut up, and as his cell was at the end of a long passage it was very gloomy and the nights there were very long.

At last came the day before the great trial, and Bulalie waited till his heart was sore to see Mr Darter. When the time came for locking up and no one had been to see him about the morrow, he could have cried out loud with the pain of his disappointment. He could not sleep all that night and when the time came for opening the cell he was weak and dazed with the hard and painful thoughts of the night.

For one short minute a great flash of happiness lighted his eyes and made his heart jump. As he passed out of the cell the Zulu warder said:

'You will not come back again.'

'No, I leave this place today,' Bulalie answered joyfully.

'Yes,' said the Zulu. 'Tonight you sleep over there.'

He pointed to the part of the jail where the convicted prisoners were, and Bulalie's hope died.

There were many kafirs to be dealt with at the great trial that day, but only a few were taken to the court, and Bulalie was among them. They were handcuffed in twos, and marched to the court, the white prisoners walking in front with their hats pulled over their eyes and their collars turned up so that the people who stopped to look should not know them.

All day was Bulalie kept shut up in a gloomy passage waiting. Two of his friends were taken to the court and tried, but his name was not called. He heard from the native guard that they had been convicted but not ordered to be flogged, so his heart was glad for himself.

Three times was Bulalie taken to the court, and on the third day Mr Darter came and took him to the end of the passage to a little room, where no one could hear them.

'You are going to be tried, today,' he said.

'When they ask you if you plead guilty or not guilty, you must say "guilty", and your punishment will not be so great.'

Bulalie could scarcely speak from surprise and anger. When he did he said:

'But I am not guilty. Is not the missis going to keep the klippie and let me go, or is what you have told me not true?'

'It is not wise for you to deny what she and all the white witnesses will say. The judge will not believe you, so do as I tell you. Am I not very wise in these things?' was all that Mr Darter would say.

Before Bulalie could speak again he heard his name called. A policeman took him roughly by the arm and partly led and pushed him up some steps, and before he quite understood where he was, he was standing in a long narrow space with a bench behind him.

When his eyes got used to the dullness he saw many white men sitting at a long table, more white men in a big box by the side of the wall, and a white man in a strange black garment sitting high up and writing in a book.

He looked round for Mr Darter, but could not see him. He did not know that the connection of his legal adviser with the case had concluded. Messrs Welcome and Barber might not stand very high in the esteem of the public, but they were not foolish enough to outrage public sentiment by attempting to avert punishment from a kafir who had perpetrated an offence against society much more reprehensible than murder by a white man. Even had they been paid by their client — or rather by the kafir whom their Mr Darter had advised in his capacity as a clerk — they would not find any member of the bar reckless and unpatriotic enough to undertake the defence of such a case. Advocates had done such things, and paid the penalty in social ostracism, and what was worse, loss of business.

Therefore Bulalie had to meet the most serious charge that could be brought against a native by committing another crime.

When formally charged through the interpreter he boldly declared that all that the missis had said was lies! Not content with openly impugning the veracity of a white woman who had sworn on oath to the truth of her statement, he accused her of theft!

'The missis has got my klippie, and when I asked her for it she screamed.' This was Bulalie's answer to the indictment.

He conducted himself and his defence in an exceedingly foolish manner. Instead of confining himself to the point at issue he contradicted witnesses, receiving their statements with absurd expressions of surprise and disapproval that kept the court in a ripple of laughter. As to cross-examining and convicting them out of their own mouths of inconsistency or the misstatements of which he interjected disapproval, he had not the slightest notion, allowing many excellent opportunities of making a point to pass, although the Judge more than once gave him a hint as to the line he should take by putting a question to a witness for him as it ought to be put.

Mrs Hopgood made a very great impression. She was handsomely dressed, and looked well. She gave her evidence with commendable absence of any bias or strong feeling, and as the newspaper expressed it, in its leading article on 'The Black Peril', next day, 'won the admiration and sympathy of every person in court by the courage with which she came through an ordeal to which no white woman would be submitted if our supine authorities had but the courage to do what, sooner or later they must — impose the death penalty for infamous offences of this character.'

When at the end of her examination-in-chief the prisoner was told he might now ask the prosecutrix any question, Bulalie convulsed the court by demanding:

'Where is my klippie? Why did you not give it me?'

Mrs Hopgood looked appealingly at judge and jury, but did not answer.

His Lordship was very sympathetic.

'Do you understand the question?' he asked.

She shook her head. 'I haven't the slightest notion what he means.'

'Any other question?' the Clerk of the Court asked.

'What is the good of asking her anything? she only lies,' was the impudent response, and — quoting the observant reporter — 'The prisoner sat down with a savage scowl, and listened to the remainder of the evidence with callous indifference, now and then making some irreverent and impudent ejaculation, but sullenly refusing to ask any further questions.'

The Judge summed up at some length, not that it was necessary, but because he was always fair to natives. The jury had long since made up their minds, and they had heard or read His Lordship's opinions on the kafir question so often that they did not need to be reminded of their duty. There was one point, however, which appealed to them. He hoped, he said, they would not allow themselves to be biassed in one direction or another by the attempt of the prisoner to insinuate that his mistress had condescended to steal something from him. They who knew the native need not be told that it was no uncommon trick to attempt to justify one wrong by imputing another to the accuser.

Without retiring, the jury brought in a unanimous verdict of guilty, and with an expression of fear that he had allowed mercy to temper justice too far, the Judge sentenced Bulalie to two years' hard labour to be preceded by the infliction of twenty lashes.

*　　*　　*　　*　　*

Had the reporter who had flattered and encouraged popular prejudice by describing and inferring that Bulalie was a callous brute who gloried in his crime, been able to see him that evening when he entered the cell, he would have felt justified in his misrepresentations. Had he been, on the other hand, a man with some knowledge of human nature, black and white, he would have seen in the light-hearted, even flippant conduct of the young kafir a confirmation of a strange but familiar paradox — that the realisation of the worst often brings exquisite relief and content.

For forty days and almost as many nights Bulalie had lived on the torture frame. The thought of the lashes in store obsessed and terrorised him. He talked lashes, thought lashes, dreamed lashes; and when, as occasionally happened, something momentarily drove the whip and triangle from thought and vision, they were brought back by the sight of some recent victim of civilisation's chief instrument limping painfully across the prison yard with head and shoulders bunched forward, and the compressed lips stifling the groans that manhood reprobated.

There are those skilled in the diagnosis of the native who profess to be able to detect at a glance a kafir or Indian who has 'passed the triangle', however far distant the event. Be that as it may, outward and visible sign of the inward agony is always so pronounced, so unlike the signals of suffering held out by any other form of physical pain, that it is not straining credulity too much to believe those who say they can conceive no torture more horrible than that of the lash in skilled hands. Certainly no victim ever passed through the ordeal unchanged mentally and physically. All this in a vague way Bulalie had learned, first in childhood from his thrice lacerated father, later from the talk of his cell companions.

The horror of anticipation had at last given way to certainty. He now was free from the torturing suspense of hope and fear, and the reaction expressed itself in childish, semi-hysterical ebullition.

He entered the cell limping, with body bent, hands on back, howling in imitation of one just released from the triangle. It was his jocular method of announcing the result of the trial. This was followed by a burst of hysterical laughter that brought the warder to the door shouting 'Tula!' (Silence!)

It was also a reminder to Bulalie that he was now a convict under strict control, not a mere *détenu*.

He squatted on the stone floor and told his companions of the trial.

There was no complaint, no whining assertion of unfair treatment, no impeachment of judge or jury, only a regret that he had forgotten to say several things that he had rehearsed. Then came a burst of jubilation.

'I called the missis a liar!' he said, 'and she couldn't say anything.'

He told this a dozen times before he slept. The recollection of that piece of retaliation atoned for much, past and to come.

'How bad is twenty?' Bulalie asked of the oldest kafir in the cell, who had passed the triangle once some years ago.

He shrugged his shoulders.

'As bad as the warder who lays them on,' he answered, summing in one sentence the whole case against the inequality and unfairness of flogging as a punishment.

The law assesses it in quantity, the warder by quality. If he be an expert – and it argues gross neglect of opportunity if he is not – he can lay on fifty without causing more suffering than that felt by a birched schoolboy; or he can cut strips of flesh from quarter-inch deep furrows with ten. The only question is, how bad or how good is the wielder of the cat.

There were to be four other victims at the triangle in the morning. Three sheep stealers had been awarded exactly the same penalty as Bulalie, by the Judge of the Native High Court. Sheep stealing only differs in enormity from the crime of assaulting white women in the opinion of the town folk who have no sheep. They are not in favour of hanging for a sheep; it would reduce the native population too rapidly, especially in times of famine and crop failure, for a hungry kafir is woefully destitute of conscience, and the more children he has the more unscrupulous.

The fourth was a young Basuto who had been carrying the racial love of the horse to the point of excess. He had collected several at various parts of the Colony and had begun to make a reputation. Three years and twenty-five lashes were his portion, and as he was the first to be operated upon he came off lightest, despite the extra five, for the warder had not got his hand and wrist in good working order until he had practised on one back.

Bulalie had been taken to the flogging place early. The doctor looked him over well, applied the stethoscope and decided that the patient was fit for treatment. He looked it. His tall, well-formed figure was firm and well covered with flesh without a wrinkle.

His quick eye showed him that his desire was to be fulfilled. It was a white man, not a kafir, who stood waiting with the cat.

He pulled off his shirt and extended his legs and arms to be strapped to the triangle without any prompting. It was the action of an old hand. The warder looked closely at the bared back for a sign. It was smooth and glossy. He laid on the first hissing outspread lash before Bulalie was ready, for he sprang upwards as far as the bonds would permit, and let out a quick gasp as one who unexpectedly receives a cold douche.

Then he braced himself rigidly, forgetting that the old Basuto had told him it made the lashes cut less deeply if one stood with the body loose. He counted up to eight, and then ceased, for he felt a scream rising in his throat that required all his thought and strength to keep down.

A tiny clot of flesh and blood flew past and settled on the triangle just where his eyes rested. He looked at it and wondered whether more would come. It must have been pieces like that which came from the back of his father and left those big furrows that he used to put his baby fingers into. Several times he had to clench his teeth and turn his tongue back in his mouth to keep back the scream that was trying so hard to come up, and once he thought he must let it come, not so much because of the agony as from shame and anger, for the water was blinding his eyes; he was shedding big tears as women do. He could hold back the scream no more; it came up, loud and broken and with it, words:

'Baas, baas, my heart is dead!' Four times more red hot wires twined round his body, then they stopped.

He turned his head to look over his shoulder, but the water would not let him see. He knew that they were doing something to his back. He felt something soft and cool, and then came a mountain of stinging, throbbing pain that could not be borne and Bulalie screamed as only strong men do at the triangle.

They untied his wrists and ankles, pulled on his shirt and led him to the cell. They were very gentle with him, for they knew that only a very small part of the punishment had been borne; that for many hours he would lie on his face in agony, while the furrows on his back healed; that every movement would bring a pang of pain sharper and more prolonged than the stroke of the lash; that he would have to take in and let out his breath slowly, and in gentle insufflations lest the movement tore apart the healing wounds; that he would suffer burning thirst but dare not move to put his lips to the water, and all this through hot days and hotter nights, while flies, mosquitos and worse, crawled over his naked body and revived the tortures of the lash. And when he would sleep because the pain was dulled for a space, his ears would be filled with the groans and cries of the others who lay beside him on the hard planks, four victims of the same hideous torture that was no throb the less because it had been earned and might have been avoided.

CHAPTER XI

THE PROGRESS OF ANNA

Few men pass through the ordeal of the solitary life of the wilds without undergoing a marked change of character. Most degenerate; some are chastened, renewed, and come back to their fellows with strangely broadened views of life and their part in it. The majority drowsily sink into the slough of physical and mental sluggishness, and yield without a struggle to the promptings 'to do as all men ever would – own no master but their mood.' The animalistic, self-indulgent man approximates yet nearer the animal; the intellectually active, destitute of the stimulant of conversation and encounter with diverse opinion and nimble wits, becomes an intellectual fungoid.

David Hyslop was saved from mental decadence through finding most of his preconceived ideas challenged by the experience of the days. Instead of coming to teach, he discovered he had first to learn, and in the process, to discard many pleasant prejudices and illusions.

It had taken him the better part of a year to assimilate these stern facts. The process had been painful, for it had revealed the state of innocence and inexperience that was his when he permitted his naturally enthusiastic and emotional nature to be swayed by what he then honestly believed to be the call to the mission field. He had dedicated himself to a task whose nature was hidden in the haze of romance.

Thrice he had resolved to act upon his conclusion that it was his duty to abandon an undertaking for which he not only felt himself unfitted but superfluous. He had actually at times questioned the utility and morality of mission work, as conducted on the lines approved and laid down by those who controlled and directed him.

But on each occasion, when the paper was prepared to receive his avowal of defeat and plea for recall, the bar across the disc of the moon, actual or subjective, had stirred him to throw down the reluctant pen with the cry, 'O, ye of little faith!'

For many weary months he had been sustained and saved from despondency by the regular letters of the little governess who found grateful surcease of sorrow from her task of trying to instil elementary intelligence and decency into the untrained children of a Cape Colonial, by writing words of cheer and comfort to the young missionary a thousand miles on the other side of the range of mountains that shadowed her home.

Alice Lister was as sincere and ardent a daughter of the Church as ever sought to pioneer the euthanasia of the religious life in the spiritual Sahara of South Africa. An orphan, brought up in an atmosphere of sacrificing piety and strict sacerdotalism, she had taken advantage of the necessity of earning her own living to gratify an ambition of her girlhood's fancy. Africa had always exercised a vague but potent spell, and when an ill-paid position as governess in the family of a Member of the Cape Assembly offered, she accepted it with delighted alacrity.

The vessel that brought her carried another religious enthusiast, and community of interest preserved by regular and unrestricted correspondence had ended as poetic justice demanded. After a twelvemonth's interchange of emotions, David Hyslop had gratified her heart's desire by asking Alice Lister to become his co-worker and wife. She had accepted without any pretence of coyness or surprise.

Time and money being a consideration, he had met his bride at Durban, where they were married quietly in the presence of the only persons known to either of them – an English clergyman and his wife on their way to England, then proceeded up country to the station at Blue Krantz.

They stayed at several farmhouses *en route*, where Mrs Hyslop captured the sympathy of their hosts completely. Her slight girlish figure, with dark hair and eyes, and the *spirituelle* face one associates with sweet young nuns, appealed to the women, whose hearts were touched by knowledge of the fate of desolate isolation that this child was welcoming with the ardour of ignorance. Few had the courage to dishearten her by hinting at the horrors of life in a native location, but one farmer's wife was not so reticent. She deplored the wilful obstinacy that would induce a girl to surrender life in a civilised town for the repellent coarseness and discomfort of association with filthy kafirs, and did not hesitate to say that while she could understand a man wanting a wife to share his loneliness, she had no patience with the inconsiderate selfishness of one who would permit a delicate young girl to sacrifice herself. As to this particular man – well, she didn't want to be rude, but she certainly thought he might be better employed than in teaching kafirs to be discontented with the lot God had chosen for them and giving them ideas that they were as good as whites.

The missionary accepted the rebuke good naturedly and made no serious attempt to reply. He was used to such criticism, but he wished it had not been uttered in the presence of his wife, for he knew the existence of hostility to missions among Christian whites would come as a painful shock to her. He tried to turn the subject, but Mrs Hyslop with surprise and grief in her expressive face began justifying by a scriptural quotation.

'Yes, my dear, I know the Bible says that. It says a good many things that we can't act up to. But wait till you know a little more about the kafir. You'll have quite enough of him on earth without wanting his company in Heaven.'

The young girl was too horrified to speak. She looked appealingly at her husband. An outburst of vulgar blasphemy would not have hurt and surprised her more.

The conscience of David Hyslop asserted itself. He was reminded that he had wilfully deceived his wife by several references to the 'hearty sympathy of his white neighbours.' He had old Boggis in his mind when he wrote that, but why did he speak of him in the plural? Simply because he was fearful of telling the truth. The young wife had several things to find out for herself that her husband had refrained from mentioning in his glowing letters.

A load was lifted from his heart by the first words she uttered on seeing the shabby mud and tin packing case that was to be her home. He had been long enough in the country to know that the first sight of a Colonial home is generally a severe shock to an English woman doomed to share it.

'What a dear little place!' was her cheering comment as she entered the little enclosure of sunflowers that formed the boundary fence, assisted by a few prickly pear bushes and straggling creepers.

He expressed his gratitude and thanks in a heartfelt kiss.

The young husband was thankful that his wife knew no word of Zulu. He tendered this as an explanation of the sullen silence with which the houseboy and the one or two natives about the establishment received their mistress. He had not the courage to acquaint her with the truth − to explain that the raw kafir, used to regard the woman as the inferior, resents the domination of a 'missis'. He can understand being ordered about by a white man, but by a woman − ow!

The young governess's experience as a resident in a civilised home in a highly civilised and long settled portion of Cape Colony had not afforded opportunity for acquaintance with the raw native. The only coloured people she had met lived in towns, wore ragged cast-off European clothing, spoke English or Dutch, and were of the ninety and nine who had no need for repentance. The kafir of Natal was as delightfully novel and unclothed as he appeared in the story books and missionary reports, and she was glad, for the educative process she was burning to begin would not be handicapped by the prior efforts of others. She rejoiced in the knowledge that she was the first white woman to take up residence in this native location.

It became a case of charity and mercy beginning at home. The reorganisation of the house engaged the attention of Mrs Hyslop for some days. Mere 'tidying-up' would have been farcical. The effects of twelve months of bachelor neglect were not remedied easily, and as young wives, whatever their qualifications, have pronounced views on the ordering and arranging of a home in which they are to be mistress, the husband had good reason for blessing the climate which permitted him to live out of doors or on the verandah while the work of domestic reform was going on under the roof.

Mrs Hyslop was prevailed upon to deal mercifully with the ten by ten cubicle which formed her husband's library, and sanctum, though only after many protests and the issuing of an ultimatum. The sitting-room and bedroom he handed over for sack and despoilment without a murmur, and after having it proved to him that a kitchen that consisted of a sheet of iron leaning against the back wall was scarcely a fit place for a young wife to prove her capacity in, Mr Hyslop joined forces with the reformer, and toilfully succeeded in putting wood and canvas walls to the hitherto open sides – a process which necessitated the sacrifice of every spare box and bit of flat wood about the place, to say nothing of the loss of skin and blood from the hands of the very amateurish carpenter who had contracted for the job.

When all was finished, Mrs Hyslop was able to write home that she had 'the sweetest little three-roomed cottage, with a lovely little kitchen outside, built by David, who is wonderfully clever with tools. There is a verandah running round three sides, two yards wide, and as there is not room in the sitting-room for David and me and all the furniture, we live mostly on the verandah, covered in with the grenadilla, which is the passion flower, only it attracts snakes. David has killed three already, and I think others that he has said nothing to me about. Of course we cannot sit out there at night, as the lamp attracts thousands of moths and beetles, which are very troublesome; also huge bats that come after the beetles and often get their feet tangled in my hair, but we are very happy.'

They were very happy. The worries and disappointments that had begun to embitter the life of the missionary lost their formidable power, when he had confided them to his companion. Her optimism and enthusiasm had not yet been blunted as his had, and the lions he saw in the path were to her as the objective of the hunter. She had come to help him fight lions, and their presence gave her an additional joy in existence.

When the house was in order and they had settled into the daily routine of a simple healthy life, Mrs Hyslop announced her readiness to begin her share of the work of the mission. It was to start with the training of a nice, good young kafir girl, who should at one and the same time be inculcated into the duties and privileges of the Christian and civilised life, and David was commanded to find a fitting subject.

Manlike he saw an objection at the outset. He had, so far, followed the fashion of the country with fair success by employing an intelligent kafir lad who had had some experience of domestic service. James the Pondo had proved impossible. Not only was he a stumbling-block by reason of the prejudice this haughty educated native excited in the kraals, but he jibbed at domestic work. He claimed to be a lay worker and interpreter for the mission, not a mere kitchen boy. After six months of petty annoyances Mr Hyslop sent him away and installed a successor who knew nothing of English but could work, wash shirts, and manage the kitchen department very creditably. He slept in a hut with the boy who looked after the horse and the garden, but it was clear that a maid servant could not be so easily accommodated. There was no room in the cottage, so the missionary sent to town for some timber and corrugated iron and walled in part of the verandah which Mrs Hyslop fitted up as a bedroom for the destined maid.

The missionary then sent for Mozulikase. The first 'obstacle' had been overcome. He was, and had been for six months, a brand snatched from the burning. Mr Hyslop had reluctantly acted upon the advice of the magistrate and obtained judgment for £7 10s., arrears of rent, interest, and costs against the sinner, who was now repentant, attended the services regularly, and borrowed boldly without false pretence. So far there had been no occasion to remind him that an unsatisfied judgment hung over him.

Mozulikase had five daughters unmarried, and as suitors were slow, or to be accurate, too poor to buy cattle to purchase wives, the girls were very much at liberty, and when it was suggested that Zoche, the fourteen-year-old maiden, should take up her residence at the mission-house, the father saw a chance of doing a bit of business.

He asked for time to discuss the matter with his wives and sons. By way of earnest of *bona fides* he borrowed half a gallon of 'palafinoil'. Next day he called to say there were reasons to believe the negotiations would have a satisfactory issue, and besought the loan of a pair of trousers as he had to ride into town to interview a son working there and get his consent to the compact.

A fortnight later Zoche was received in triumph by Mrs Hyslop to be her maid for twelve months, in consideration of the sum of five shillings per mensem, half of which was to go towards the extinction of the father's debt of £7 10s., the other moiety to be equally divided between the girl and her father. No mention was made of the 'palafinoil' and trousers. They were written off as bonsella, otherwise commission on the transaction.

Zoche was renamed Anna, pending her formal christening and reception into the Church. Mrs Hyslop had originally chosen 'Mary Anne', in ignorance of the difficulty Zulus have with the letter r, so Anna was hit upon as a judicious blend of Christian and native nomenclature. Anna was put into a print frock and cap, and, according to her mistress, looked so sweet that that enthusiast sat up half the night writing an account of the beginning of 'the conversion of Anna – my first convert.' It appeared some months later in the missionary page of a religious paper in England, and brought many parcels of useless articles of clothing and improving literature for Mrs Hyslop's *protégée*.

When Anna had broken half the crockery through getting her feet mixed up in the unaccustomed skirt, her mistress reluctantly yielded to the girl's earnest prayer for permission to resume her native girdle by a compromise. The skirt and petticoat were fastened to about the level of the knee during working hours, and let down during the hour devoted to mental instruction. At bedtime Mrs Hyslop acted as tiring woman and undressed her maid to make certain that the girl did not sleep in her clothes, and for some time she found it equally necessary to assist at the morning toilette to prevent Anna serving the early coffee in native costume.

Gentleness and patience brought the usual reward. Within a month Anna was sufficiently advanced to 'do for herself'. She progressed in many things, and Mrs Hyslop was particularly pleased at finding the girl's bed nicely made before breakfast every morning, until occasion took her to the room late one night. Anna was invisible, so was the neat little carpet square that usually covered the floor. The mission staff was turned out to search for the missing maid, and Anna crawled from under the bed to help in the quest.

The secret was out. Anna was in the habit of wrapping herself in the carpet and sleeping beneath the bed, because, as she explained, it was more homelike, and saved the sheets, which latter was true, but the neat print frock was ruined.

Mrs Hyslop was too broad in her catholicity to restrict her efforts as a pioneer of civilisation to her own home. As she grew in knowledge of the vernacular under the tutelage of her husband, who was rapidly attaining proficiency, she visited the kraals, and dispensed sweetness and light. The care and treatment of babies was a subject on which she claimed an authority that rather surprised her husband. She washed and physicked the ailing piccanins on the lines laid down in the 'Mother's Guide', and spent much time in making queer little garments and flannel bands, but abandoned her maternal offices when she found that the mothers invaribaly administered emetics to nullify the effect of white medicine as soon as she had gone, and cut up the bandages to make lamp wicks.

The little woman was sadly depressed and discouraged by the almost catastrophic result of her last attempt at civilising kafir babyhood. A friend of the mission sent a large wax doll with beautfiul blue eyes that closed, and a squeak. Mrs Hyslop invited a crowd of mothers and juveniles to the house, regaled them with bread and jam, and suddenly produced the doll. She laid it tenderly across her knee to show how the eyes closed, extracted a squeak, and was startled to hear it echoed by twenty agonised screams. The mothers' meeting dissolved with a jerk. Black piccanins were snatched up or dragged by the arm, and the mothers rushed off the verandah yelling 'Tagata! Tagata!' (Witchcraft!)

It was a terrible blow to the mission, but worse followed. One of the babies that had been doctored and coddled by Mrs Hyslop, died, and her growing reputation as a white witch attained its apotheosis. She insisted that death was the result of removing the flannel bandages with which she had swathed it, and with feminine insequence used the case as a triumphant vindication of her theory that all babies required flannel bands. The fact that until she had shown the proper method of rearing infants none had died in the location for a year or more, or that infantine mortality was practically non-existent in the kraals, weighed for nothing against the statistics given in her handbook. They showed that a third of the infants born in London slums died within a year. A kafir hut was much more salubrious than a London slum dwelling, where the district visitor and church nurses helped to inculcate the correct principles of child-rearing. How, therefore, could the ignorant kafir mother expect to bring up her progeny successfully amid her squalid surroundings and without peptonised infant food and flannel bandages?

Her husband mildly hinted that the birth-rate in kafirdom was the highest in the world, and the mortality so low that the population question was becoming a serious menace to the future of the whites.

'Then all the more reason that the mothers should be taught civilised methods of rearing a healthy family,' was Mrs Hyslop's reply.

She yielded to the pressure of her husband, backed by old Boggis, and suspended hostilities in the kraals till public feeling had been reassured by the survival of the remainder of the infants. In the meantime she devoted herself to the Anglicising of Anna.

The girl was prone to fits of meditation in seclusion, and obesity. As these were not qualities admired by the young bachelors of his tribe, old Mozulikase had felt less repugnance at the idea of sacrificing his daughter for fifteenpence a month, and the extinction of a debt that had hardly begun to worry him.

The qualities, however, which prejudiced Anna's matrimonial prospects facilitated the process of Anglicisation. She was too lazy to rebel against the innovations and experiments of her mistress, who interpreted stolid passivity into charmed and grateful assent. The tendency to horizontal expansion was a distinct advantage. Most of the clothing sent out by friends of the mission had belonged to adults and required no 'taking in'. It was easier to shorten a skirt by pinning it up than to widen a bodice by letting in a piece of material sliced off the skirt. Mrs Hyslop had tried to qualify the bulginess of Anna in the region of the blouse by squeezing her into a corset, but as it had to be got off with the scissors at bedtime it was put aside; and a large white bib apron would have reduced the bolster-like appearance above the waist, but Mrs Hyslop's injunctions to keep it clean became so irksome that Anna used to tuck the lower part of the apron into her bosom to ensure freedom from contaminating contact with the pots which she always carried dangling against her dress.

Mrs Hyslop was a marvel of patient perseverance. She talked at her pupil in fluent English and dislocated Zulu all day, and adjusted and readjusted her disordered dress with a mildly deprecatory 'O Anna! You *do* look such a guy!'

Anna submitted to be dressed and undressed, altered and repaired, with the unprotesting submissiveness of a sedate pug dog 'dressed up' by the children in the nursery, and her mistress rejoiced that the work of civilisation progressed.

The story of 'The Progress of Anna' was continued in the missionary magazine.

'A delightful and encouraging incident occurred the other day,' she wrote. 'I have noticed with pleasure that Anna has shown no desire to return to her heathen friends and companions. On several occasions when natives from the kraals have visited the mission the dear girl has made excuses to remain busy in my bedroom to avoid speaking with them. On Tuesday a great marriage feast was to be held in a neighbouring kraal, and I was surprised that Anna had not asked for leave to attend it. I told her that she might go if she returned before sunset, and wore her second-best frock, when to my delight the child replied, "No, dear mistress, I prefer to remain with you. I have no desire to mix with my people." Truly the seed has fallen on fruitful ground.'

Which shows how the pure and simple-minded always put the best interpretation, even on things obscure. Had Mrs Hyslop been more at home with Zulu idiom she would have known that the true interpretation of Anna's refusal should not have been expressed in the stilted language of the polite letter writer, but that a more accurate and less free rendering would have been:

'No fear, missis, I'd rather stay here than be a guy among my own people.'

It is possible that if Mrs Hyslop had been taken, *nolens volens*, by some masterful enthusiast on dress reform, and tricked out in grotesque garments, she would have found something to occupy her in a remote part of the house when friends called, and like Anna, preferred the company of her gentle tyrant to exhibiting herself in a mirth-provoking costume at a wedding breakfast.

CHAPTER XII

THE PREPARATION OF THE LEAVEN

The husband watched the progress of Anna with interest and did his best to conceal his own absence of optimism as to the result of the experiment. Experience and opportunity for thought free from the biassing influence of sympathetic souls had brought about, if not a change, a distinct modification of many of the views on missionary duty and endeavour that he had brought with him to Blue Krantz. The time had arrived for the preparation of his annual report, but he had procrastinated anew each time he sat down to refresh his memory with the mass of notes that formed the skeleton of the document that was to be the record and account of his stewardship.

He read them in a fresh light, and modified or eliminated so freely that the original scheme had almost disappeared.

He had fondly hoped that the sympathetic presence of his wife would stimulate and inspire him to the discharge of a task that he had shirked again and again; that her whole-hearted enthusiasm would establish revivifying contact with his own negative current, but the effect was the reverse of what he had hoped.

He had not dared to tell her that the experiments she was trying on her *protégée* were not only futile but unwise, because they were based on the false premise that change of heart was best effected through change of clothing. He had come to the conclusion that the native was less susceptible to spiritual influence when taken out of his natural environment. He had begun to believe that there was something in the Colonial suggestion that a native who would throw over the outward sign of the race traditions of ages for a suit of clothes and the trifling material advantage derivable from association with a mission, was not likely to prove an influence for good and leaven of righteousness when he returned to his own people. The original desertion stamped him a Renegade, and as such he could never again have part or lot in the kraal.

For some time the doctrine of the leaven had cheered David Hyslop greatly. 'It is true,' he thought, 'that for some reason of unfitness I have failed to touch and stir the spiritual in these poor people, but it is impossible that my lessons and example of industry, cleanliness, truthfulness and material usefulness cannot leave an impress.'

He had cultivated and encouraged this line of thought many months, and had sketched out a very telling argument in favour of making spiritual teaching subordinate to the material when he ran against a fact.

There had come to a kraal in his mission district, one Tom Malief, a kafir who had for a period of nearly twenty years been in the employ of a firm of builders in Maritzburg. Tom was the civilised kafir *par excellence*. He was skilled in the use of the tools of blacksmith, carpenter and builder. Indeed he was the equal of many a white mechanic, and but for his colour would have worked with them on terms of equality. He had saved nearly two hundred pounds, and at last had listened to the call of the veld and returned to his childhood's home.

The missionary had heard of Tom and rode over to make the acquaintance of one whom he hoped to enlist as a useful exemplar of the advantages of the Christian life.

He saw a native, naked except for his loin cloth, sitting at a fire of cowdung, heating a nail stuck in a cleft stick. With the nail he bored holes in a withe, slowly and laboriously, to pass through them a strip of leathern thong to hold down the thatch on the roof of his beehive-shaped hut.

'Is Tom Malief here?' the missionary asked in Zulu.

'I am Tom, baas,' came the answer in excellent English.

Mr Hyslop looked at him in amaze.

'You, Tom Malief – the carpenter – boring holes with a hot nail like a raw native!'

'I am not a carpenter any more, baas. I am at home. I do no more work.'

'But you are working – working foolishly, boring holes with a nail when you know how to use a gimlet. That job will not be finished tomorrow.'

'There are plenty of tomorrows in the kraal, baas.'

Tom was the leaven, but he had been absorbed by the lump instead of leavening it.

After twenty years of daily contact with the heirs of all the ages – after absorbing as many Christian virtues and vices as his enlarged mind had room for, after wearing white men's clothes so long that he could not don the moocha without assistance, he had within an hour resumed the life of a naked savage, and moved in his native element as easily and congenially as a captured fish returned alive to the river.

Among the thorns that afflicted the flesh and spirit of the young missionary were certain flippant criticisms of himself and his work that appeared at intervals in the 'Notes from Blue Krantz', published in one of the daily papers. Rumour accredited them to Mulligan, the Sheriff and Court Messenger, whose acquaintance he had made on a memorable occasion. They were always spiteful and captious. The missionary was never referred to by name; generally as 'a young skypilot', a 'black polisher', a 'kafir disintegrator', and cognate phraseological combinations of contempt and humour. They were mostly mere vulgarities, but they were edifying to their subject, inasmuch as they afforded a clue to what might be the popular attitude and state of mind towards missionaries.

One paragraph made a lasting impression upon the victim. He had pasted it in his scrap-book and frequently read it.

It referred to an incident at one of his services for natives held near the magistracy when a kafir put several questions to the preacher. At the time Mr Hyslop was struck by their logical astuteness, for he did not know what was now clear that the enquiries had been prompted by a white man – probably the writer of the paragraph.

'A kafir Disintegrator who indignantly denies that he preaches the doctrine of Black and White equality had an opportunity of proving it the other day,' said the paragraph. 'He was holding forth on the duty of the kafir to attend church, when he was asked by a cute native if, when he got to Heaven, he could sit among the white baases or would he have to sit among the coloured people. The Disintegrator, not seeing the trap, walked in, and boldly answered that before God White and Black were equal. Then asked the boy, "Is a Christian native as good as a Christian white man?" and the reply was "Certainly." This Disintegrator doesn't teach equality of the races, oh dear no!'

The missionary had taken precautions to prevent his wife seeing these discouraging criticisms, but he was not successful in suppressing one which had special reference to her. It was written in the usual cumbersomely satiric-comic vein, and ran:

'People who visit the abode of skypilots must not run away with the notion that they (the skypilots, not the people) are living in luxury because they keep kafir maids rigged out in all the panoply of the parlourmaid of an English duke. The intombi is simply being trained for her future career as the wife of a drunken, lazy kafir. She is learning how to hand round cups of tea instead of kafir beer, and to open the door of the hut and say, "Not at home," to the police when they call for dog tax.'

The paragraph proceeded to give a burlesque description of the reformed methods of life in a kafir hut, '*á la missionary*,' and concluded thus:

'Do these foolish people, we wonder, ever pause to think what is to be the future of kafir girls who are taken from their kraals, tricked out like monkeys and made objects of contempt and loathing to their own people? Does this guileless young skypilot know what is the invariable fate of ninety-nine out of every hundred kafir girls who discard the blanket for the petticoat?'

Mrs Hyslop had a good cry when she read the brutal jeer. Her husband sought to soothe her by describing the presumed writer as one who had an objection to missionaries, probably because they reduced his earnings as Court Messenger by discouraging kafir litigation.

The explanation was accepted, but the distressed young wife noticed that her husband had made no attempt to answer the question of the writer. Something warned her not to ask him to do so.

The report could be delayed no longer. David Hyslop sat down resolutely one morning and completed it. He read it to his companion in the evening. She was enthusiastic in her applause. It was beautiful, she said, and so clever.

It was not vanity but full knowledge of the circumstances that impelled the author to agree that the document was clever. With an infinitude of pains he had succeeded in producing a statement of his year's work that, without being optimistic or the reverse, concealed the keen sense of disappointment and dissatisfaction of the writer. Instead of enlarging on apparent success or minimising unmistakable failures, he kept uppermost the idea that he was but a private soldier carrying out in the battle such duties as fell to him, ignorant whether his shots told, but content to know that they were fired in conjunction with those of others, and that it was the volley and not the single shot that counted in the total result. Time alone would decide whether he had shot well or ill.

The day that the report was dispatched an event happened that was destined to influence very considerably the next account of his stewardship drawn up by the Rev. David Hyslop.

Old Boggis arrived at the mission-house to announce that his long meditated removal from the district was settled.

His friends were genuinely grieved, for the old man's visits had become a much appreciated fixture. He was the only white man in the vast district who had shown any friendliness, and they had found his advice and many helpful deeds extremely acceptable. But above all he was sympathetic and interested in their work with the natives.

'I want you to do me a favour, parson,' the old man said, when they had exhausted the main subjects of conversation. 'I've got a very decent kafir. I can't take him with me and I should like him to get into the hands of some one like yourself who would treat the boy well. It isn't a matter of money. I have only been giving him a stray shilling or two a month, and he is quite contented, but he is in a great state about my quitting the camp as you can understand when I tell you he's an escaped convict.'

Mrs Hyslop gave a little cry of alarm and her husband looked grave.

'Rather a serious thing to harbour a – run-away, isn't it?' he asked.

'Well it is and it isn't. All depends upon the circumstances. You are not supposed to know that he is wanted by the police; no employer wants to know that, and I wouldn't have told you except to explain why I ask you to take him. You mark my words, parson, you can make a good boy of this Bulalie. My advice is, keep him and use him to practise on. He dare not run away. You'll have a cheap servant and he'll be a help and a credit to you.'

Mr Hyslop hesitated, he did not like the idea of holding a servant by fear, and said so.

'Lord bless you, if that is your objection you must get rid of Anna. Do you think her father would let her cut herself off from her people if he had his own way? Don't you hold him in the bonds of debt? Do you think kafirs give their services for love? No, sir, fear and profit, mostly fear, because if they didn't earn money they couldn't pay hut tax and that would mean something to be afraid of. You find a job for Bulalie and you can quiet your conscience by knowing you are making of him a light to lighten the Gentiles. You can let him loose among the kafirs in the compounds of the Transvaal after you've loaded him up with Gospel truth, and he'll be a sort of Apostle. I tell you he's a darned smart boy. You can teach him anything, and what's more, he wants to learn. He asked me to teach him to write, the funniest thing I ever heard. You take him on, parson.'

The missionary took the night to consider. He looked at the matter from all points of view that presented themselves, and thought he saw in the proposal a plan of relief. He had been oppressed by a sense of effort too widely dissipated. His teaching was scattered over too great an area, he had been firing wildly into the air on the chance of hitting a passing bird instead of aiming at one.

He was fascinated by the half jocular suggestion of Boggis that this native could be transformed into a light to lighten his fellows. In spite of the sneers and insinuations of the anonymous correspondent against Mrs Hyslop's experiment, in spite of the case of Tom Malief, he would persevere on the lines of concentrated effort. His work on its present lines would not be interfered with, and if the experiment failed it would not be a disaster, for some influence for good must remain.

He turned the pages of the diary he kept with business-like care and regularity to see when the service ended of the boy he would have to displace to make room for Bulalie. Each day was provided with a text. That for the day the new boy would take up his duties ran:

'Therefore, brethren, be steadfast, unmovable, always abounding in the work of the Lord; forasmuch as ye know that your labour is not in vain.'

When Boggis left next morning David Hyslop rode several miles with him, and heard as much of the story of Bulalie as the old man knew. He returned to his home satisfied, as Boggis was, that the boy had been unjustly convicted and resolved to render back to this victim of white oppression 'large service in the truth' for the wrongs he had suffered.

CHAPTER XIII

FREEDOM

Bulalie had been nearly six months in jail and had become inured to the not too strenuous life of a kafir convict. He had long since ceased to feel angry and sore when he thought of the wrongfulness of his conviction; even the memory of the terrible lashes was growing faint, and had it not been that the signs and sounds in a certain corner of the jail yard were a too frequent reminder, he would not have shuddered and felt the hot blood run from his heart to his brain so often.

He went out with the road gang at times, and preferred it to working in the prison, for there was always something to see, and sometimes something to pick up. He had more than once had a banana or orange, and even a cigarette thrown to him by a sympathetic kafir, who had probably known what it was to have to do without luxuries for years, and now and then he was selected because of his tallness and strength to help in the government offices and private houses of officials. This meant much more freedom than fell to the lot of many prisoners, and as every day that passed brought the day of freedom nearer, Bulalie was not unhappy, and prison was not the terrible place that he had at first feared.

One day Bacheta came into the jail. He had been working with a labour gang in another part of the country and was glad to get back to Maritzburg, for country jails are not so desirable. He had learned of the fate of Bulalie, for, whether in prison or in kraal, natives hear much news.

Bulalie told him in small pieces the story of the fate of the klippie, but not knowing what had become of the gold things in the bag, he thought them still in the care of Sekoos.

Bacheta was very sad, but not angry when he heard of what had befallen the diamond, and when in the course of many days Bulalie heard the full story of how it fell into the hands of Bacheta, he understood much that was before a mystery.

He learned that Bacheta had worked for a good baas called Jack Hodson on the Vaal River Diamond Diggings. The baas was always kind to Bacheta and paid him well and honestly for any stones the boy found, which all diggers do not. Bacheta did not know the complete story, but he knew that his baas was in great trouble because 'The Company' wished him to leave and give his claim to another. There was much lawyer work, and the baas one day went to Court. When he came back he told Bacheta that he was ruined, that the company was coming to take away his claim and all that he had, because he had no money to pay the lawyers. Being in great trouble he did as white men do – drank so much brandy to make him happy that he became very ill, and stayed all night in the canteen.

Next morning Bacheta saw strange men coming to the camp, and knowing they had come to take away all that belonged to his master, he ran to the tent and dug up from the hole beneath the bed the little tin box in which the baas kept the stones he found. Bacheta also took a leathern case in which were the gold things that Sekoos now held, and as many small things as he could put into a handkerchief. Then he went away and hid till the strange men had gone.

It was long before Bacheta dared come out of the donga where he had been hiding and go to find his master to give him the things that he had saved for him, for he was afraid lest the strange men should see him and take away his master's property. So he first hid the things carefully in a hole in the side of the donga so high that the water would never reach it, looked very hard and carefully so that he might know the place again, and went to the canteen. His master was not there nor could Bacheta find him in any of the camps, though he walked long and wearily all next day. Then he met a kafir who told him that his master had gone away in a Cape cart and was going over the blue water to his kraal in England.

Bacheta found another baas on the diggings, and stayed many months, hoping that his old baas might return, but the white men all said, 'No, he dare not come back. The company will put him in prison if they find him, for he has gone away without paying them.'

Then Bacheta, when it was dark, went to the donga and took away such things as he could carry without much danger, but he was afraid to touch the diamonds for he knew that if he were found with them he would be sent to prison for many years.

Then he travelled many days and nights till he got back to his kraal and was soon called out to work with the road party where Bulalie met him.

'And now,' said Bacheta, 'I am waiting till they let me out of prison. I have on a piece of paper the name of my baas's kraal where he is living. I met in the jail at Bulwer a kafir who had worked on the diggings and had often heard his own baas say he came from the same kraal as Jack Hodson, and he wrote it down for me. When I get out I shall go to a kafir I can trust who can write, and send a letter to my baas to tell him where he can find the klippies I have hidden, because he was a good baas.'

'Why did you bring away the stone that you gave me to keep?' Bulalie asked, and Bacheta told how he did not take it from the tin box but found it among the small gold things.

And Bacheta and Bulalie became great and good friends. By reason of his great wisdom and knowledge in the ways of prisons Bacheta was able to show Bulalie how to make his lot soft and keep from many things that would bring punishment.

One day Bacheta told Bulalie, 'We are going to see our own land. Tomorrow we go to work in the Blue Krantz,' and it came true, as did most things that Bacheta said.

About fity prisoners were taken on the train, then marched for one day and a half till they came to the Magistracy at Blue Krantz where was a new jail building. They could see many places that Bulalie knew, and his heart was glad, though when he thought of his kraal and the night so long ago when he left it, he was sad, and wished he had not come.

On the fourth day a white warder and a Zulu took six prisoners, among whom were Bacheta and Bulalie, a long way to dig out a wagon that had sunk deeply into a soft piece of the ground by the river. It was a very hot day, and the warder who sat with his back against a big stone and his gun on his knee nodded his head on his breast and went to sleep.

Bacheta whispered to Bulalie, 'Shall we run? We know the country and can hide in many good places in the mountains. The warder and the Zulu dare not come after us lest the others run away also.'

Bulalie's heart gave a great jump, for he had been looking at the mountain not far away that hid his kraal, and he was thinking how good it was to be among his people, his sisters and his mother, with no work to do, nothing but lie in the sun and have no Zulu warder come striking with his kierie to make him work faster.

'Come on,' said Bacheta, and he started to run. Bulalie followed and then came a great shout. The Zulu had seen them, and was following. He carried three assegais and was a famous thrower, but he was big and fat, and could not run very fast.

Then came the sound of the warder's gun, and a bullet struck a stone a long way in front of them. Bacheta ran on without speaking, Bulalie keeping a good distance to his right so that if a bullet missed one it might not hit the other.

Four more shots came, but though they were very near each time they did but put fastness into the legs of the two.

Presently Bacheta spoke. He had looked back over his shoulder.

'They have gone back lest the others run away,' he said, and Bulalie saw that it was so and rejoiced.

Bacheta ran up a low hill that was all that lay between them and the sugar bush and thorn country where they could run and not be seen. He turned to look once more to be certain the warder was not following when the gun sounded, and Bacheta felt a stinging pain at his shoulder.

'Come fast, Bulalie,' he said, 'for I am hurt and may not run much farther. I know a cave where we can rest, and if they come after us we can keep them away by throwing down rocks. It is high up, but I can get there before my pain grows too great. If they catch us they will lash us, Bulalie. Do you want more lashes? Lashes! lashes! Run, Bulalie!'

The thorn bush covered them so that even if anyone followed they could not see them, but Bacheta would not stay and rest although the blood fell in a big river over his breast and back, and his breath came out with a harsh sound.

'No, I will not stay to be caught. If they shoot me on the mountain I shall not cry out, but I should scream at the triangle. They tell me you did not scream till it was over.'

Bulalie was very proud that Bacheta should say this, for though they had talked of many things since they met in the jail Bulalie had never mentioned the one thing he was wishful to forget. Now he was almost pleased that he had been lashed because Bacheta had learned that he was a man and no intombi.

They had a long and wearying climb up the sides of the mountain, not because it was steep, for it was not, but rose up slowly and slowly under the thorn bushes. At last when the breath was coming from Bacheta more noisily, they struck the narrow path that led to the steep krantz where was the cave that Bacheta knew of, and the trouble began, for it was a goat path, and so full of loose rocks and steep places that even Bulalie, strong as he was, had sometimes to pause to get back his breath. Then came a still more narrow path sloping sideways like the roof of a white man's house and narrow as the tin trough that catches the rain; then thick bushes and a dark hole big enough only for a man who crawled. Bacheta went in on his hands and knees. A big black mamba (snake) wriggled out and fell in coils like a heavy rope past Bulalie into the bush. Bacheta cried out:

'Bulalie, I am going to die. The snake carried away my life. Did you not see that he could have bitten me easily but he would not?'

Bulalie crawled into the cave, which was only big enough to hold an ox lying down, and looked in the face of his friend. The death colour had come into it, and the blood was coming out of the corner of his mouth. Bacheta was sitting with his back at the side of the cave, and the light of the sun shone on him; yet he was cold, for he shivered.

'Find the bullet-hole, Bulalie, and put my shirt into it,' he said. He spoke little bits of words only, for the blood in his mouth was choking him.

Bulalie sought and found a very small round hole behind the shoulder, that looked as if it might have been made with a nail. On the left breast was another, but much larger, where the bullet had come out.

Bulalie tore his own shirt and pushed a little piece into each hole. The blood still came out, but not so fast, but more came from the mouth.

'Is there great pain, Bacheta?' asked Bulalie when his friend had not spoken for some time, but hung his head on his breast and held both hands against his chest.

'There is pain like the stabbing of a little knife, Bulalie, but there is more sorrow. I shall not now be able to tell my baas where the klippies are, and he is thinking that I stole them.'

Bacheta could not say this all in one piece, but in little words.

'I will find him and tell him,' Bulalie answered.

Bacheta smiled and tried to speak; but the blood came faster from his mouth, and he leaned his head deeper down and signed to Bulalie to put his ear close, which he did. After a long time, and with much close listening, he heard words that he resolved never to forget, for they told how the baas might find the donga where the klippies were hidden in the tin box. Bacheta signed to Bulalie to feel the band of the prison trousers. He did so, and knew that the paper was there that told where to find the baas's kraal.

There was long, long silence; then strange noises came from Bacheta's throat, and twice he said very weakly 'Manzi' (water), but Bulalie knew that there was none except far, far away through the thorn bush at the bottom of the krantz.

So he sat and watched Bacheta die.

When the blood came from the mouth in big clots he thought of the day when he was tied to the triangle and lumps of blood and flesh came from his back, leaving red hot pain. He stooped and looked at his friend's face and knew there was no pain for his mouth was open.

'Bacheta,' he said, 'be joyful, you have finished. They cannot lash you any more, there is no more pain, Bacheta. You have been a good brother to me, Bacheta. There is no pain, is there?'

Bacheta had made a strange noise in his throat; his head fell forward, and he clutched the wrist of Bulalie, and then was still — so still that Bulalie could hear the drops of blood falling very slowly on to the dry leaves.

A big fly settled on Bacheta's mouth, then another. Bulalie put up his hand to drive them away, and the body of his friend fell forward, then sideways, so that he could see the face. The eyes were wide open, and the chin was falling: Bulalie knew that his friend was dead.

He took the piece of paper from the waistband of the trousers, then went out of the cave to gather stones to lay upon the body. It was the time of the moon, so that he could see to travel; so also could the police, if they were coming. He must leave the cave quickly. As he went back with stones he saw the black snake going into the cave, and knew that it was the spirit of Bacheta, and that there would be no need to cover the body, for the snake would guard it.

And Bulalie turned his face toward the spot where the sun had gone into its hole, and travelled all night.

When the sun came back in the morning it shone on a white tent a little way up the hill where Bulalie had lain to sleep in a patch of long grass. An old white man was lighting a fire near the tent, and Bulalie knew by that he could have no boy to work for him. So he went up boldly and said:

'Saku bona, baas. I want work, and I am very hungry.'

CHAPTER XIV

THE EDUCATION OF BULALIE

Three months' careful observation had satisfied the Rev. David Hyslop that old Boggis had not erred in his recommendation of Bulalie as a 'darned smart boy, a help, and a credit.' He had proved all this – minus the darned – and promised to be even more. Mrs Hyslop had taken to the boy; her natural tenderness had been touched by the story of his wrongs. The missionary had made some enquiries, cautiously and discreetly, had read the reports of the trial, and spoken with several persons whose opinion carried weight. These without committing themselves to a declaration of faith in the innocence of the accused did not hesitate to express a belief in the extreme probability of a miscarriage of justice, but, as one put it, 'It would have been expecting the impossible that a Natal jury should deliberately elect to believe the denial of a kafir against the sworn testimony of a white woman of known respectability.' It was a case of branding her as a perjurer or inflicting a mild punishment on a raw kafir. There could be no possible alternative. The boy had admitted that he had had an altercation with this mistress, and that alone justified some punishment. The sanctity of the white woman must be preserved and impressed upon the native at any cost. If Bulalie had been wrongfully punished, he was unfortunate, but better fifty kafirs be wrongly flogged than rudeness and violence to a white woman be condoned once.

Mr Hyslop went back strengthened. He had been provided with a powerful argument in support of his faith in the civilising process. The more the kafir was enlightened – the nearer he was brought to moral and intellectual equality with the white – the less likely was he to be a 'Black Peril.' What a magnificent triumph for the cause it would be if he could transform into a civilised and moral being one who had been the symbol and exemplar of all the white man feared in the native! It was a work worthy a life's devotion, and he fervently thanked God for giving him the privilege of the effort.

He had begun the educational process carefully and judiciously, striving to make it imperceptible and gradual, avoiding pedagogy, and particularly refraining from creating an impresson on the mind of the boy that the lessons were tasks or part of the price he had to pay for being saved from the vengeance of the law. Under the pretext of learning Zulu from Bulalie he began a course of English, and early in the chapter had acted upon the hint of Boggis that the art of writing was a desire of the boy.

When questioned, Bulalie said he only wanted to be able to write one letter to a white man on behalf of a dead friend. He was too cautious to reveal the nature and occasion of the intended communication. He had not forgotten that disregard of Bacheta's advice about showing the klippie had brought imprisonment and lashes. He had resolved to make atonement by carrying out the behest of Bacheta. He would learn to write well enough to send a letter to Bacheta's baas informing him where he could recover the property that his faithful servant had saved for him. The piece of paper bearing the name of the kraal of the baas was as carefully concealed about him as the klippie once had been; but this would be revealed to no man, black or white, not even to the preacher.

The harbouring of a convict native likely to be recognised by the police was fraught with many disadvantages. Bulalie had to be kept practically a prisoner on the mission reserve. He could not accompany his master on his expeditions to the magistracy or to any place frequented by the police. Enquiry had been made for him at the mission, fortunately some time before his arrival, and old Boggis had had to defend his *protégé* by concealing him and lying on two occasions. Direct search had long since been abandoned, for the authorities knew that sooner or later they gather in their lost sheep without expenditure of effort.

The very propinquity of the mission station to the police headquarters was, however, a safeguard. The young troopers on patrol duty rarely honoured Mr Hyslop with a call, for he kept no whisky on the premises and had no spare bedroom.

Life at the mission station seemed to go much more happily since the arrival of Bulalie. He provided the one thing that had before been lacking – a direct incentive and objective. The result of the sporadic civilising propaganda in the scattered kraals was not always visible; the progress of Anna and Bulalie was. The jibes and sneers of the writer of 'Notes from Blue Krantz,' ceased to irritate and discourage; the contemptuous or patronising bearing towards him of the casual white men encountered on his excursions, did not now inspire feelings of isolation and Ishmaelism. He even fancied that many people were not so much aloof, for he was scarcely conscious of an improvement in his own demeanour. He was more frank, brisk and communicative – less the parson and more the man; more ready to resent rough badinage with good-natured chaff than to smile meekly and sit silent as of yore. He felt the confidence of success and asserted and justified boldly, even pugnaciously, what before he had advanced with apologetic diffidence. Twice on visiting the Magistracy, he had deliberately sought a verbal contest with Mulligan, the Court Messenger, and scored heavily by turning the laugh against him, eliciting by a subtle process of Socratic questioning that the erudition of the oracle of Blue Krantz was derived from odd volumes of an antique encyclopædia which only dealt with subjects embraced between the letters F and L. The subjugation of the Court Messenger was complete, and though the victor had to pay the price by an increase in the vitriolic pungency of the 'Notes from Blue Krantz,' he was content, for the exposure of Mulligan made a strong friend of Mr Flemming, who had writhed for years under the sarcasms and misquotations which his educational limitations brought upon him.

'Look 'ere, Wiseacre, this 'ere subject don't begin with any letter between F and L, so you don't know nothing about it,' became the old farmer's weapon of defence and offence, and he used it freely.

His gratitude to the missionary was not expressed in words. He sent him a present — a crowing hen that Mrs Flemming refused to keep or eat because it was unlucky. 'But it's a good brooder,' he explained in extenuation.

The educational process proceeded with system, husband and wife entering into friendly rivalry with their respective pupils until Mrs Hyslop realised that the system of scoring points would have to be amended. Anna required a very different method of treatment to Bulalie. To begin with, the girl was abnormally dull and phlegmatic; praise and blame were accepted with the same wooden grin. She never apologised for or sought to excuse her manifold sins and wickednesses, but repeated them or failed to repeat them by bungling into the right path, till her patient instructress grew tired of the monotony of her own stock of deprecatory ejaculations.

Anna unconsciously adopted the army regulation which ordains that the last order given nullifies all precedent. She had carried in two lumps of sugar with the bedside coffee every morning for months, till one piece was once sent back unused. This she interpreted as a new rule, and one lump became the regular ration in spite of remonstrance. When Mrs Hyslop temporarily departed from her customary tidiness by placing a pair of shoes on the dressing-table, Anna promptly adopted it as the legitimate boot rack.

Had she possessed any sympathy with the Darwinian theory Mrs Hyslop could have deduced from a day's observation of the vagaries of her maid, twenty suggestive evidences of an apish origin. A useful act Anna ignored; a casual and unpremeditated blunder was imitated and repeated, *ad nauseam.* Capacity for independent initiative was absolutely non-existent. The simplest action would be performed with mechanical repetition although there might be fifty obvious variations on the method of treatment. Having once had to repeat the wiping of a plate, she invariably went over the lot a second time till her mistress began to feel that there was some justification for the perpetual complaining against kafir servants which is the staple subject with all Colonial women.

The husband found his pupil a little more amenable to deductive reasoning than Anna, but there was a disappointing absence of anything like enthusiasm or expressed interest. Bulalie did his work at day and his lessons at night with as obvious a desire to be through with them as any 'kept in' schoolboy. He failed entiriely to come up to the touching picture David Hyslop remembered to have seen in his callow days – a picturesque black of the 'Uncle Tom' type with a big Bible in his hand and tears in his eyes appealing to a missionary to teach him to read.

Bulalie started very keenly on learning to write, but when he found that he would not be able to acquire the art in time to get his letter off by the next mail he seemed to lose interest. Reading, he explained, he regarded as superfluous; he was nothing if not practical, and he had no use for books, unless they contained highly coloured pictures. Black-and-white art did not appeal to him. He was never quite certain that he held the picture right side up till he had studied it for some time, and the laughter this induced in other natives annoyed him and led to fights. However, he persevered with the pothooks and hangers, and figures.

These last interested him greatly. They were practical, and conveyed tangible ideas, for Bulalie could count up to two hundred with comparative accuracy, and gloried in his ability to express numbers on paper.

His instructor saw in this predilection a short cut to writing. He reverted to the symbolism of the Egyptians and Phœnicians, inventing a kind of picture shorthand to enable Bulalie to keep his stock-book. A stroke like a yoke stood for an ox, a curly tail for a pig, a tiny circle for a bag of mealies, and a larger for potatoes. By placing the figures before the sign, Bulalie was able to open a day-book and stock inventory. He was delighted with the new weapon, and having catalogued everything about the mission that had a sign to stand for it, he extended his labours to the kraals, and trouble began.

Kafirs share with old-time Boers a superstitious dread of anything that suggests a numbering of the people, or the people's belongings. It had been duly advertised, mainly by Bulalie, that he could now write like a white man, and when he somewhat ostentatiously proceeded to prove it by counting the kraals' oxen, goats and fowls, and writing the computation in a book, it became evident that he was an agent of the missionary, who was a secret agent of the Government, and that fresh taxation was the objective.

So they threw Bulalie out of the kraal and confiscated his book, destroying any malefic power it possessed by sticking it through with an assegai steeped in blood of a goat.

Bulalie declared war against the kraal in the name of the missionary, and in the course of half-an-hour wiped out the effects of eighteen months' Evangelising.

There were other worries to follow in the trail of Bulalie's too facile pencil. When it was understood that he could write, he was beset with applicants requiring bogus passes authorising storekeepers to supply them with liquor. He was able to avert a humiliating exposure of the hollowness of his pretentions to scholarship by assuming a tone of withering morality. He refused to be a party to the perpetration of a serious crime, even for a reward of a shilling and two drinks of the illicit rum. He confiscated the passes brought to him as a model. Mr Hyslop found them later. Bulalie had been practising the difficult art of copying characters he did not understand.

'Baas, I want to learn to read,' he delighted his teacher by declaring one day when the writing lessons had advanced to words of two syllables.

Bulalie was introduced to print characters.

'I know what they are for,' he said, jubilantly. 'They are on the passes and the papers the policemen bring when they take kafirs to jail.'

'The symbols of enlightenment are to the native the symbols of authority and punishment' the missionary remarked that night in his diary.

It was not till Mr Hyslop began to direct his pupil's attention to things not of the earth that he began to appreciate to the full the real difficulties of mission effort. Bulalie was the first honest pagan he had met – a splendid agnostic, as free from any suspicion of faith or spirituality as of views on bimetallism. Therefore a more promising subject, since there was no old belief to impede the assimilation of a new one, no prejudices to overcome, no sentiment to outrage and kill, no old idols to break. Bulalie had not even picked up any of the phrases and tricks with which the native who has enjoyed the blessed privilege of town life uses with sufficient skill to deceive the very elect. It had been the missionary's fate to fall very early to the lure of the kafir hypocrite. He had championed a native charged with several objectionable forms of crime, going into the witness-box and sending the Court into convulsions of laughter by expressing his utmost confidence in the boy's integrity 'because he was a most devout student of the Scriptures, and prayed fervently.'

David Hyslop forgave the laugh and the caustic comments of the press when he was compelled to admit the record of his *protégé* as a notorious impostor who made a speciality of victimising missionaries and religious people by his hypocritical pretences to conversion. The reason the rascal had not spent the best part of his life in jail was that his victims were too merciful or too sensitive to ridicule to prosecute.

This experience had made Mr Hyslop cautious, and the stray kafir who arrived at the mission carrying a sample of pious literature was placed in moral quarantine before being admitted to the privileges of Christian fellowship.

It was startling at first to the missionary − the frank unreticence of Bulalie in dealing with matters sacred. He asked questions about the persons of the Trinity singly and collectively with less show of awe than characterised his references to the police and the jail warders, and received with amused incredulity the assurance of a future existence. When the earnestness of the teacher brought something like conviction, Bulalie looked very grave and thoughtful.

'Poor Bacheta! I told him that he would have no more lashes,' he remarked regretfully, and it took many lessons and much talk to satisfy Bulalie that life beyond the grave was not controlled by the police.

The question that caused the missionary the greatest trouble was whether Jesus Christ was a white man. He had expected and dreaded it, for he knew that an answer in the affirmative must conjure up in the mind of this innocent, a white baas who would demand from kafirs the same subservience exacted by other and less influential white baases. He had not the courage and resource of the Portuguese missionary who painted the religious pictures black. He had prepared a line of retreat by confusing the issue. He endeavoured to convey to Bulalie that colour was only relative, that there was practically little difference between white men, yellow men, brown men and black. It was weak and inconclusive. Bulalie evidently thought as much, for he countered with a staggering blow.

'Jesus is a white man; then all his indunas and head men must be white men. White men can't work, they must have kafirs to work for them. You are one of Jesus's indunas, and you have kafirs to work for you, and it will be the same always.'

The Rev. David Hyslop abandoned a long-cherished project − the translation into Zulu of sundry English works likely to benefit natives. He began to collect material for a 'missionary's handbook; being hints on meeting heathen arguments and objections.'

Bulalie taught his teacher very much and the teacher recognised and appreciated it. If in return he had not succeeded in making of his pupil a

Christian quite up to the standard required by the missionary reports, he had at least succeeded in producing a very manly, clean-minded sample of the semi-civilised native, and he was proud of him, both as a man and a pupil. He was a little disappointed but not discouraged by his apparent failure to touch the spiritual which he knew lay dormant in the subject. He was thankful that he had been permitted to proceed so far in preparing the dwelling for the habitation of the spirit that would come. It was only a matter of time, faith, and energy.

CHAPTER XV

THE BLACKBIRDER

A year had passed since Bulalie had entered into the life of the missionary and given him hope and a new aim and objective. Matters had never gone so smoothly at the mission before, and he was looking forward with delight to the time just a week off when he could leave the mission house and its flourishing little farm and garden in the loyal conscientious charge of his henchman Bulalie while he journeyed to Durban to bring back his wife and the son and heir that had come still further to brighten the life of the happy home.

It was an hour before sundown when a young man in worn but well-cut riding costume rode into the station. Visitors had not been quite so rare of late, and the missionary was not so elated at the prospect of entertaining a white man, particularly when he recognised his visitor as Weldon, late a police trooper attached to the Blue Krantz detachment.

He was at his best not a desirable type of the young Colonial, and least of all a credit to the police force from which he had recently resigned by way of anticipating his discharge.

He swaggered up to the missionary, after giving Bulalie noisy and emphatic instructions as to the care of his horse and shook hands effusively.

'I know you don't keep anything in the house,' he said, throwing himself into the host's favourite chair on the verandah, and producing a pocket flask.

'If you'll tell the boy to bring me a glass I shall be obliged. I haven't had a nip since I left Bob Dando's place.'

The missionary thought it must have been a very stiff one, or Weldon had travelled surprisingly fast. His face was flushed, eyes watery and speech thick – as usual.

'Suppose you know I've chucked the police? No good staying on, no prospects for a chap who wants to go ahead.'

'You have something that suits you better I suppose,' Mr Hyslop suggested for the sake of saying something.

'Rather. I'm a native labour agent. Getting boys for the Rand mines. Good business, I can tell you. I took up a batch of boys last month – thirty-seven – and got two quid each for them. That's better than police patrol, eh?'

'Where did you get them? Over the Zambesi?'

Mr Weldon laughed. 'Not much. Think I'm fool enough to risk fever and horse sickness when I can get boys in Natal?'

'But surely recruiting for native labour in Natal is forbidden by the Government?'

'So are a good many things. More ways of killing a dog than hanging, you know. I'm not taking any risks. I've got funny little ways. I've been in the police, you know. You learn a thing or two there. My boys go up to the border on their own account; nobody can stop them if their passes are in order, and I see to that. I follow on and take charge of them as soon as they get into the Transvaal and then, there you are, don't you know.'

Mr Hyslop had heard that the provision against recruiting was evaded like all laws that interfere with profit-making out of natives. He took advantage of the vulgar boasting of this latest addition to the law breakers to learn how it was done.

'I don't mind telling you,' he said, 'because I don't suppose you'll want to cut in at the game. You know enough of this country to know that there ain't many laws and regulations a man can't get over if he's smart, and don't play the giddy goat. The regulation against recruiting forbids touts going to a kraal and persuading natives to go with them to the Transvaal. It doesn't say anything against a man like me who talks kafir like a native and knows them meeting the chief outside the kraal, filling him up with liquor and promising him five bob a head for all the boys he orders out to work. I don't appear in the business till I'm over the border. Then the storekeepers are very useful. They always have a list of natives who owe them more than they can pay, and it doesn't need much pressure to get a father to send his son to the mines to keep the old man out of jail for debt or being sold up. That's what comes of knowing the ropes. I can get almost as many boys as I want right under the noses of the R.M. Did you see that bit in the paper the other day? Somebody wrote that native labour agents were recruiting in Natal. The Minister for Native Affairs got his rag out and went for the papers for giving currency to falsehoods damaging to the Colony. "Recruiting is strictly forbidden" he said, and didn't I laugh!'

Mr Weldon believing he had an appreciative listener proceeded to furnish other evidence of his qualifications for the work he was engaged in. He narrated instances of rascality and deception practised upon natives which would have justified the missionary in kicking him off the verandah; but Weldon's character as a boasting liar was known to his auditor. The thing that hurt Mr Hyslop was the knowledge that though Weldon might not have perpetrated the injustices of which he boasted they sounded too circumstantial not to have been practised by some one.

A few minutes later the missionary was quite satisfied that he was committing no wrong in believing the worst possible of the ex-policeman.

'I don't like taking away any man's servants,' Weldon began, after several obvious efforts to introduce an unpleasant subject; 'but I've got to take that boy Bulalie.'

Mr Hyslop started. He had sufficient self-control to say quietly, 'I hope not.'

'You know who he is, don't you?'

Weldon looked at the missionary meaningly.

'He's a very good boy,' was the intentionally evasive reply.

Weldon, who was alcoholicly courageous, pulled himself together with an effort. He was preparing himself for a scene.

'Look here, mister. You know that boy is an escaped convict. I spotted him a month ago, but said nothing. I could take him with me now, and you dare not obstruct me. The thing is, do you want him taken back to jail and flogged with six months put on his sentence, or shall I take him to Johannesburg?'

'Why should you do either?'

'Simply because I want him. I may as well get two quid for him as hand him over to the R.M. at Blue Krantz.'

The brutality of the proposal sent the blood into David Hyslop's face.

'If that isn't slave dealing, I should like to know what is,' he said indignantly.

'Slave dealing, eh? You talk of slave dealing, and you have been taking all you can out of this boy for nothing, knowing that he dare not run away!'

Mr Hyslop was stung.

'It is altogether false,' he said with asperity.

'False, eh? Can you look me in the face and say you didn't know you were illegally harbouring an escaped convict?'

There was silence.

The missionary realised that this blackguard was master of the situation. He endeavoured to compromise.

'You say you will get two pounds for the boy. Leave him and I will pay you that.'

'Couldn't do it. You see it isn't the two quid. I've got to make up a batch. I contracted to deliver fifty boys and I'm three short. I must have him.'

Weldon spoke firmly.

'But you said a short time ago you could get all the boys you wanted,' the missionary reminded him.

'So I can – all I want, but not always when I want 'em.'

Mr Hyslop dropped his mandatory tone and condescended to plead. He offered three pounds, four, five, and with each advance the face of Weldon broadened with a smile of malicious glee.

'I should like the fiver,' he said, 'but I'm a man of honour and must stick to my bargain. Besides, they will soon know at Blue Krantz the boy is here, so he had better get away with the skin on his back – what there is of it, for I hear they've marked him well.'

An idea occurred to Weldon.

'Tell you what – send for the boy and I'll ask him whether he would rather stay with you or go with me. I'll bet you he prefers me.'

Mr Hyslop called Bulalie. He came up wearing his customary good humoured smile that set off his magnificent teeth.

Weldon addressed him.

'Will you go to Johannesburg and work on a mine? Plenty puza, plenty skoff, and five sovereigns a month.'

Bulalie looked at his master and laughed.

'Ikona, baas.'

It was an emphatic negative.

'Would you rather stay here till the police came and took you back to jail and lashed you?'

Bulalie's smile died. He turned a grave enquiring face to the missionary. He paused awhile as if weighing his reply.

'I will stay here till the baas tells me to go.'

He spoke as one who fully appreciated the consequences of his decision – firmly and quietly.

The missionary felt a throb of delight. This was no acting, but absolute sincerity.

Weldon played his trump.

'Then they will take you to jail and the baas too for hiding a kafir who has run away.'

Bulalie looked at his master. 'Is that true, baas?'

'Perhaps, Bulalie.'

'Will they take you if I go to Johannesburg?'

'Perhaps – perhaps not.'

Bulalie came close to his master, and spoke earnestly.

'Baas, you must not go to jail. Ow, baas! it's a bad place – dark! No, baas. I go to Johannesburg, you stay here.'

'I told you he'd come with me,' Weldon remarked sneeringly.

'Do you mean to take him?'

'Why certainly. What do you think?'

'I think you are a heartless blackguard.'

Weldon laughed insolently. 'Not bad for a parson. But, be civil. It's not too late to drop a hint to the R.M. You know how he loves you. It would do your mission a lot of good if you were prosecuted for harbouring runaway convicts, wouldn't it?'

The missionary winced.

There was no occasion to remind him of this. He was quite alive to the risk he ran of being involved in a damaging scandal. He had no choice but to avoid irritating this soulless creature, for even with the departure of Bulalie, danger was not removed. The fact that he had harboured the boy for over a year could be easily proved.

Weldon wanted to carry off his prize at once, but agreed to stay till morning if he could have a 'reviver.' He was dying for the want of a drop of brandy, he said.

'Why not send to Dando's store? You can have Bulalie and my horse. Write an order and I will send him. He can go there and back in a couple of hours.'

Weldon grinned. 'There are very good reasons why I don't. First I haven't got half-a-sovereign, secondly if I had and sent it, Bob Dando would stick to it on account of a little bit I owe him, and thirdly, as you parsons say, I'm not going to let Bulalie leave till I go with him.'

Mr Hyslop restrained his indignation. He was cowed by this vulgar brute – fearful lest he might provoke him to act upon his covert threat and bring about an exposure of his relation with Bulalie, which would, he knew, do incalculable damage to the mission. He ordered the kitchen boy to saddle up, gave him half-a-sovereign and wrote the necessary authority to supply the bearer with one bottle of brandy. Without an order signed by a white man it is a crime to supply natives with liquor.

There were two farmers at the store when the boy presented the order.

Bob Dando read it out, emphasising the signature.

'I knew it would come to this,' he said. 'The missionary's wife is away, and he wants a comforter. In a couple of days the boy will be back for two bottles, and within a month I shall be supplying three bottles a week. He has started a little sooner than I expected, but better early than late. I shall lay in a stock of bromide. These amateur drunkards fresh out from home are strong on bromide till they get used to a big head in the morning.'

Within a week several farmers within an area of three hundred square miles had heard on the authority of people who had been shown the signed orders, that the missionary at Blue Krantz had taken to drinking to the extent of three bottles of brandy a week — sometimes four.

Mr Hyslop took advantage of the deep sleep that overcame Weldon within an hour of the arrival of the brandy to go to Bulalie's hut and have a long farewell talk.

'Remember all I have taught you, Bulalie. Never drink puza, never tell lies or take things that belong to other people. Do what the white baases tell you, and give all the money you can save to the Protector of Natives to send to me and I will take care of it for you, or buy cattle that shall run on the mission farm and increase, so that when you come back you will be early rich.'

Unfortunately Mr Hyslop's knowledge of the real evils and temptations of life on the mines was very limited; his advice therefore was of a wide and general character, and consequently not calculated to make a great impression.

Bulalie took the addressed envelope and writing paper with which he was to get 'Mahlick' (Marwick, the Protector of Natal Natives on the Rand), to communicate the name of the mine that had absorbed him, and three sovereigns which the missionary could ill spare.

'Baas only owes me ten shillings,' he said.

It was explained that the overplus was a bonsella.

Bulalie put his hand to his mouth and ejaculated the 'ow!' of astonishment.

'Baas is the first white man who ever gave me a bonsella,' he said. Then, handing one of the sovereigns back, 'That's a bonsella for the little piccanin that's coming,' he said.

There was a friendly dispute. It ended in Bulalie tying up the three sovereigns in the little bag that held the letters and his treasured writing book.

Then the missionary said 'good-bye' and shook hands with Bulalie. It was the first time he had ever done such a thing. He was afraid to outrage Colonial prejudice by taking the hand of a kafir in the presence of Weldon; that was why he got over the leave taking in the privacy of the hut. Besides, he was not certain that he would be equal to the ordeal of seeing his first fruits taken to market.

He saddled up the tired horse, rode out into the veld and tried to sleep.

When he returned to the house in the morning it was very lonely.

CHAPTER XVI

TO THE MINES

Weldon had lied, after his manner, when he represented that he could obtain as many recruits as he wished. He was but a beginner at the business, little known to the natives, and disliked where he was known. Therefore, he had to be content with the leavings of more reputable labour agents and the fruits of his cunning, or as he expressed it – his 'funny ways.'

His victims were mainly raw natives allured by lying assurances of impossible wages, deserters from domestic service, boys recruited in some such manner as Bulalie had been obtained, and now and then a *bona fide* volunteer – probably an old mine hand too well known to be recruited by others.

As an ex-member of the force which is sometimes occupied in seeing that the elastic legal restrictions on recruiting in Natal are not flagrantly violated, he was familiar with the art of evading official interference – his only qualification for the work – and though his initial efforts had not been sufficiently effective to justify his continuing a business that pays handsomely.

It was not true, as he had said, that he had a contract to supply fifty or even fifteen boys; but the mine manager to whom he had sold his last batch of thirty had intimated that he could 'do with as many more at the same price' – a premium of one pound a boy. He had refused to do what was customary when dealing with reputable agents – advance something on account for railway and other expenses, for the very good and sufficient reason that he did not place any reliance on Weldon. Consequently the labour agent found himself in a difficulty about transporting his batch to Johannesburg. He had borrowed from a speculative storekeeper enough to carry the thirty odd boys by rail over the border, where they would be safe from interference by the Natal authorities. The remainder of the journey – a matter of 140 miles, would have to be done as in the pre-railway days, on foot, though there was just the chance of his being able to borrow the railway fare off some banker of the road – a canteen keeper.

Bulalie met his new baas by appointment at a railway siding, where he was given a pass and railway ticket. Other boys were picked up in due course, and by nightfall Bulalie was one of a gang of thirty-two natives *en route* for Standerton, which place they had been severally instructed to declare as their objective if questioned. Weldon occupied a first-class carriage, and got out at every station to count heads, but he refrained from associating himself too closely with his freight.

He breathed freely when the border was passed. He felt as a contrabandist must when he has safely passed the scrutiny of the customs officers. The gang were now completely in his power. They could not return, except on foot, unprovided with food or money for the long tramp back to their starting point. To be found in the Transvaal as passless kafirs without a baas or employment to go to meant arrest, fine, and imprisonment and even lashes, or what might be quite as bad, seizure by some Boer, who, under threat of doing his duty by handing them over to the police, would intimidate them into engaging to serve him as farm hands for an indefinite period for problematical pay. The tramp kafir is not encouraged in the Transvaal. A paternal Government has made perfect arrangement to prevent the scandal of an out of work proletariat. The jails are frequent and free, and the doors opening inwards run on well oiled hinges through constant use.

There was one little bit of what Mr Weldon called 'stony patch' to be crossed before he could feel that his troubles were all over. He had to explain or rather avoid explaining, why his undertaking to carry his capture to the mines by train was not carried out. With the bulk of the boys there would be little if any trouble, for they would accept his assurance that the mines were 'just over the mountains yonder.' But four or five of the gang had travelled and knew that they were two days in the train after passing Majuba. As the accepted guides and mentors of the ignorant majority they imparted of their knowledge freely.

Mr Weldon was quite prepared. He singled out the most voluble agitator and asked him what he had been saying.

'We have got off the wagons too soon, baas,' said the boy.

Mr Weldon grew sarcastic.

'Very well, as you know the way, off you go to Johannesburg. Go back to the station and tell the station people they have made a mistake and must send you on further.'

The boy grinned.

'Got no ticket and no money, baas.'

'No, but you have got that and that.'

'That' was two good, well-aimed punches on jaw and neck. The boy put up his hands to protect his face and stood meekly waiting for the rest.

Weldon threw one quick glance at the crowd and knew that the lesson had sunk in as he intended it should. He gave the boy a kick behind, and to the gang the order to march.

They fell in in groups of twos and threes with bundles on head or shoulder and marched, silent at first; then some one laughed and the irrepressible bubbling stream of kafir talk began to flow freely.

At the end of five or six miles, when they had nearly reached a bit of rising ground that would give a view over the mountain and show no sign of the mines, was a wayside store and canteen.

Weldon practised a piece of adroit diplomacy. He halted his ragged regiment of incipient mutineers and purchased bread, biscuits and tinned meat. The feast cost him a sovereign, but it was money well spent.

He made a little speech while the boys fed, consisting of well turned Zulu phrases depicting the joys awaiting the weary pilgrims in the City of Delight, Johannesburg. Puza, first; money, more puza; skoff (food), unlimited skoff, with sheep meat, bullock meat, every day; puza all day. Intombis (girls). Then fights with Basutos, Shangaans – dogs of every tribe whose heads they could break with their kieries – dogs who could not throw an assegai, or knobkierie. A kafir paradise!

He repeated the pæan with judicious variations, flourished his sjambok, made cuts and thrusts, stamped his foot and uttered old tribal war cries, till the boys, their mouths bulging with baking-powder-inflated bread, took up the cries and hailed him Inkoos! (Chief).

Weldon had not lied when he boasted that he knew kafirs. He did know them, their weakness, their docility, their credulity and their easily stirred enthusiasm.

The storekeeper who had been looking on amused, and understanding the game, took a part. He patted Weldon on the back, and lauded him in Zulu, loudly, but of course with no intent that his words should reach the crowd.

'Good baas, best baas that comes along the road. These boys do not know you as I do – as the thousands of boys you take to the mines know you. They are lucky boys to have such a good baas.'

And the two went inside and opened a bottle of whisky, the best in stock, not the brand supplied to casual customers. It was almost good enough to drink when well diluted with ginger-ale.

'You'll do,' the storekeeper remarked, with the approving assurance of an expert. 'If I could spare the cash I'd advance you the fares and go halves. It's jolly rough to have to hoof it, but you'll have better luck next trip. A chap who can bamboozle 'em as you can ought to be able to get all the boys he wants. Break the journey when you come back and give me a look up. I shall be able to talk business then. I happen to know there is going to be a big demand for mine boys presently when half-a-dozen mines are pushed ahead. The companies will be only too glad to pay fifty or sixty shillings a boy within three months. I can see you know how to gather the right sort and keep 'em sweet, and you can rely on me for any cash you want up to a couple of hundred on third share terms.'

Before the pair retired for the night Weldon had persuaded his prospective partner to go a little farther and agree to advance the money necessary for the fares of the gang if the manager of the New Yankee mine to which they were going would undertake to reimburse him on receipt of the boys.

The gang was halted for the night and accommodated in the out-buildings of the store.

Early next day the telegraph was set to work, a satisfactory reply obtained, and the afternoon train from Standerton took westward a gang of thirty-two boys consigned to the New Yankee mine by Weldon and Hacker, labour agents, at a premium of two pounds for each boy delivered.

This was the genesis of the famous firm of labour agents who in five years, from date of their agreement to the death of Weldon from alcoholic excess, sold forty thousand pounds' worth of natives to the mines of the Witwatersrand.

Weldon's luck was in. He delivered his parcel, received his cheque and celebrated in Rand fashion by going on a glorious spree of a week's duration. Not being altogether a fool, he pulled himself together before he had expended his return fare and sufficient to pay for a telegram to Hacker, explaining that he had been laid up by a severe attack of the scourge of Johannesburg – pneumonia.

CHAPTER XVII

A MODEL COMPOUND MANAGER

Sidney Dane, Compound Manager of the New Yankee Gold Mining Company, Limited, was, of course, a Natalian. The mine compound is as much the preserve of the Natalian as the engineroom of a steamship is of Scotsmen; for the very sufficient reason that the youth of the miscalled 'Garden Colony' are the only South Africans who learn native languages.

Dane had acquired his position by virtue of his intimate acquaintance with the kafir, and, incidentally by paying his predecessor two hundred sovereigns in cash and ten pounds a month for five months, which was a fair premium to pay for a billet carrying a salary of £40 per mensem, and considerably less than the sum asked by the compound manager of an older and larger mine for which Dane had negotiated.

Mine magnates, if asked why it is the custom to buy and sell these appointments, would probably express surprise, and even deny that such a traffic existed; nor would their ignorance be improbable. A mine is a large community, containing a much greater area and population than many a Colonial village. To expect directors who reside in Johannesburg, and probably spend less than fifty hours a year on their property, to know all that was going on there, would be unreasonable. If they did know of these transactions, they would have a ready and simple explanation. Life on a mine at £40 per month with quarters can be as nearly idyllic as anything in the sordid, ugly environment of the Rand. The compound manager is less subject to irritating supervision than any other employee. He is practically his own master; his comings in and goings out are not recorded in a time book, and so long as the required number of boys are turned out to go on shift, that almighty personage, the mine manager, has no occasion to talk business or otherwise assert his authority.

Then there is another great attraction, which appeals to the thrifty, careful young Natalian. He can save money. There have been compound managers who have saved a hundred pounds a month out of their salary of forty or fifty; but that has necessitated very strict, almost grinding economy and self-denial; consequently they are the exception rather than the rule. But he would be unworthy the traditions of his class who did not know how to limit his expenditure and restrain his desire for luxuries sufficiently to save nearly all his salary.

Sidney Dane was not of the stingy, cheeseparing type. He was free with his money, but not extravagant; content to possess a smart trap, pony, and riding horse, attend the local races, join a shooting party up country for a week or so during the season, and spend a modest fiver on a Saturday night's amusement in Johannesburg. What was left after paying his board and liquor bill, he put away and never grumbled if it was not more than thirty-five pounds.

That happened to be the amount he had estimated to pay in to his deposit account the day that Weldon brought his batch of boys and received a cheque for sixty pounds, but he found himself nearly ten pounds short. Being a man of action, Dane went into 'camp', as most of the old hands still call Johannesburg, and hunted up the labour agent. He found him in the bar of the Grand National Hotel, 'sobering up' on small brandies and large sodas. The young man looked annoyed, but invited the compound manager to join him in a drink.

'I was coming out to pay you, old chap, but have been awfully seedy,' he began volubly.

Mr Dane took his drink to a table away from the crowd and beckoned Weldon to follow.

'Now, Mr Weldon,' he began, 'I don't know what you call this, but I tell you straight these games won't go down with me. You got your cheque three days ago, and promised faithfully to let me have my bit as soon as you had cashed it. I want thirty-two five-bobs, which is eight sovereigns, and I tell you that if this is the sort of business you do, you sell no more boys to the Yankee or any other mine, for I shall just pass the word round to the other compound managers, and your game will be finished. Let's understand one another. This is our first deal, but it looks like being the last. You are not the only labour agent in the country, so don't you forget it.'

Weldon did something very unusual. He told the truth. He had got drunk, he said, as soon as he cashed the cheque, expressed contrition and paid over eight sovereigns.

'Now have a drink with me and listen to what I've got to say,' Dane said, as he signalled to the barman.

'Our people will be taking a thousand boys during the next two months, and they are prepared to pay two pounds a head. I don't want to be greedy, but as it rests with me to accept or reject, I expect something for my trouble. These are my terms: Four shillings for every boy up to fifty, four-and-six for all over that number, cash down the day you get your cheque.'

Weldon was disposed to haggle. Dane finished his drink and got up.

'Take it or leave it,' he said with the air of a man who meant it. 'I get those terms from the other agents, and they are quite satisfied. Mind, I pass no boy into my compound for a penny less.'

Weldon capitulated.

'While I'm in camp I may as well pay exes,' Dane soliloquised as he left the hotel. 'I'll give Ikey a call.'

He walked to Commissioner Street and turned up a passage leading to the side entrance of a shabby but obviously prosperous bar, entered and called for a whisky which was not served to him.

The barman nodded and indicated with his eyebrows a private door. Dane walked into a small room, furnished partly as an office, partly as the proprietor's snuggery. A well-dressed young man of Jewish appearance sat at the table, busy with a pile of invoices. He greeted the visitor cordially and took down a whisky bottle and box of cigars.

The opening remarks were casual, bearing principally on matters horsey. Then Mr Ikey Bernstein changed the subject abruptly.

'Everythink goin' right?'

'Yes. We had one of our directors on the property on Monday. He was a bit curious to know how many boys were off work. I had about two hundred of 'em getting sober, but as luck would have it they were mostly quiet in their quarters. I had shut the doors in case of stray prowlers, so the old chap didn't see anything. I told him there were too many off for my liking, but that things were improving. I gave him a hint that what liquor got into the compound was supplied by Barzinsky.'

Ikey grinned. 'We mustn't shove Barzinsky off, you know. We ain't afraid of him. I suppose we sell ten bottles to his one. Let him have the credit of supplying the lot. How about the police?'

'Blind as owls in the sunshine. I gave two kafirs into custody for drunk and disorderly yesterday. We mustn't be too lenient. I've got to study my character as a strict manager, you know.'

Both men laughed. Mr Bernstein had taken something out of a cash-box and pushed it with his be-diamonded finger towards Dane.

'That'll help to pay exes in town tonight,' he said.

Dane carelessly slipped the ten sovereigns into his waistcoat pocket.

'Thanks. Are you satisfied?'

Mr Bernstein put out his hand. Dane shook it and rose.

'You might give a hint to that new man you've got in the canteen not to be so cocky with the kafirs. He has knocked several of my boys about, and they don't like it. The beggars are artful as monkeys. They know that the police are on the look-out, and they might turn spiteful and speak too loud. I just mention it as a hint. We can't be too careful. The local newspaper has been saying things lately about the Sunday drunks.'

Mr Bernstein nodded knowingly.

'It's all right. They're only playing up for a bit of sugar. They'll be sweetened presently. We're going to give them a big advertisement of our bottle store in the township.'

'That's right. I can't afford to have them on my track. One of my directors has got the illicit liquor business on the brain just now. I suppose you saw his speech at the last meeting of the Chamber of Mines?'

Mr Bernstein nodded and winked, and put out his hand again.

Mr Dane shook it and helped himself to a cigar.

'Take a dozen, man.'

He obliged, and said good morning.

As he passed out of the passage he felt and recounted the coins in his pocket.

'A darned sight freer with his cigars than his quids,' he thought, 'but the quids are good; that's more than his cigars are. Never mind, I can give them away at the smoker tonight.'

'The genial Sid Dane,' as the local newspaper invariably described the compound manager of the New Yankee, was to take the chair that evening at a smoking concert on an adjacent mine. The circumstance was unimportant, but significant as an evidence of the popularity of the cheery, frank, open-handed C.M. In the ordinary course the compliment should have been paid to John Fraser, who held on the Belmont the corresponding position to Dane on the Yankee, but Fraser lacked the geniality of his rival and was in every respect his antithesis. Dane's motto was 'Make things as pleasant for everybody as you can,' and he acted up to it consistently. The result was that things were made very pleasant for him.

The tradesmen who held contracts for the supply of food and such material as was required for the compound agreed in regretting that there were not more managers like Dane. He never fussed or wrote letters threatening to 'inform my chief' if the bread or meat happened to be a few hundred pounds short of weight or not up to sample. At the worst he would call in at the office and remark, in his casual, jocular way, 'Awful rotten stuff that last parcel; I reckon you didn't lose much on that deal.' Or to the bread man, 'I fancy there's something gone wrong with the multiplication table you use; I'm about a thousand rations short on the month.' And the butcher would explain that he had picked up a carcase or two very cheaply as it was a bit off, and playfully ask Dane to accept a fiver for calling attention to the poor quality, while the baker would express astonishment and regret and beg to be allowed to reimburse Dane to the extent of a few sovereigns for having the trouble to call.

Fraser having none of the tact of Dane, and being too petty-minded to act up the 'live and let live' axiom, never failed to count and weigh everything before signing a receipt, and had no scruples about keeping the delivery man hanging about the compound while he checked and doubly checked the consignment. When remonstrated with for wasting the valuable time of other people's employees he would reply in his sneering way that he was studying the interests of the tradesman by making sure that he was not wronging himself by delivering more than he would be paid for.

In the little amenities of neighbourliness Dane shone conspicuously. If one of the contractors wanted the use of a few boys for nothing, the loan or gift of a bit of timber, coal or other trifle, Dane could always be relied upon to oblige, while Fraser was as certain to rebuff the applicant by a curt excuse to the effect that he could not give away the property of the company − a company with a capital of half a million and paying dividends of thirty and forty per cent., unable to spare the use of a few of its kafirs or a paltry load of wood from the piles on piles encumbering the ground!

The same mania for magnifying trifles was manifested by Fraser in the handling of the details of the compound. When an unusually heavy rainstorm had made a bit of a mess of the boys' sleeping quarters, Fraser worried the manager by alarmist pictures of flooded floors and leaking roofs into spending a couple of hundred pounds on repairs. Even then he was not satisfied, but coolly attributed a slight outbreak of pneumonia and typhoid that occurred about a week later to the dilapidated condition of the compound. The rather heavy mortality among the natives was commented upon by one of the papers, which sent a reporter to interview Fraser. Seeing a chance to get a little cheap notoriety, instead of ordering the man off the premises, he showed him round. The result was a scandalous article under the senational heading, 'How Mine Kafirs are Killed. Housed worse than Pigs.' Fraser pleaded that he was not responsible for what the reporter wrote; that he had only given him permission to look round for himself. The directors very generously accepted this feeble excuse, but warned him to be careful. His show of studying the interests of the company had had its desired effect in persuading some of the board that they had a conscientious servant in Fraser.

Sid Dane's treatment of the matter was in keeping with his light-hearted disposition and systematic refusal to go half way to meet trouble. When the kafirs went to him and complained that the rain fell on their sleeping places and drenched them, he laughed good-humouredly, and pointed out that they had received a good washing which they much needed, and if the roof was broken in parts it was an advantage, as they would know when it rained without the trouble of getting up and going outside to look.

Dane was rarely worried by the complaints and imaginary grievances of his boys. They knew him too well to emulate the whining schoolboy. A new hand now and then would go to him with some nonsensical story of oppression, but he rarely went twice. A new cook after a week's experience of his duties had the temerity to suggest that the meat supplied by the contractor was many pounds short.

'What have you done with it?' the manager asked.

'Never had it, baas; every day boys come to me and say they have not had enough. Often I cannot give them all meat.'

'I think your memory is a little bit out of order,' Dane replied; 'I must try to mend it.'

He put the cook in the stocks, with a native to stand by with a sjambok to see that the victim did not endeavour to relieve the strain on his muscles by lying on his back.

The inventor of that ancient form of mild restraint has never received proper recognition of his ingenuity in producing an instrument of torture so innocently harmless in appearance that its application has always been regarded as a fit subject for humour. What could look less like a tortured creature than a man sitting on the ground with ankles merely passed through two large holes that do not pinch or compress the flesh half as much as a pair of handcuffs? Nobody but the victim notices that the ankles are raised six or eight inches from the ground, forcing the body into a position that strains the muscles of the back and brings on excruciating pains that last for hours, even days after release.

The stocks at the New Yankee had been designed by Mr Dane, who had introduced a great improvement. The holes for the ankles were placed six, twelve, eighteen, twenty-four and thirty-six inches apart. As the intensity of the torture is increased by widening the distance, the degree of punishment could be regulated to a nicety.

The cook was given the maximum stretch, and two hours in which to test its efficacy as a mnemonic stimulant.

At the end of that time he declared with many groans and moans he remembered that he must have used the meat without noticing it. An hour more of the torture and he would have remembered and admitted having eaten the missing four hundred pounds at one surreptitious meal.

The implied imputation against the *bona fides* of the meat contractor having been withdrawn by the frank confession of the real culprit, he was released, and went about his work for two days with body bent at an angle of sixty.

Nobody who knew the genial Dane would ever accuse him of cruelty. He was firm, because he 'knew kafirs', but, as he often said, he did not believe in brutality. That is why he rarely handed over recalcitrants to the police. Magistrates were so absurdly official. They expected every statement made against an accused kafir to be borne out by a witness, which meant taking boys, and even white men, to town to waste the day hanging about the court over a case which probably ended in the infliction of a fine the kafir could not pay, and had to work out in jail, and a remand for further evidence, or even an acquittal. The latter was fatal to discipline on the mine. The triumphant boy would return to boast of his victory and put on airs and consequences that invariably resulted in Dane having to take the impudent rascal into a quiet shed and convince him, by two dozen from a sjambok well laid on, that his acquittal was a mistake and jubilation premature.

The natives have a name for every compound manager on the Rand, always descriptive, generally amusingly accurate. By it the owner is known in every kraal in kafirdom that yields its overplus of manhood to the mines, and thousands who have never seen him are familiar with his personality and characteristics, even as the British peasant in some remote village knows well political celebrities whom he has heard of only through the descriptive reporter. 'Genial Sid Dane' was famous by a name difficult to write and impossible of pronunciation by Europeans. It meant the man who is a gentle fawn by daylight but a tiger-cat by night.

CHAPTER XVIII

IN THE COMPOUND

If within two months of his arrival in the compound of the New Yankee, Bulalie had been called as a witness before some commission of enquiry as to the condition of natives on the mines, his testimony and appearance would have satisfied the most prejudiced that the compound was a branch establishment of whatever may be the kafir's concept of Paradise.

Bulalie was truly happy, with the happiness of a healthy, high-spirited child suddenly enfranchised with freedom from control left to do as it liked amid new and attractive surroundings. Compared with life in the kraal and mission station, that of the compound was as the bustling gaiety of London to the youth fresh from the drowsy village; domestic service in Natal was irksome imprisonment.

Bulalie smiled at the innocence which had led him to believe throughout his childhood that Umgungundhlovu was the most wonderful place of the white man on earth. Now he knew it for a sleepy, barren place of wide, empty streets, white-faced and shrill-voiced missises, and policemen who lived to 'run in' kafirs. Here on the mines was wonder on wonder; in the streets of Johannesburg men and women as plenty as mealie stalks in a big garden, and in the shops − ow! That was the only word that described them − ow! drawn out long and lingeringly through the fingers held over his mouth.

Even the kafirs were more plentiful and varied than he had ever seen − kafirs of tribes whose names he only recalled with an effort, kafirs with speech and customs so different to his own that he would look over at the corners of the big compound where they kept aloof with almost as much wonderment as he first regarded the Indians he saw in such vast crowds in Maritzburg.

Little wonder that Bulalie, like most of his kind, was delighted with the new life. He neither knew nor cared to know that the conditions amid which he lived were unique, abnormal; that they represented only the sordid, brutal side of the white man's civilisation, as unlike the phase of existence the philanthropist imagines when he talks of civilising the native as the London viewed through the atmosphere of an East-End slum is like the city of luxury and refinement pictured by the romantic village maiden with the aid of a 'high-life' novel.

Baas Weldon's lurid description of the joys of the compound had not proved altogether overdrawn. Much had been realised; what had not doubtless would be.

Bulalie was receiving fifty-three shillings a month. He never had seen so much in one handful, and spent half of it at the kafir truck store in childish unnecessaries before he had quite counted it all. Of course he bought cooked meat, almost every day, cakes, jam and sugar, eating the mealie pap supplied freely from the compound cookhouse only when he had no white man's food. One thing he would not buy – puza, rum, against which the missionary had warned him. He had touched it but once since that night of foolishness when he had talked too much to Dick. Besides, Bulalie was not a fool. He saw every day what happened in the compound through the puza – how kafirs quarrelled with and fought their brothers, shouted and sang till the compound manager would come slashing his sjambok and dragging off the noisiest to be put in the stocks or locked up in the dark place where the bad kafirs were put, to come out next morning with dry lips and eyes that bulged, and bodies sore from the cuts of the baas's sjambok or the sticks of his head boys.

There were awful things talked about that black hole, the inside of which Bulalie had never seen. He had heard kafirs crying out, some through the sickness that came after too much puza, many because the baas was squeezing the calves of their legs by kneeling on them, or twisting and punching parts of their bodies that would not show any marks.

He was very clever and cunning in making pain without showing it, was Baas Dane. He could twist a boy's arm till he shrieked as if touched with a hot iron; and when the shriek came out he would look so surprised and say, 'What's the matter with the fool? I haven't touched him yet.'

He was very fond of that arm twist. Boys always tried to pass him on the right hand that held the sjambok, for it was with the other that he stung like a scorpion that hides in the hollow and dark places.

Bulalie as yet knew these things only by sight and hearsay. Fortune had smiled on him. He was with a gang of surface workers that never went down in the cage to the mine, but were employed in the varied work of pick and shovel, loading and unloading stores under a white foreman.

Dane had many qualities to justify his reputation as a successful compound manager, and not the least of them was his knowledge of how to humour the prejudices and stimulate the predilections of his boys. He knew, apart from tribal considerations, who were best for underground or surface work, and

Bulalie was at once marked out as a future bell wether among the surface hands.

There was another reason for his regarding the boy favourably. The New Yankee was one of the show mines of the Rand. Its directors rather encouraged the globe-trotting visitor to go over the property, for it would bear strict investigation – at any rate such scrutiny as a casual non-technical person was likely to give it.

Sid Dane efficiently backed up his manager in this particular, and the compound of the New Yankee was probably the most visited, quoted and photographed on the Rand, and its manager as skilful a showman as ever bluffed an audience.

In his early days at the mine, Dane was disposed to resent the intrusion of visitors. Like most Colonials, he could not conceive how any white man could be interested in kafirs, even making allowance for the simplicity which all Natalians are agreed is the characteristic of an English tourist in South Africa.

One day a lady visitor asked, among other absurd questions, whether any of the natives in the compound were still cannibals, and exhibited such genuine disappointment at learning they were practically vegetarians from birth that Dane resolved that future visitors should be provided with information more in harmony with what they wanted than prosy fact. Opportunity soon arrived, and within a few months Sid Dane was known in mining circles as the most ingenious and daring player of the game known as 'spoof'. He had coached several intelligent kafirs to play up to him, and practice had made chief actor and supers adepts.

'You would never think that a year ago that kafir' – pointing to a sedate and cleanly native in trousers and flannel shirt – 'was killing and eating his enemies,' he would remark casually when escorting a party of visitors over his domain.

'Come here, Zogo. How many men have you killed and eaten?' he would ask in Zulu, then in English.

Zogo would hold up both hands two or three times and try to pronounce in English 'thirty-six.'

If the visitors were interested in this type of civilised savage, Dane would call up 'the son of Chaka the Second, the most blood-thirsty chief in kafirdom,' or 'Malulu, the famous chief of the Bulongas, deposed by the Government for his atrocities, and now earning his bread as a Christianised mine boy.'

If the gentler aspect of native life appealed more, Dane would show the son of Dr Livingstone's favourite body servant, Emin Pasha's ex-pipe bearer,

Stanley's first recruit, or even Mungo Park's tent boy. Now and then the subjects refuted the story obviously by youth and appearance, or not noticing that the visitors included one who had previously toured the compound, Dane would introduce the converted cannibal of the previous visit as Mungo Park's tent boy. This enforced the necessity for more careful stage management and rehearsal. But success, and the applauding laughter of those in the secret, induced recklessness and the cultivation of the art of improvisation.

A soulful young lady deeply interested in mission work was entranced by learning on the authority of the compound manager that the most severe and effective form of punishment he could and did inflict on wrong-doers was forbidding attendance at church on Sunday, and the story duly appeared with approving comment in a very serious and simple publication.

'What are they singing?' another enquired, indicating a group of kafirs sitting on the ground and chanting, to the accompaniment of rhythmically beaten paraffin tins, a native indecency.

'That is the choir of the Zolonga Native Church practising the kafir version of "Shall we gather at the river?"' was the straightfaced reply.

An inspection of the compound manager's private album was generally accorded to a particularly gullible set of visitors.

An amateur photographer in the assaying department was fond of making up studies of the grotesque and absurd with the aid of a large assortment of incongruous garments. A big, burly, middle-aged kafir in a baby's bib and cap, a boy in a corset and lady's hat, another wearing his legs through the arms of a soldier's tunic and similar improbabilities would be shown the delighted visitors, with the bland assurance that 'they often come from the kraal like that.'

There were many things that visitors did not see in the compound of the New Yankee; the manager did not parade them, for the very good reason that they would probably not be accepted with such approving interest as the romances. They would also require explaining and justifying, a task for which Sid Dane had neither the desire nor ability. English people newly arrived in the country held such absurd notions about kafirs that it was waste of time to attempt to correct them. Dane was quite content to abide by the verdict of results. He was baas of 3 000 boys, and it was his business to see that a fair percentage of them earned their wage. As a matter of fact he was well aware that an undue percentage did not, but thanks to his skill in handling time-sheets the fact that from fifteen to twenty-five per cent were frequently incapacitated by drink every Monday after Sunday's debauch did not appear on the record in such naked bluntness. Other mines had even a larger average, and this fact he did not let the directors forget when the liquor curse came in for deprecation, as it regularly did.

Dane admitted with regret that too many of his boys were victims of the illicit liquor-seller, but he would point with pride to his having been instrumental in procuring the conviction of several kafirs caught in the act of selling liquor in the compound, or that a poaching Peruvian not in the illicit 'ring' had had his shebeen raided by the police, and the manager, specially engaged to take such risks, sent to prison for three months. The result, Dane would aver, was a marked diminution in the length of Monday's list of drunk and incapables. He did not comment on the noteworthy circumstance that, though other places were raided, the proprietors, somehow, were never caught. Apparently they were warned in time by kafirs not desirous of having their sources of liquor supply cut off.

Bulalie had not been in the compound long before he learned that his knowledge of the ways of the police, gained by his long watchings against sudden invasion of his father's kraal, was useful. Almost imperceptibly he was exalted to a recognised position as scout and spy for the Zulus of his compound. He had quickly acquired the knack of recognising a 'trap' boy sent by the police to worm out the secret of the 'underground passage' by which bottles of liquor were conveyed from the shebeen to the compound. His association with clever convicts in jail, and their stories of successful outwitting of white men were producing effect and reward. Within three months Bulalie was the cleverest of the small gang of natives who earned threepence and even a shilling a bottle by smuggling in liquor for others less skilful and cautious. He found very early in the chapter that he had nothing to fear from Baas Dane, so long as he did not awkwardly run up against him while carrying liquor only partially concealed in blanket or coat rolled into a bulky bundle. If he was foolish enough to force the baas to notice him, he ran the risk of a smart thrashing on the spot, the smashing of the bottles, and further thrashings from the disappointed clients for whom he was acting.

But only very rarely did Bulalie blunder. Whether it was that he had absorbed it from his baas and missis at Blue Krantz, or whether it was part of the natural smartness that had won the appreciation of Baas Boggis, Bulalie possessed a remarkable amount of tact. He had no need to be told that Baas Dane was purposely blind to the regular importation of the loved and prohibited liquor; that his loud threats of severe punishment, when he could not help seeing a parcel in transit, were only so much acting, since he never said a word against the smuggling unless the directors or other white men were about.

Dane's observant eye had fallen on Bulalie, and the boy recognised that a great compliment had been paid him when the baas, after a few months, selected him out of many score candidates for a position about his person. Bulalie was picking up English very quickly, and could be trusted to convey messages to white men – a duty which gave him many agreeable jaunts into town or to adjacent mines. His knowledge of the shady side of mine life increased by leaps and bounds. There was not a trick practised in the compound that he did not know; not an illicit liquor-seller's agent or police 'trap' boy that Bulalie could not recognise; and he was cautious in displaying his knowledge. The advice of Bacheta never to display all one knows had become a life's axiom, and 'Long Bulalie', or 'The Shadow', as he was labelled, became a trusted agent of all who had shady transactions with the compound of the New Yankee, and their name was legion.

To Sid Dane he was invaluable. He could put Bulalie to check the baker's or butcher's delivery on behalf of the cook, knowing that the tactful checker would not make a fuss and cry 'Hold!' when the baker counted ten loaves as twenty. If he was sent as escort to half-a-dozen boys illegitimately lent to oblige a friend, Bulalie could always be trusted to give a satisfactory explanation to any inquisitive official who wanted to know more than was good. If a present was to be conveyed from some contractor bent on conciliating the compound manager, Bulalie knew how to transport it to his baas's quarters without ostentatious display, and his quick perception and ear for English enabled him to overhear many casual comments by white visitors that were not intended for Dane's ear.

In short, Bulalie had, by force of circumstance and capacity, developed into a useful jackal, scout and general aider and abettor of as clever and unscrupulous a compound manager as ever waxed fat at the expense of employers, employees and contractors, not to mention the illicit liquor sellers. Towards them Dane's attitude was officially hostile, privately passive. Their requirements were extremely simple: they only asked that his blind eye should be most often turned in their direction.

As Bulalie grew in wisdom there came the understanding that knowledge was power and pelf. The money he was able to save by rigorous abstention from liquor at five and six shillings a bottle he did not remit after the first month or two to Mr Hyslop. He invested it in loans at cent per cent. He could generally be depended upon to make up the three or four shillings lacking to complete the pool being engineered among a dozen impecunious habitual drunkards yearning for a stiff 'soupie'. As Baas Dane had the handling of the wagecards, Bulalie had no anxiety as to repayment; even failing that guarantee, he could always fall back upon his strong right arm and his acknowledged strength as the baas's boy; and it is to be feared that having a giant's strength he rarely failed to use it like a giant. The example of the tyrannical authority of which he had been a victim had not been lost upon Bulalie.

Alcohol excites and carries in its train many vices which are not the exclusive prerogative of white men, and Bulalie found the business of the procurer quite as profitable as that of liquor agent. The 'white' creatures who owned the houses found no difficulty in tempting Bulalie to act as their representative in the compound, and it is but just to Mr Sid Dane to acknowledge that he did not demand from his confidential boy any share of his wages of sin derived from this source. Mr Dane drew the line at the illicit liquor scoundrels; the other could not be touched by white hands.

One night the quarters of a batch of fifty Zulu drill boys, known for their sobriety, general steadiness and thrift, were rifled during their absence on shift, and their savings, variously estimated between two hundred and three hundred pounds, disappeared.

Bulalie got a bad scare. He took up the plank underneath his stretcher bed in the cosy little ten-by-six iron shed that his master had assigned to him, and extracted a jam-pot.

Sid Dane was not usually surprised at anything a kafir did, but he was astonished when Bulalie poured a chinking little torrent of gold from the jam-pot on to the table, with a request that the baas would put it on to the telegraph wires and send it on to Preacher Hyslop at Blue Krantz for Bulalie, to buy cattle – red ones, for preference.

A few days later the Rev. David Hyslop was astounded by receiving a draft on the Natal Bank at Maritzburg for one hundred and seventeen pounds, with a formal letter signed 'Sid Dane, Compound Manager, New Yankee G. M. Co., Ltd.,' requesting an acknowledgment per return of amount in favour of Bulalie.

The money represented the savings for thirteen months out of a wage of fifty-seven shillings per *mensem*.

CHAPTER XIX

THE IMPEACHMENT OF THE MISSIONARY

'Alice, this decides me. We go to Johannesburg.'

It was the ultimatum of the Rev. David Hyslop, after he and his wife had read, re-read and discussed Sid Dane's curt letter, and brought their combined limited knowledge of 'perfectly good' paper money to bear on the bank draft.

That a kafir receiving a wage of fifty-three shillings per month should be able to save the enormously disproportionate amount of one hundred and seventeen pounds in a year astounded him. It did more. It opened up very unpleasant suggestions.

The missionary had but the vaguest notion of the life of a kafir on the mines, and though he had reason to believe that vices in many new and alluring forms assailed the native there, he had never associated them with money-getting.

When, after two small contributions, Bulalie ceased to send money to be hoarded the missionary sadly conjectured that his pet pupil had joined the majority as a reckless spendthrift and was living up to his income. He deeply regretted his inability to convey a warning word. Now his duty, he conceived, was to discover the secret of this unexpected development of acquisitiveness, and not merely warn against it, but repress it, for the more he regarded the puzzle the more certain was he that Bulalie's wealth was ill-gotten.

He did not purchase cattle with it; neither did he invest it. He went to Maritzburg, consulted a reputable lawyer, and under his advice placed the money in the government Savings Bank fully and unequivocally secured to Bulalie through the joint trusteeship of himself and the solicitor.

Mr Hyslop had very good reason for this precautionary measure.

Events of the past year had rendered it absolutely essential that he should walk circumspectly. He was now a marked man, surrounded with enemies, active and passive, spies and informers.

Fate had decided that he should become the popular embodiment of all that was attackable in the missionary. The Rev. David Hyslop had had fame thrust upon him, and he had been for many wearying months fighting single-handed on behalf of Missiondom. His comings out and goings in, his words and actions – all were recorded in spoken or printed words, sometimes briefly and contemptuously, at others with all the weight and importance that the combined arts of the imaginative reporter and the clever sub-editorial headline inventor could bestow.

Like many great events, the notoriety of the Krantz missionary grew out of a trifle.

The trifle was the snub-nosed, red-headed Afrikander-Irish Court Messenger of the Magisterial Division of Blue Krantz.

The famous 'Notes from Blue Krantz' had won universal fame. That is, a third of the twenty thousand white adults in Natal who read read them – not so much because they mainly retailed the trivial gossip of an insignificant spot on the map, but because the writer had a gift of racy, vulgar humour of a type that appeals to that large section of the public who delight in seeing someone in the pillory being pelted with offensive missiles by a skilful marksman. As everybody passed through Blue Krantz in the course of a year, a mischievous imp with a catapult need never be at a loss for a mark. 'Q. Q.,' the anonymous author of the famous notes, shot freely and frequently, and as he had the tact never to make himself objectionable to popular and influential personages or public officials, he was permitted a licence and freedom in 'tickling up' others that maddened the victims as much as it delighted the exempted onlookers. Naturally in a community so small his subjects were limited; but like a singer or actor with a limited *repertoire*, he had to ring the changes and extract all and sometimes more than seemed possible from them. Thus it came that the most trivial sayings and doings of his chosen butts were of necessity expanded and distorted with immense ingenuity.

Chief of his stock characters was the 'Kafir Disintegrator', who had become as much a feature of the notes as the mother-in-law or inexperienced young wife are to the alleged comic journalist. To the public at large he was the missionary of popular prejudice – a foolish, pretentious, money-grabbing hypocrite, who posed as a martyr to principle, and exploited the kafir for his own profit and glory. One phase was always kept uppermost – the political. The 'Disintegrator' was systematically presented as a teacher of the detestable doctrine of Black and White Equality, *ergo* a creature as dangerous as the scoundrel who makes a fortune by 'gun-running', and helps to expedite the great racial war that is the dread of the serious and responsible, the secret hope of the unthinking, Colonial South African. As an abstraction, the invention of a humorous writer, 'the Disintegrator' amused its thinly-veiled original. When David Hyslop realised that he was personally associated with the character, and privately and publicly accused of saying and doing the foolish things attributed to his stage impersonation, he began to regard the matter as beyond a joke. He laughed as heartily as anyone when he found himself made the hero of stupid stories of missionary fatuity collected from ancient sources and localised; he picked up from them many a useful hint and suggestion on what to avoid in his intercourse with black and white, and frankly admitted the cleverness of many of the quips and cranks. But this persistent blackening of himself and inferentially of all other missionaries as stirrers up of racial strife was doing serious harm to the cause. In self-defence he sent a protest to the Government reminding them of a regulation forbidding civil servants contributing to the press.

The 'Notes from Blue Krantz' suddenly ceased. In their stead appeared at intervals letters to the editor from 'Anti-humbug', 'Scrutator', 'Old Colonial', and others whose phraseology and literary style were strangely similar, asking questions and propounding hypothetical cases that to the uninitiated looked perfectly natural and innocuous, but became very grave libels when read in their intended application to a real person.

There were rumours of native unrest at this time, and the Colony was in a humour to accept blindly the suggestions that the growing assertiveness of the kafirs was the direct result of missionary propaganda.

Mr Hyslop determined to trace some of the stories against him to their origin and bring the authors to book.

He was horrified when he looked over the list of charges made at various times, and believed and passed on by nearly every person with whom he came in contact. They began mildly, but increased in virulence as the list lengthened.

First he was accused generally and specifically of teaching the kafirs that they were as good as whites, and consequently justified in resenting white domination.

This being a stock charge against all missionaries, he did not feel called upon to make any heroic or special effort to rebut it. He was content to allow results to supply the contradiction, and, if challenged, to cite Colonial history in support of the fact that Christianised kafirs had never figured largely in native risings.

The second count in the long indictment was apparently based on an exaggerated and distorted version of the affair of Mozulikase, the kid, and the daughter. It took the form of a story of ruthless oppression and proselytising. He had taken a mean advantage of the indebtedness of the father to seize his only kid and hold the daughter as a hostage, for payment of an impossible and iniquitous rent. In the meantime the girl had been compulsorily Christianised, and in consequence cut off from her own people, and her father deprived of his right to sell the girl as a wife to a kafir who was prepared to pay the old man's debt. A later and enlarged edition of the story told how Anna had been sent into domestic service in Durban, and had become an outcast.

The third charge was the familiar one of exploiting the labour of converts. The missionary, it was alleged, by threats and persuasions induced natives to till his land and toil like slaves without wage.

'In that case,' Mr Hyslop remarked, 'I deserve not abuse but a public testimonial, for it seems I have been able to get for nothing what Colonials fail to obtain for payment – hard work from a kafir.'

It was true that he did now and then succeed in persuading a few natives to work off arrears of rent and assistance in cash and kind received in time of need, but the balance was still heavily against the mission.

Charge four was a rehash of an old slander against missionaries. He was accused of having refused to distribute among the natives sundry articles sent out to them by English supporters of the mission, and selling them to the storekeepers.

'I plead guilty to that,' he remarked to his wife, who was listening to the reading of the impeachment with tearful indignation. 'They are referring to your baby bandages and night caps, dear.'

Mrs Hyslop's slight sense of humour was roused. She lay back in her chair and laughed hysterically as she recalled her first attempts at introducing civilised methods of baby rearing.

Before the experiment prompted by her artless enthusiasm had proved a disastrous failure, Mrs Hyslop had written to her lady friends at home a glowing and probably too optimistic account of her labours. Next month's mail brought a large parcel of flannel bandages, baby caps, bibs and tuckers, and a score of other articles of everyday use in English nurseries, but supremely superfluous in a kafir kraal. By this time the young reformer had realised the meaning of the ancient jest regarding the despatch of fans and ice-creams to the Greenlanders, and muffs and sleeping socks to the Tropics. She shed tears over the evidences of a futile labour of love, and passed many anxious hours in drafting a letter of thanks to the generous donors that would express that gratitude which marks a sense of favours to come without prejudice to those received.

The disposal of the gifts in something approaching the conditions of the bequest was for long a stock subject of discussion between husband and wife, till an opportunity came for turning them into cash, and the proceeds were expended on articles which more ripened experience had shown to be better adapted to the needs of the kafir nurseries.

So far the charges had not greatly annoyed or hurt the missionary. The knowledge that they were of a stock character, and belonged to the familiar type of vulgar invective which labels lawyers thieves and doctors quacks or poisoners, diluted their biting bitterness. Even some of those who repeated them to him did so with a laugh that expressed amused incredulity. But, as generally happens, he was long in learning the more serious imputations. People who chaffed him as a kafir trader in mission stock, or a lucky and much-to-be-envied controller of cheap native labour, hesitated to tell him that he was a reputed drunkard. That this was added to his suspected crimes was unguessed and unsuspected until a Christian friend, 'having the cause at heart, and being actuated only by the highest and most friendly motives,' wrote him a letter which presumed the charges true, and expatiated on the folly of anyone placing himself in the hands of the enemy by sending documentary proof of his indiscretion and weakness by a kafir servant to a storekeeper notoriously hostile to missionary endeavour.

He recalled with a spasm of horror and vain regret the several occasions on which he had repeated the friendly office that the ex-policeman Weldon had first extracted from him. Perhaps half-a-dozen times he had been pressed by casual visitors to allow the use of his name for the purpose of obtaining liquor from Bob Dando's store. On each occasion the pretext had been a bold avowal that an outstanding account rendered it improbable that the liquor would be sent if Dando knew his customer. Mr Hyslop remembered that the tempters were generally police troopers or minor officials from Blue Krantz. He could now see the hand of the Court Messenger in the business. It was part of the scheme of vengeance he had openly threatened.

The missionary rode over to the store and demanded the return of the damning documents.

Bob Dando was polite but firm. He refused to surrender them.

They were his only protection, he said, against any spiteful person or teetotal crank who chose to accuse him of having broken the law by supplying liquor to natives. Of course he denied having shown the passes to any person, and explained the public knowledge of their existence to the presence of white men in the bar when the missionary's kafir had presented the orders.

Mr Hyslop left unsatisfied and with a disagreeable suspicion that he had done a foolish thing, which would have been reduced to a certainty had he heard Dando's comments when telling the story.

'He fitted the cap,' he said. 'People don't worry themselves over charges that have no foundation. It was worth a fiver to see his face when I refused to give him the passes.'

The next published version of the liquor story was that the missionary at Blue Krantz had offered Dando five pounds a-piece for the return of orders for liquor bearing his signature.

The casual critics who accuse Colonial farmers of being credulous overlook the well-established fact that the solitary life, particularly in a mountainous country, tends to the cultivation of imagination.

The last charge, so far as the missionary had evidence, alleged against him the civil crime of harbouring escaped convicts. The farmers as a body did not unduly emphasise this.

They were disposed to symapthise with one who availed himself of an opportunity to obtain the free services of a kafir. The subject was a delicate one, and could only be openly discussed by officials who lived too near the jail to harbour a convict without detection.

The knowledge that all these despiteful things were being uttered against him did not disturb the subject the less because his conscience was clear. It was for the cause that he mourned. That white men should believe and circulate such stories was saddening; it was heartbreaking to know, as he did, that the slanders were repeated to natives in other districts. He had been publicly jeered at as a drunkard by a kafir on another location. Then came the horrifying discovery that his sweet, patient wife was included in the attack. He heard that she was in the habit of brutally beating her maid.

Unfortunately there was, as with most of the stories told against himself, a mole-hill to form the basis of the mountain.

When the baby came to the mission station the young mother persisted in performing for it every office, till there came a time when want of strength overcame indiscreet devotion, and she allowed Anna to share the labour. One awful day the girl was set to watch the infant lying in its little cot on the warm verandah while the mother snatched much-needed rest. Something, maternal instinct perhaps, brought her out in time to find the child black in the face from futile effort to dislodge the banana which the attentive Anna had forced down its throat in unsophisticated kindness.

When the danger was over, and the mother had partially recovered from the shock that was more severe than that suffered by the cause of it, Anna began an explanation, which was the nearest approach to an apology ever extracted under any circumstances.

'I have often put bigger bananas into baby's mouth,' she remarked, in a tone that to the alarmed mother implied a readiness to do it again.

For the first time in her career as an exemplar Mrs Hyslop allowed the woman and mother to overcome the Christian.

She seized a small garden rake that Fate had cruelly ordained should be near her hand, and brought it with unscientific inaccuracy across the head of the petrified maid, who stared stolidly at her demented mistress, while the blood trickled down her fat, unlovely face from an ugly scalp wound.

Next instant the mistress was crying and sobbing hysterically, atoning by lavishing care and caresses.

CHAPTER XX

THE UNFINISHED SERMON

The difficulty of procuring prompt and proper medical attention for mother and babe had necessitated a sojourn in the capital. While there Mr Hyslop was invited to occupy the pulpit at a Nonconformist church whose enterprising Pastor had been stirring the dry bones by a series of 'popular' and unconventional services with sermons or addresses by 'men who had something to say,' or tried to say something a little off the stereotyped model.

Mr Hyslop hesitated before accepting, till the motto on the handbills and advertisements attracted and inspired him – 'Addresses by men who have something to say.'

'I have something I should very much like to say to the face of a congregation of Colonials,' he remarked, when the Pastor asked his subject. The only question is whether the people and you would like me to say it.'

The Pastor looked uneasy.

'Of course we cannot give an opinion until we have heard what it is,' he said. 'It had occurred to me that you, as a comparatively new-comer to the country, might very appropriately say something that would point out the good cause for rejoicing and thankfulness Colonials have in being blessed by residence in a country free from the intolerance, bigotry and narrowness that obtain in the older civilisations, where the shadow of dead creeds still overhangs; and how it behoves them to avail themselves of their glorious privileges to —— to ——'

'To extend that privilege to others,' Mr Hyslop suggested.

'Exactly. I think it would please the congregation. We have some very influential people at our services, and they like to have the Colony well spoken of.'

The church was crowded by a representative throng, not because of the preacher; they came as they had every Sunday evening during the series because the musical portion of the entertainment was good and not conspicuously 'religious.' Some were there expectant; one or two of the 'men with something to say' who had occupied the pulpit had been worth listening to. This missionary was a stranger, therefore presented an element of novelty. A few, very few, who had heard faint echoes of the strife proceeding in the Blue Krantz district came to see a man of whom they had heard queer stories. About a tenth of the congregation near the doors left when the musical portion of the service was over, but that was no reflection on the preacher – it was their custom.

The incident, however, was noted by the missionary. His sensitive soul saw in it a reflex and repetition of the boycotting of which he had been a victim for many months. It gave him an opening that arrested the attention of his listeners from the start, and doubtless stimulated them to an acuteness of perception that might otherwise have required much prefatory effort and eloquence.

'I am sorry,' he began, 'that even the few who have left the building just now should have done so. First, because I am going to say things tonight that it might be good for them personally to hear; secondly, because, large as this assembly is, I am in need of all the testifiers and recorders of my words that I can get, for I shall probably never have another opportunity to speak to you, and I am speaking to the Colony through you.'

His next sentence was destined to prove a thousand times more important than the speaker either guessed or intended. It led to a bitter war of assertion, denial and recrimination, and in the end, though not immediately, finished those 'popular' services.

'The subject I purpose dealing with tonight was suggested to me by your Pastor, and I heartily thank him for it.'

The Pastor smiled decorously, and enjoyed a flash of momentary happiness that was to be the last he would know that evening.

'He has reminded me of what I, as a stranger, might have overlooked, that you Colonials are the proud inheritors of the traditions of generations of religious ancestors – which may be true.'

There was a perceptible flutter – that vague rustle like the passage of a zephyr across a cornfield; a stirring of the warm air of a church that proves that the congregation are not asleep.

'He has also remarked to me that you are blessed by residence in a country free from the intolerance, bigotry and narrowness that obtain in the older civilisations.'

He paused like a good actor before speaking his most telling line.

'I wish I could believe him.'

The zephyr expanded to a breeze. The audience was moved – mentally and corporeally, for faces were turned towards the face adjacent and eyes sought the

Pastor. He was squeezing his bearded chin, and trying to look as if he quite understood and appreciated an unflattering avowal. He waited anxiously for the sentence to follow, which would, he was sure, explain away cleverly and effectively a severe piece of censure, uttered only to be qualified prettily.

'I am sorry to have to say that it has not been my good fortune to experience what has apparently been the fortune of my friend. I will not, at present, say anything of intolerance or bigotry. What I will speak on is narrowness; and I say, with due regard for the weight and meaning of words, that narrowness is the one transcendental characteristic of Colonial Christianity. So narrow is it, that it allows no standing room for your fellow. It is more exclusive than the narrowest Calvinism, more selfish than the greed of the most sordid grasper of treasures that rust. And what is worse, you make a virtue of your narrowness, and attempt to justify it by open, glaring, impious disregard of the very main principle of the religion you profess with such unction.'

A gleam of relief passed over the face of the Pastor. After all, Hyslop was only leading up to a strong denunciation of hypocrites and sinners in the style of the fervent Evangelist. Still, it would have been in better taste had he differentiated somewhat; that 'you' was too general and sweeping. Why did he not attack those who did not come to church, and be a little more considerate of the feelings of those who did?

The next sentence of the preacher sent the blood into the pale face of the Pastor. He dared not again look up to mark the effect on the congregation.

'Almost the last words spoken by Christ on earth were a command: "Go ye into *all* the world, and preach the gospel to *every* creature."'

He emphasised the adverbs.

'I have come to preach the gospel to some of the creatures in this part of the world, – to obey that distinct and unequivocal command, and what do I find? An organised, universal hostility to me and those like me – missionaries. We are despised and rejected, our work openly deprecated and flouted; "Christianised kafir," the most damning and opprobrious term you can use against those whom your Master commanded should be taught to share His kingdom with you who despise them. Is that narrowness? bigotry? prejudice? More; I ask you, and challenge your reply: Is it Christianity, or is it anti-Christianity?'

Then came an enhanced flutter, stir, frou-frou, sibilation. Descriptive reporters use the word 'sensation', in parenthesis.

The preacher saw and heard.

He paused pointedly while two influential members of the congregation left their seats and walked out.

The Pastor perspired, mopped his turned-down face furtively, and looked at his watch. At least fifteen minutes more of this awfulness was probable! – time for all the influential members of the congregation to follow the example of the forerunners! He yearned for the courage that would enable him to rise and give out a hymn.

The retreat of the dissentients stimulated the young missionary. He felt certain that others would go. He commenced to fire the shots he had intended to reserve for later in the attack. If the enemy would not face his rifle, they should not escape without feeling some of his heavier metal. He let himself go. He taunted the 'self-called Christians' with selfish neglect of their heathen brethren; challenged any master of native servants to declare that he had ever given one thought to the welfare of the soul of his charges; to deny that he regarded the kafir otherwise than as a beast of burden, to be exploited for his own selfish ends.

'The only men who have not directly opposed me,' he said vehemently, 'have exhorted me to preach to the native the gospel of the Dignity of Labour. Why? That the kafir may benefit by his toil? No; that it might be made cheaper and more available for you. Do you care whether the native's work is dignified or debasing to him so long as you profit by it? You – a few of you – pretend to encourage the missionary to "convert" the native. Convert him to what? To a pliant uncomplaining labourer for your own sordid ends. In the words of our Lord: "Ye compass sea and land to make one proselyte, and when he is made, ye make him twofold more the child of hell than yourselves." I say, and I challenge contradiction, that the soul of a kafir is jeopardised by contact with his white "superiors."'

He uttered the last word with withering, long-drawn-out contemptuousness and obvious irony.

Four, five, six – a small crowd of men and women got up and walked out, making comments loud enough to be described as 'disorder'. The Pastor had lost his nerve. He stood up, looked appealingly at the congregation. No more left their seats.

The preacher resumed.

'These are hard words, I know, but you who know the native need not me to remind you of what is the general result of his mixing with white men. You yourselves say hard things about him, and to an extent you are justified.'

The Pastor breathed freely. The congregation, now tense and expectant, leaned forward to catch the next sentence.

'I admit that the civilised native is an unattractive object – to those who do not understand him. He is a parody of civilisation, a pathetic specimen of incompleteness, but he is what you white men have made him, not the missionary.

'You accuse us of teaching the native that he is the equal of the white. If you took the trouble to find out what we do teach, you would know that our one great aim is to warn and prevent the native from imitating most of the whites they meet, because the model is such a bad one.'

There came another stir, and two 'influentials' with their wives and daughters rustled out.

'I have said that you professing Christians are hostile to mission work. It may be that I have misjudged you.'

The Pastor nodded an emphatic assent.

'There may be good reason for that opposition. You pride yourselves on being a practical people. Is it that your opposition comes from your honest belief that missions to natives are superfluous?'

From the young men crowding the back of the church came several distinct 'Hear, hears.'

'I am disposed to agree with you if, as it seems, you think that. I will tell you why. I hold in my hand the calendar of criminal cases to be tried at the forthcoming circuit; also a return of the convictions of white persons for the past year. I find twenty-two different crimes, only three of which are known among natives. Need I tell you, who pride yourselves on your intimate knowledge of the native, that unchastity is so rare in the kraals as to be practically non-existent; that petty theft, larceny, false pretence, slander, and crimes actuated by sordid greed, hatred and malice are rare; that nine-tenths of the stock thefts are the result of hunger rather than covetousness; that crimes of violence and the occasional murders are directly traceable to the infamous liquor introduced and sold for profit by you whites? There is no need to remind you of all this, or that the jails are filled with natives whose principal crimes are offences against artifical laws and restrictions made for the sole purpose of keeping them in abject subjection. Yes, I am disposed to agree with you that missions are largely superfluous. The missionary would find greater scope for his labour among you than among the natives – You, their masters and evil exemplars.'

A chorus of distinct 'Oh's!' came from the end of the church. People got up in threes and fours in the body of the building. Those who had previously left had been occupying seats at the ends of the pews, so that retreat was comparatively easy without disturbing others. Now the exodus began from right, left and centre. The Pastor was deathly pale. He had lost all self-control. He stood up underneath the pulpit, turned his head up at an awkward angle, and said something to the preacher which nobody heard. Numbers of the congregation stood also as if expecting to witness a scene between Pastor and preacher, for their heads had approached and a loudly-whispered colloquy was interrupted by the organ striking out into a loud voluntary.

David Hyslop gave one look at the moving, excited crowd, then left the pulpit.

As no reporters happened to be present, their accounts next day were full and graphic, and were augmented by the letters of 'A Disgusted Sympathiser with Missions', 'One Who was Present', and a fervid denial from the Pastor of the 'unwarranted assertion' that he had suggested the subject to Mr Hyslop.

The editorials were more dignified than the reports. They deplored the 'discreditable scene', spoke of 'misplaced enthusiasm', 'mistaken ideals', 'youthful want of tact', and 'execrable bad taste', but did not combat the charges.

The author of the sensation wrote a letter which was inserted with very little editing. He made but brief reference to the 'scene', neither apologised nor justified, but simply remarked that no editor or correspondent had ventured to traverse a statement he had made, but had confined themselves to objecting, each after his own manner, to the introduction of the subject. 'From this I infer, as every intelligent man must, that my charges are incontrovertible,' was his Parthian shot.

The Rev. David Hyslop had become the most prominent missionary in the country; his fame, or folly, was known from the Zambesi to Cape Agulhas, and his letter mail became inconveniently large. Letters of abuse, brotherly counsel and Christian remonstrance, which was more virulent than the abuse, came in packets, relieved now and then by an encouraging note of approval from a correspondent who wrote to express his admiration of pluck, or wishing 'more power to his elbow' for having 'smitten the hypocrites hip and thigh.'

But the crowning blow, and most painful, came from the local Head of the Mission. He wrote in terms of grave reprobation, regretting that his dear but misguided brother should have prejudiced mission work in the eyes of Christians by interference and assertion of a kind it was most desirable that missionaries should avoid. 'If you cannot interest them in our work, do not declare your lack of sympathy with theirs,' he wrote, and wound up by expressing his 'deep regret that the unfortunate incident should have occurred during the presence in this country of our esteemed and valued friend and wholehearted supporter, Mr Amos Drysdale, the philanthropic Christian who purposes visiting your station in the course of his tour of the country.'

Mr Drysdale duly arrived, – an elderly, serious person, whose appearance suggested the successful tradesman raised to the dignity of a chapel deaconship.

He spoke in ponderous sentences that generally began with a negative presumption, and ended with an interrogative 'eh?' and an expression of marked pain and surprise that his assumption should prove correct.

'I suppose you could not persuade the converts to build you a church, eh?' was his first query on finding that the mission possessed no building to be used as church or school-house.

The missionary explained that a church would be a work of supererogation in the strictest sense. During the rainy season the natives did not leave their kraals to travel; in the dry season they preferred to sit in the open to be preached at.

'Dear me; a very great pity. The mission church is such a picturesque adjunct to a mission. Our friends at home expect a church. It is very disappointing.'

'I am afraid our friends at home expect many unpractical things,' the missionary responded. 'They create their own ideals of what a mission should be like, and rather resent the reality.'

'I suppose there is not a heathen temple, or place of idolatrous worship about here, eh?'

'I am very sorry to have to disappoint you, but heathen temples and idols are not to be found in this or any other district that I have heard of. All I know of them is through pictures and stories.'

'Dear me; that is very –' He was evidently going to say 'disappointing', but amended it to 'delightful'.

'But I don't suppose they are without some form of pagan worship, eh?'

'The South African native may have some form of worship. So far as I have been able to discover the only object of their worship is cattle.'

'Dear me, how very interesting. Quite like the – what do you call them? Really, I ought to remember, for I have been a subscriber to that mission for years. *They* worship a bull.'

Mr Hyslop thought it better to explain that he spoke allegorically, then regretted it, for Mr Drysdale seemed very disappointed.

In short, the old gentleman was an obviously disappointed man; and after half-a-dozen other 'I don't supposes' had been justified, he honestly confessed it.

'When I visited the station at –' (he mentioned a rival sect's outpost), 'I was received by a party of converts who sang hymns and behaved in a charmingly Christian manner. It was truly refreshing.'

Mr Hyslop was piqued by the comparison. He was a missionary, and even missionaries are not superior to professional jealousies, though they prefer to speak of them as 'laudable emulation'.

'I do not keep anything on show,' he said. 'I prefer that the little that is to be seen here should be in its normal, natural condition, not as a carefully rehearsed spectacle got up to impress the unwary.'

Mr Drysdale replied with some asperity.

'But I assure you I was not unwary; I took most careful notice. I questioned many of the converts, and they told me that they were very happy, and thanked the Lord for having brought them out of darkness into light.'

'I was not aware that you spoke Zulu.'

'O dear no! I spoke with them through the missionary who interpreted.'

'Exactly,' was all Mr Hyslop said.

Mr Drysdale went on: 'They were all in European clothes – men, women and girls. I notice that the women in your location do not wear – dresses.'

'No; and perhaps you may have noticed that at this mission station there is nothing equivalent to a foundling hospital.'

Mr Drysdale looked puzzled.

'I don't think I quite understand,' he said.

'No; it is a matter not so well understood as it should be,' Mr Hyslop answered, and changed the subject.

CHAPTER XXI

CAPITULATION

The decision of Mr Hyslop to go to the Transvaal was the outcome of much anxious thought.

His position at Blue Krantz had not been prejudiced by the famous sermon so far as his influence on the natives was concerned; but something had occurred directly after the visit of Mr Drysdale to change the attitude towards him of the head of the mission. He was plainly not giving satisfaction. There was a too frequent demand for what the missionary described as 'a showy balance-sheet', too many hints and suggestions that it was souls he had to deal with rather than bodies. His invariable reply was that the house must first be prepared as a fit dwelling place for the spirit, and that process was not to be performed in a year or two.

A great change had come over him. He was no longer the ardent religious enthusiast who believed that the scattered nations were to be gathered under the banner of Christianity by beat of drum and the uttering of war cries. He knew that at best a change wrought by working on the feelings of a childlike emotional race was only the transient alteration effected on a mirror by breathing on it.

He had learned in the painful school of experience how easy it was to provoke hypocrisy. Had he continued the simple, trusting enthusiast that first came to Blue Krantz, he could have filled pages of the missionary magazine with touching stories of heathen who had, under skilful cross-examination and leading, professed 'change from darkness to light.' He had twenty natives who could howl what passed for native hymns, and as many more who would attend two consecutive services without asking for a 'bonsella' as a reward for their pious devotion. But David Hyslop no longer mistook symptoms. He had studied the native mind, and, rightly or wrongly, had arrived at the same conclusion regarding it as many other equally earnest and sincere Christians. That every fruit was the product of a special soil; if fruit other than that indigenous to that soil was to be raised from it, a long and skilful process of preparation and adaptation was necessary, and even then the result was not assured.

These views he tried to impress upon his chief. The reply was, 'What other men have done, men can do.'

His retort was, 'I am not satisfied that other men have done it.'

'But we have a man who has and can.'

'Send him on. I will make way, not in any spirit of pique, but in the earnest hope that he may succeed where I have failed.'

A month after the receipt of Bulalie's draft, the Rev. David Hyslop installed his successor, a quiet, suave man of settled age, who had contracted that indescribably dejected languid air which comes of life in an enervating climate. He was the Rev. Arthur Woodburn, well known to students of missionary literature as the author of numerous inspiring narratives of harrowing experiences that were always crowned with triumph. His fame rested principally on that faith-testing story, 'The Regenerated Hottentot; or, Brought to Grace from the Jaws of the Lion.'

He had, as the Head of the Mission suggested, been peculiarly blessed in the practice of instantaneous conversions.

It was, in the times before missionaries lived so much under the electric light of local criticism, almost a monthly occurrence for a ferocious chief, with an impi of bloodthirsty followers, to raid Mr Woodburn's mission bent on rapine and slaughter, and leave with a heap of Bibles he could not read and an invitation to the impregnable missionary to 'come and preach to my sinful people.' In the course of quarter of a century Mr Woodburn appears to have Christianised a dozen kafir Constantines; but after the manner of great men, they failed to leave descendants equally gifted with their own virtues.

David Hyslop specially commended Mozulikase to the care and efforts of his successor, and sadly said good-bye to Blue Krantz – the scene of so many hopes, fears, partial successes and entire failures.

His plans were vague. The health of wife and child rendered a trip to the homeland advisable; the year of their absence, he thought, might be profitably spent in a species of freelance missioning among the natives in the compounds of the Rand mines. Since he had learned a little of their character he had often dreamed dreams of utilising them as centres whence the leaven of righteousness might be distributed throughout the length and breadth of kafirdom by the home-returning natives. He had interested a wealthy friend at home in the project, and knew that he had only to announce his readiness to obtain the necessary financial support.

He still believed in the ultimate efficacy of the leaven, though his youthful impatience to see results had been tempered by experience and sounder judgment. He was prepared to watch the slowly-spreading growth, if need be, for years, so long as he had one tittle of evidence that his labour was not in vain. Therefore he yearned to see Bulalie, the first object of his serious prayerful care − longed, yet dreaded, for an opportunity to see the answer to his oft-asked question, 'What will the harvest be?'

*   *   *   *   *

On the advice of friends with whom he was staying, Mr Hyslop discarded clerical uniform for his visit to the compound.

'The natives will talk more freely to you than they would if they know you to be a missionary,' was the explanation, which a year or two before would have puzzled him. Now he knew that natives do not care to be identified with missions. He was aware that the taint prejudiced them in the eyes of employers of domestic labour, but it came as a painful surprise that the same objection should hold good on the mines.

He put on the suit he usually wore when cycling, and, armed with a letter of introduction to the mine secretary, rode out to the New Yankee.

He was desirous of making a surprise visit; he had become uneasily suspicious of formal shows. For that reason he resolved to avoid making himself known to the compound manager till the last thing.

But the heads of department on the New Yankee knew their business too well to be surprised. In the first place no visitor ever saw more than he was permitted to see. Not that there was anything to hide in the general control of the property − at least, no more than the managers of any business had the right to exclude from prying eyes. Such secrets as were not desirable to expose belonged to the department of Mr Sid Dane, and he was quite able to guard himself against unwished-for intrusion.

The mine secretary, like most of his clan on the reef, was polite and affable, despite the chronic infliction of visitors, and handed Mr Hyslop over to a member of the staff who was about to escort a small party over the property.

They made the round of the show places, stared at the vast head-gear, the huge engines and machinery, asked the usual foolish and unanswerable questions till taken to the battery-house, where the roar of the stamps rendered speech but facial contortion, and the entire party deaf and silent for some time after.

The missionary was duly and properly impressed by the ponderous vastness and unintelligibility of all he saw, but his eyes were more receptive for the human aspect of the colossal monument to man's ingenuity. It was the teeming life of the reef that interested him − the hundreds of natives busily and cheerfully occupied all over the thousands of acres that constituted the property. He withdrew from the party, and mounted a tramway embankment that gave a view not only of the extensive surface of the New Yankee, but eastward and westward, as far as the sky line, of other mines, many yet larger hives of black industry. Here, within easy reach, were a hundred thousand representatives of nearly every tribe of the sons of Ham in the sub-continent, who, in the course of a few months, at most a year or two, would have returned to their native kraals to spread the story of the vastness of the white man's work, power and – what else?

The answer he knew, but hesitated to express.

He was startled from his reverie by the sound of an angry voice shouting in guttural Northumbrian accent.

Then came the sound of blows, more shouting and foul oaths.

He stepped up the bank and saw a burly white man belabouring a kafir with a pick-handle. The boy was standing erect, his head covered with his arms to ward off the blows.

Mr Hyslop shouted 'Hi, there!' and ran forward.

The man stared at the interrupter sullenly and stopped using his bludgeon.

'What has he done?' the missionary asked.

'Done? Nothing. He's a fule, that's what he is. Can't understand a damned word I say; but I'll learn him. Voetzak, you –!'

He gave the boy a helpful kick down the embankment.

'Did you speak to him in Zulu?' Mr Hyslop enquired amiably.

'Zulu? No fear. English is good enough for me. Are you on the staff here?'

'No; I am a visitor.'

'O, then you mind your own business, and let me look after mine.'

There were several superfluous adjectives in the sentence.

A mechanic passing along the tramline jerked his head towards the retreating Northumbrian.

'The old story,' he remarked, laughingly. 'Those chaps have been bullied by their own bosses in the mines at home, and when they find themselves bosses over kafirs they take it out of the poor devils to revenge themselves. That chap cripples a kafir twice a week on an average. He'll get laid out one of these days, and serve him right.'

The missionary caught up with the assaulted kafir and spoke to him in Zulu.

'Why did the white baas beat you?' he asked.

'I don't know, baas; because he was angry, I suppose. He speaks strange words that no boy can understand, so he beats and kicks much.'

He gave the boy sixpence. It was accepted in the matter-of-course manner which has probably earned for the kafir his reputation for ingratitude.

The boy looked round, apparently to see if his task-master was in sight, then ran towards a disreputable tin building about which a number of kafirs were standing, most of them eating.

The missionary followed up. The place was a sort of store and eating-house. He could see kafirs being served by a Jewish-looking man and a native at a counter, but could not detect what the comestible was. He advanced nearer.

A tall native, in grey shirt, smasher hat, riding breeches and gaiters, came out, roughly pushing away a kafir who obstructed his path.

'Don't push me, if you *are* nearly a white man,' said the offended one, with ironical emphasis.

The tall kafir turned and struck viciously with a sjambok. The victim ran behind the building.

'Man, white or black, dressed in a little brief authority!' the missionary soliloquised.

'Baas! Ow!'

'Bulalie!'

The tall kafir suddenly drew himself erect like a soldier sharply called to attention. The ejaculatory 'Ow!' of astonishment was checked in its growth, and the hand came down from the mouth.

The missionary noted the action and interpreted it. The boy was endeavouring to restrain the instinctive impulse of his pristine nature. He was emerging from the chrysalis.

He stood, grinning and laughing, pleasure and embarrassment struggling and alternating.

'Are you glad to see me, Bulalie?'

'Yes, baas.' Then, as if an afterthought, 'If you don't take me away.'

'You are happy and wish to stay here?'

The magnificent salt-white teeth gleamed and the big eyes opened wide.

'Yes. I am my baas's head boy. I make lots of money. How are my cattle?'

'There are no cattle, because I have left the mission station, and am not going back. But your money is in a place where it grows.'

Bulalie's face showed intense disappointment.

'No cattle?'

He looked pensively at the horizon and flicked his gaiters with his sjambok.

'How does my money grow?'

'Every sovereign grows a sixpence in a year, and becomes a sovereign and a sixpence. Do you still know how to write figures?'

' 'Musa!'

The native ejaculation expressive of extreme vexation came out long drawn, with no effort at repression.

'Only one sixpence for a sovereign! Ow! I can make one sovereign grow into two between paydays. I must have my money. Baas, you have treated Bulalie badly — bought no cattle! My sovereigns make only sixpences!'

Had the missionary been bluntly accused of misappropriation and general fraud he could not have experienced a keener sense of astonishment and humiliation.

He stood gazing at Bulalie, and took in rapidly a fearsome impression.

The boy had changed marvellously. The quiet, modest simplicity that had been his charm of old had given place to an assertive, perky insolence of bearing — the vulgar aggressiveness and conscious ostentation he had seen in young white men placed in positions of affluence and authority for which their training and qualifications did not fit them — an attitude described colloquially as 'putting on side.'

As he mused, a raw kafir passed very close, grinned and greeted Bulalie familiarly.

A sharp cut from the ready sjambok across the naked calves sent him hopping off.

'Why did you do that, Bulalie? That is two boys I have seen you strike. That is not the way to make friends. They will hate you,' the missionary remarked gravely.

'I don't fear them; they fear me,' was the reply, given with contemptuous emphasis.

'Why should they fear you?'

'Because I am Bulalie, the baas's head boy. Besides, that "ishanga" (rascal, villain) owes me four shillings.'

'Has he refused to pay you?'

Bulalie laughed, as if the suggestion was absurd.

'No; I get it when he is paid on Monday and two more shillings.'

A light flashed across the missionary's mind.

'You lend money! So that is how you were able to send me one hundred and seventeen sovereigns?'

'More. I sent you one hundred and thirty. Baas Dane sent them for me, and you sent him a letter saying you had them. He showed me your writing and I knew it was yours.'

Bulalie spoke with his old-time frankness, and the missionary believed him.

'I must see your baas; there is some mistake,' he said.

The boy interposed sharply.

'No, you must not see him; he must not know you are here. You may have the other money. You have been good to me. Give it to the missis for the piccanin.'

'He does not believe me,' the missionary ejaculated; then, in Zulu: 'Bulalie, do you think I would lie to you? Tell me, why must I not see your baas?'

'Because he knows you are a preacher, and he will think you have come to take me away. Baas, let me stay; I cannot come back to the kraal. Come tomorrow; I will speak to you under the wall of the big dam. I must go now. Tomorrow, next day, any day, at the dam wall after the big whistle has called the boys to go on shift.'

He ran off towards the compound without even a farewell.

The hours that David Hyslop passed until he again saw Bulalie were full of the bitterness of unsatisfied hope.

The boy was punctual, but not eager at the appointment.

'I want you to tell me truly, Bulalie,' the missionary said when they were walking up and down the footpath at the bottom of the lofty embankment that held in millions of gallons of water. 'How did you make all the money you sent me? Quite honestly, I hope.'

'Yes, baas; I make it by buying liquor for the kafirs who have not enough money to pay for a bottle. They pay me one shilling for each two shillings I lend them, sometimes more. Then the white baases who sell the liquor out of bags in the veld give five shillings, sometimes ten shillings when they sell much.'

'Why should they pay you?'

'Because I know all the police-trap boys, and the good time for selling when the police are not likely to come or when my baas is away in town or sleeping in his room.'

He made the confession of his complicity in the crime scourge of the mines without demur, apology or extenuation. His old mentor listened and grieved.

'But you know you are doing wrong, Bulalie. You know the liquor makes the kafirs sick and quarrelsome, so that they fight and get into jail.'

'Yes, I know that; they know it also. But they drink the liquor, I do not. You always told me not to drink.'

There was some compensation in the knowledge that one precept had borne fruit.

'You must not do this wickedness any more, Bulalie.'

Bulalie drew himself up, and spoke with genuine surprise.

'Wickedness? Where is the wickedness? Why should not kafirs drink as well as white men? Do they not work very hard and pay big money for the puza?'

'But the law says you must not do this wickedness.'

'The law and the police say many things that are not true. Did they not say that I did wrong to my missis at Maritzburg and give me lashes?'

Was this evolved out of the boy's own mind, or was it the conscience-stifling suggestion of the unscrupulous whites who used him as their tool? A simple question might provide a clue.

'Does not Baas Dane tell you it is wicked?'

Bulalie looked at his questioner as if to probe the meaning and object of the query.

'Baas Dane does not know that the boys buy liquor. He takes it away and breaks the bottles when he sees them. He will not have puza in the compound.'

Mr Hyslop looked the boy searchingly straight in the eyes. They quailed and dropped to the ground. He knew that Bulalie was repeating a lesson. He sprang another trap question upon him.

'Did Baas Dane know how you got all that money he sent to me for you?'

'Yes, baas.'

'Then he does know that you bring in puza.'

Bulalie saw his blunder. He began to flounder.

'It is bonsellas. The baas knows that I get bonsellas,' he volunteered, hesitatingly and lamely.

'What for? From whom?'

'Baas, please baas! I must not tell you. Baas says I must not talk to you.'

'Then he knows I am here?'

'No, baas; but he thinks you will come some day.'

'Bulalie, you know that is not true. How should he think that I should come all the way from Natal? You have told him I am here, and he has told you what to say and what not to say. Speak truly, Bulalie.'

'Yes, baas, that is so.'

The shamefaced avowal delighted the missionary. It was an evidence that his influence over his old pupil was not quite dead. He made a moving appeal to him.

'Bulalie. You said yesterday I was always good to you. Do you still say so?'

'Yes, baas.'

'As good as Baas Dane?'

There was a pause.

'Yes; but you did not show me how I might make money.'

'Bulalie, it was because of what I taught you that you are now head boy here. Is not that the same as showing you how to make money? And did I not hide you for more than a year when the police wanted you to take you back and lash you?'

Bulalie was touched.

'Yes, baas, you did all that,' he said submissively.

'Then do you not think I am as much your friend as Baas Dane?'

'Yes, baas.'

'Then, Bulalie, I want you to show that you think I am your friend by answering some questions I am going to ask you.'

'They will not hurt me with Baas Dane or the police?'

It was the missionary's turn to hesitate. Before he had framed a satisfactory reply, Bulalie had got up hurriedly from the ground, on which he had been squatting native fashion. The missionary followed his frightened glance.

A fair, good-looking, thick-set man of about thirty-five, in a lounge suit, was standing on the embankment above them.

Instinct told Mr Hyslop that he was about to have an interview with Baas Dane.

CHAPTER XXII

THE CHRISTIANISED KAFIR

'I suppose I ought to apologise for interrupting you,' the compound manager said laughingly, as he came down the embankment and extended his hand. 'I guess who you are. We have had financial relationship regarding that rascal Bulalie. I wonder whether he gave you as much trouble as he does me. I followed him up just now expecting to find him at his old games – gambling. Clear off to your work – if the baas has done with you,' he said to the boy. Then to the missionary: 'You will come over to my quarters and have a chat. You can see Bulalie there as often as you please.'

There was a charming frankness about the man which produced on the missionary the same favourable impression as on nearly everybody. Dane was not labelled 'genial' ironically.

'I am surprised at what you said about Bulalie's gambling,' the missionary remarked, when seated with a pipe and cup of coffee in Dane's comfortable snuggery.

'Gambling? He's a demon at it. That money I sent you for him was mainly picked up at cards. He is very smart; about the "slimmest" kafir in the compound. I can't imagine where he learnt it. I sometimes fancy he must have spent a long time in jail, but he swears he has never seen the inside of one. He has been lashed, I see, and badly, too. He tells me they were laid on by his baas when he was with a road party. Has he ever been in jail, do you know?'

Mr Dane glanced furtively at his guest over his whisky glass.

'I always found the boy very truthful,' the missionary answered.

'Let's see if his character has altered much. Come here, Bulalie.'

'You have never been in tronk, have you?' Dane asked.

The boy smiled, as if conscious of being made fun of.

'You know, baas. I told you about Maritzburg and the lashing. You said you knew all about it.'

'That will do. Voetzak!'

When the boy had gone, 'That's the fourth or fifth version,' Dane remarked laughingly. 'Strange that he can never stick to a story. He has a magnificent imagination. As a matter of fact, I keep the rascal principally because he amuses me with his lies.'

Mr Hyslop expressed surprise and regret, but did not keep the subject open. He had read Dane, and knew that this cumbersome attempt to brand Bulalie as a liar had an object; further, that the man was most probably aware of the harbouring of the escaped convict, and meant to use his knowledge in his own time and manner if the missionary proved too inquisitive and troublesome. He quietly remarked:

'What a fuss the Natal officials made when they found that Bulalie had been living at my mission station after his escape from jail! I wonder they did not take action against me.'

Mr Dane was surprised and annoyed at the bold exposure of the cards. He was fully aware of the reputation of the missionary as a kafir champion, and though he had no fear of him because of anything he might see or say, he objected to him with that unreasoning prejudice which practically every South African Colonial feels towards any man who takes sides with a native, and particularly missionaries.

The ghost of an idea had been flitting through Dane's mind. It would be a magnificent score if he could work up a sensation for the benefit of the parson – a hoax of some kind that would make him ridiculous, and then spring on him the knowledge of his lawbreaking as a harbourer of escaped criminals; but the victim's bold avowal of his share in the matter had shown that he was not to be frightened with that bogie.

A more subtle and brutal form of torture occurred to him. He would let the missionary see the fate that usually befell the Christianised kafir.

'Bulalie was one of your best mission boys, I believe,' he remarked insinuatively.

Mr Hyslop assented, without emphasis or enthusiasm, for he had a presentiment that Bulalie's advancement had been in spite of rather than because of his brief connection with the mission.

'I spotted him as a mission kafir from the first. That is why I made him a head boy. They are splendid for positions of authority. They hate the raw kafir, and jump at the opportunity of getting even for the snubs and insults put upon them in the kraals. There is not much chance of a raw boy taking advantage of me or the shift baas if a Christian kafir is about.'

'They are much more intelligent, are they not?' the missionary interjected, rather pleased by the testimony.

'I wouldn't say that,' Dane answered thoughtfully. 'I should put it another way. They are like a woman who has a grudge against another woman. She may not be more clever, but she is more keen on using an advantage against her victim. You mustn't forget that the kafir who chucks his people and customs for Christianity isn't loved by those he has left. They make it very hot for him, and it's only natural that when he gets the chance he wipes something off the slate. It's a treat to see Bulalie lording it around. He lends money in a small way. A Jewish usurer with a Christian debtor isn't in it with your Christianised kafir.'

If the missionary had been disposed to suspect Dane of gross exaggeration, or even invention, the little incidents of tyranny of which he had been an eye-witness must have removed such suspicion. He could not deny the moral deterioration of his *protégé*; he could only find relief in a discovery of the cause.

'You surely wouldn't suggest that a mission boy is more likely to be addicted to acts of viciousness than a raw kafir?'

'No; but he has greater provocation. He is more or less an outsider. He is suspected and boycotted by the majority, and the only way he has of punishing them is by showing his authority if he has the chance; if not, he must do something by way of proving himself cleverer than the rest, and the shortest cut is by breaking the law in some way that a raw kafir isn't up to. Our cleverest smugglers of illicit liquor are Christianised kafirs. Of course you are aware the drink is the curse of the compounds. I dare say Bulalie makes five or six pounds a month by bringing in liquor.'

'Then, knowing this, why do you not stop him?' the missionary asked, indignantly.

'Because I'm not a fool. I know that so long as Bulalie can make money at the game, he will take good care no one else has a look in. He is a finer detective than all the police employed by the Government and the mines. For every bottle that he passes in, I reckon he is the means of keeping out ten that would be got in by others. It's a case of checking and regulating a flood that you can't stop altogether.'

'Do you think it right or kind to encourage natives to act as you say they do?' Mr Hyslop asked, after listening to several stories of cunning, treachery and criminal astuteness on the part of alleged Christianised kafirs.

'If you turn out material suitable for a certain class of work, you mustn't be surprised if it is used where it is likely to be most useful. I'm not in love with this part of my business, but if I have dirty work to do and find that Christianised kafirs are best qualified for it, I should be a fool not to use them.'

The speech sank into the missionary's heart, and he pondered it long and painfully. Dane had effected his purpose. He had wounded the missionary on his tenderest spot.

'Instead of assisting in the regeneration of his fellows Bulalie has become a potent instrument for their degradation, and it is my training that has fitted him for his infamous work.'

This was the wail and moan of the Rev. David Hyslop.

He took advantage of Mr Dane's invitation to make himself free of the compound, and talked much with the boys.

They were not eager in responding to his friendly overtures. As soon as they found that he had nothing to give but advice, and was opposed to the introduction of liquor, they shunned him. He was only a preacher; the other white men who came to the compound nearly always had something agreeable to sell, or suggest; or, what was better, would buy bead work, knobkieries, or copper-wire bracelets. The preacher not only would not buy these things, but told them they were foolishness fit only for very young girls.

A few days after Mr Hyslop's first appearance in the compound two kafirs were caught by the mine police bringing in liquor. The bottles were smashed, and the boys taken to the compound lock-up and thrashed by Baas Dane.

Someone suggested that the Preacher was responsible, regardless of the fact that boys had been similarly caught and punished frequently. It may be that the rumour was originated by a Peruvian who supplied liquor secretly at night from a quiet spot in the veld, where he had twice been disturbed by the appearance of Mr Hyslop.

That was the suggestion offered by Mr Fraser when, a week later, the Preacher was thrown violently from his bicycle by a kafir lying at the side of the path. The rascal inserted a stick between the spokes of the wheel and disappeared in the fast-gathering darkness.

Mr Hyslop had made a special effort to cultivate the acquaintance of Fraser of the Belmont. He was anxious to know a man of whom all spoke, if not in terms of approval, in unreserved acknowledgment of his honesty. He was said to be bribery-proof. Why, was not very apparent. That he had some motive outside mere honesty stood to reason; no man rejected fifty pounds a month on the Rand unless the self-restraint brought an equivalent or greater reward. Therefore it was obvious that Fraser was playing some subtle game. As to his being a teetotaller and abstainer from the indulgences which his salary would justify, that proved nothing, except his characteristic meanness. It was only a matter of time. Those who lived the longest would see the most. Fraser would soon show up in his real colours, as every paragon of virtue on the reef did.

The missionary gladly accepted the invitation to 'come in and have a crack when you feel that way,' and spent many hours very agreeably. Fraser was intelligent, as all young Scots of his type are, and not having many companions, read a great deal.

But Mr Hyslop was a little disappointed when he began to talk negrophilism. Fraser was not exactly antipathetic; he was scientifically analytical and utilitarian rather than altruistic. He accepted the allusions to his bold attitude towards the corruptors with indifference and made no pretence of being actuated by any motive higher than the bare performance of the conditions of his contract with his employers.

'I don't refuse bribes, or "bonsellas" as they prefer to call them, on any moral ground,' he admitted to Mr Hyslop. 'I should like to be able to double my salary, but I know that there is such a thing as paying thirty shillings for a sovereign. If I accepted the tips offered me, I should be tied hand and foot, as Dane is, to these rascals, who would not hesitate to sell me any moment if by chucking me over they could make sure of an increased profit. It's very tempting and very hard to resist the chances of making an easy tenner; but I've been long enough at the business to see a good many go under. If a man could make ten or fifteen thousand in a couple of years and clear out, I might be inclined to take a hand at the game; but one can't. The profits are niggling – just enough to gratify one for the moment, but not enough to make a splash with. Dane and the rest of them are like a clerk who is fingering the cash. They steal a lot in trumpery amounts, but when the time comes to make a bolt they haven't enough to provide half a wing. No; I tell you honestly I don't object to making a bit; what I do object to is having to hand myself over to the bribers. The squaring business on the Rand is so comprehensive and universal that no one dare make an open stand against it for fear of compromising his best friend. Therefore I go slow and say nothing.'

'There is one subject which is a great puzzle to me,' the missionary said, encouraged by the candour of the Scot. 'We constantly see the heads of the mining industry denouncing the liquor traffic among the natives, yet there is no really serious attempt to crush the business. I think you will agree with me that if you and I, with our knowledge of how this thing is managed, had the power the mining authorities have, we should soon wipe out the illicit liquor dealer. Are the mining people really sincere in their complaints?'

'The matter isn't quite so easy as you think. It isn't a question of whether they could stop the liquor, but whether it would be policy to do so. I believe that most of the mining bosses who have so much to say against the liquor business are sincere enough. There may be a certain amount of playing to the gallery and to the goody-goody people, who like to believe that directors' meetings open with prayer and close with the singing of the Doxology; but on the whole these chaps mean what they say. But the worst of it is they are not all agreed. There are experienced mine managers who believe in letting the kafir have his tot, and I'm

with them to a very large extent. If we could make certain that the poor brutes
were not poisoned by the awful stuff these infernal Peruvians off-load on to
them, I should say let the boys have all they wanted, but flog 'em well if they got
drunk.

'The point on which most of the mine managers can't agree is this: — They
know that the knowledge that they can get drink is a great inducement to many
boys to come to the mines. A large percentage are regularly incapacitated
through drink for a day or two. This is, of course, a loss to the mines. The
question is whether it doesn't pay better to allow the liquor into the compound,
and have from ten to fifteen per cent of your boys drunk on Mondays, than to
forbid the liquor and always be short of labour. It's purely a matter of
economics.'

'And what about the welfare of the kafirs?' the missionary asked.

Mr Fraser smiled. 'A compound is not a reformatory. We undertake to house
and feed a native and give him a reasonable — in fact, a good wage, in return for
a certain expenditure of physical energy on his party. If by drinking or any other
form of debauchery he depreciates as a working machine, we clear him out. We
cannot afford to keep him in repair. He is too cheap. If he were a slave costing a
hundred pounds, it would be policy to look after his morals a bit.'

The missionary made a gesture of horrified dissent.

Fraser laughed — not brutally or aggressively, but as one laughs at the
astonishment of the simple and innocent.

'I know all this sounds very brutal. When I first came to the country I held
much the same ideas as you and most Britishers do about our duties to our black
brother, but they got knocked on the head very soon; and you find yourself
taking the Colonial view of the kafir as a superior ape before you realise it. You
know I have a reputation as a good and humane manager of kafirs. The fact is, I
am a weakling. I can't thrash a kafir any more than I can kill a tame rabbit. It's
not that I disagree with flogging: I think it absolutely necessary; but I shirk it.
The result is the kafirs despise me. They respect Dane. They say he is a man; I
am a woman. They come to me, not because they love or respect me, but
because I am weak and lenient; or if you like to put it in another way, because I
am considerate.'

'I don't think that is the word,' said the missionary. 'If you were considerate
you would make an effort to prevent the introduction of alcohol which is killing
the native off by hundreds — '

'Say thousands. You evidently have not got up your case. What are
pneumonia, dysentery, and half the officially described causes of death but the
last and natural stage of alcoholism? Take away the puza from whites and

blacks as well, and the Rand, instead of having the highest death rate of civilisation, would have the lowest. But then comes the question, would it be better for the native to have the mines more attractive?'

Mr Hyslop looked up astonished.

Fraser was amused. 'I can see that you have only nibbled at the surface of this subject,' he said. 'Let me try and show you my view of it. Tell me honestly, so far as you have seen life on the mines, do you think the experience is likely to improve the kafir morally and physically?'

The missionary was weighing the question. He was apprehensive of a logical trap.

Fraser took down and opened a big book.

'Perhaps this may help you to form an opinion,' he said. 'This is official, duly checked by the doctor and the Government inspector. There were discharged from the Belmont last year as medically unfit 348 kafirs, and of that number I can answer that three hundred took back with them some form of incurable and unnecessary disease. About eleven hundred returned to their kraals in the ordinary way, and probably a third of them had disease in a more or less virulent form, which is certain to leave its effects on future generations, and probably ninety per cent have taken back a craving for puza that will end in the creation of a crowd of dangerous drunkards. Now, Mr Hyslop, do you honestly believe that the moral condition of the native is worse in the kraals than in touch with civilisation in the compounds? Would you feel justified after what you know in advising a kafir to come to the mines?'

'I must confess that I am surprised and pained by the horrible materialism I have witnessed in the compounds.'

'Why is it that you missionaries and moralists are such dodgers round disagreeable facts? Why is it one can never get a straight answer to a simple question? You are all the same. Now tell me this: Can you honestly say that you have ever met a kafir in this country who was a better creature for having been in contact with whites?'

'Really, Mr Fraser, that is a difficult – an impossible question. Unless I knew exactly what the native was before his contact, how can I say?'

'Well, I won't press you. I'll just confine you to one case you ought to be in a position to know something of. Take that boy Bulalie of Dane's. I believe he was one of your mission boys. Is he the better for association with whites?'

'He certainly has acquired certain undesirable characteristics since he has been here.'

'Perhaps you don't know him so well as I do. I'll tell you what I know of him. He is a liar, a petty tyrant, an unscrupulous usurer. He is in the pay of the illicit liquor people, and assists in passing in hundreds of bottles for the physical and spiritual damnation of his fellows. He is always ready to bear false witness; several times to my knowledge he has committed gross and hurtful perjury as a witness in the Courts in assault cases, and he has always been on the side of the white oppressor of his people. I have also good reason to believe that he is engaged in the most odious form of traffic that human beings can take up. In short, he is a blackguard and a source of pestilential corruption. Was he like that in the kraal and at the mission station?'

'He certainly gave no sign of a disposition towards that degree of depravity.'

Mr Hyslop, after eliciting an assurance that Fraser was not overstating the case, made one or two guesses at an explanation.

With Scottish logical insistence Fraser forced him to admit that the evil must have been of white origin and instigation.

'Therefore,' Fraser concluded, 'the effect of white domination over the black is pernicious.'

'Some whites,' Mr Hyslop pressed as an amendment.

'And now here is another view of the matter. Has it ever occurred to you that association with the black is prejudicial to the white?'

'Some whites, no doubt. But explain.'

'It may have occurred to you that the majority of whites in this country are not precisely the type of men one would cite as fair samples of civilisation or Christian manhood.'

Mr Hyslop assented with a sad smile.

'These men, finding themselves in authority over a subordinate race, are not likely to exercise that restraint and thoughtful consideration that the strong, righteous man should show to the weak. In other words, they take advantage of their opportunity to assert their instinctive tyranny.

'I am not preaching at others. I speak for myself. I know that I swear at and kick a kafir for things that I would not let a white man see annoyed me. Then my natural cowardice is excited in the presence of a native. I will hit a fellow big and strong enough to eat me because I know he dare not resent it. It is human nature. And the sight of means to do ill deeds makes ill deeds done. My theory is that as no man can touch pitch without being defiled, so no average white man can associate with an inferior and servile race without moral deterioration. It's all very well to talk of what we ought to do in the way of setting example, being just, remembering your own manhood, and all that high-falutin piffle. The class of men who come to mining camps are not overburdened with the finer moralities. They have left their morals at home, and mean to put them on with their dress suits when they go back with a pile. Out there they are in their shabbiest clothes – moral and actual. The native only sees the worst side of a white man; he tries to imitate him, and shows his own worst side. No, Mr Hyslop; the history of the ages is on my side. Wherever white men have had close connection with an inferior race, both have suffered. Instead of trying to preach morality in the compounds, you go back and preach a crusade against them in the kraals. Make it your business to teach the kafir to avoid the white man as he would the smallpox, and you'll do good. The chances are you'll get knocked on the head or have your moral character tarred and feathered; but if you are looking for a short cut to eternal glory, there's your road.'

'There is much in what you say,' the missionary agreed. 'But the logical extension of your theory would be to leave the kafir alone in his native heathenism.'

'Exactly so. Did you ever hear the story of the old woman and the fish? No? Well, it's very simple, but I think it has a moral. She was very sympathetic, and particularly fond of all sorts of dumb creatures. She was a victim to rheumatism, and couldn't stand cold water. So her heart went out to people and things that had to do much with cold water. She kept some gold fish in a globe, and one cold day while sitting over her cosy fire she thought how selfish she was to enjoy so much comfort and warmth while the fish were half freezing. So she poured in hot water and stood the bowl by the fire. She extended the privileges she enjoyed to others. Does it fit?'

CHAPTER XXIII

CONVERTING THE MISSIONARY

Patiently, slowly but surely, the Rev. David Hyslop qualified for his heart's desire – to know all that was knowable of kafir life on the mines. He had learned and digested thoroughly two important preliminary lessons, applicable alike to casual sporadic spectator and the man whose stay in the country may be long.

One was the deceptive dangerous character of first impressions; the other, the unwisdom of making any display of zeal or enthusiasm. No one made a hit by earnestness – outside the money-making circle. Zeal for anything that did not bring in money was proof of latent insanity. The reason the few philanthropists and moral reformers the country had produced have not yet been placed under restraint is simple. Their friends are giving them time to prove that their professions of love and concern for their fellow men are only lures to distract criticism from the real game they are playing.

Mr Hyslop resisted the frequent temptation to champion the cause of some outraged native or denounce the persistent winking at the liquor infamy by officials and mine authorities. He realised that if he began to make himself a nuisance, or even a suspect, every compound would be closed to him, and his hoped-for career of usefulness effectively stopped. He, therefore, not without some qualms of conscience, made friends of the mammon of unrighteousness, and studied to avoid act or word that would accentuate the universal prejudice against his profession. He affected, not unsuccessfully, the man-of-the-world parson who never talked 'shop' out of business hours, and if anyone manifested any curiosity as to his hauntings of compounds and the places where natives most did congregate, he referred vaguely to 'a sort of mission that might be started some day in connection with a kind of philanthropic institution.' He displayed no particular interest, but conveyed an impression that the scheme whatever it might be was very much in the air at present.

Within a couple of months 'the Preacher chap' was quite well known on the Reef. He had made several rather good unparsonic speeches at mine 'smokers' and the perennial presentations to mine officials, who were either leaving or had been testimonialised as a hint that they ought to leave; was on the committee of a mine athletic club; and – strangest, but most important of all – was frequently seen in the company of Sid Dane, who publicly described the parson as 'not half a bad chap.'

The compound manager of the New Yankee never did anything without an object; and this sudden discovery of a liking for the company of a parson betokened a deep and serious scheme.

He was cautiously converting the missionary, and was not without hope of making him a useful and valuable ally in the furtherance of a cause.

Sid Dane was the trusted aider and abettor of an influential clique of mine magnates who have been steadily pressing towards that much, but secretly desired goal – the institution of the compound system.

They have for years kept before them the delectable vision of a time when every native employee on a mining property shall be a source of profit apart from his labour. The hundreds of thousands of pounds yearly drawn from the company's coffers are distributed among storekeepers along the reef and in the town. Why should not the mineowners be also storekeepers, and the native be compelled to patronise their philanthropic establishments by the simple expedient of keeping him on the property, as at the diamond mines of Kimberley, inside a barbed-wire fence?

Now and then a feeler has been thrown out in the shape of a casual observation to the effect that the welfare of the native demands the protection of the wire fence; but the trading community have responded with a howl of dissent, and the suggestion has been adroitly explained away.

But there are able and far-seeing diplomats among those who direct the destinies of the great industry, and they understand the art of educating the public – by leading rather than driving.

'Every drunken kafir who commits an excess outside the area of the mining property is a living argument in favour of compounding.

'Every kafir who dies from the effect of drink in the compound is an eloquent and unanswerable argument in favour of reformation by cutting off the means of access to liquor.

'It is true that we should add thousands of pounds to our profits, but that is mere dross compared to the moral and physical welfare of our guileless native employees.

'Therefore, do not attempt to minimise the extent of the liquor curse – rather declare it upon the house-tops. Let a sympathetic simple world know that our compounds are antehalls to Hades, and the people who have nothing to lose by the change will say, "Let the philanthropic mineowners protect the native against himself, by confining him in a compound where he will find every inducement to expend in useless if harmless unnecessaries the money that would otherwise go to enrich the liquor-seller."'

It was Fraser who thus epitomised the theory of the compound system for the benefit of David Hyslop.

The quiet, caustic young Scotsman had vastly attracted the missionary, who appreciated his brusque criticisms and philosophisings because they seemed sincere, and not the outcome of a vain desire to pose as mentor. Mr Hyslop had begun to understand one striking trait of the Colonial – his unreticent outspokenness. He had ceased to be ruffled by candid if untactful suggestions and comments on his own conduct, and, unpleasant though the truth often was, he was bound to confess it was more wholesome than the insincere flatteries of less frank and fearless commentators.

He had confided to Fraser his darling ambition – to become an authority on native and general life on the mines – and he found the advice and criticisms exceedingly helpful.

Fraser always talked with a grumpy hesitancy, as though the effort had been dragged from him. He was fecund with parable and simile, as if he would compensate for a too free expression by a dose of cryptic vagueness. One of his illustrations produced a marked effect upon his pupil. Mr Hyslop had announced his intention of accepting an offer of Dane to show him something of the illicit liquor selling.

'You must do one thing before you knock round among whites on the Reef,' said Fraser. 'You must get out of that collar. Nobody tells the truth to a parson. He thinks he hears and sees a lot, but everybody is more or less on their Sunday behaviour when a parson's around. There's old Bill Scrivens, the finest swearer on the Reef. They say he has paralysed a religious chap with a couple of his best explosive phrases, and when he offers to stand a drink in a bar the other man generally orders a large Condy. Yet as soon as a parson comes in sight, Bill works at low pressure. A white choker is like that ring they put round the necks of the fishing pelicans to prevent their swallowing their catches. You leave it at home, and you'll find you'll swallow more in a night than you'd see in a year with that thing on.'

Under the pilotage of Dane Mr Hyslop visited liquor shebeens, and saw the ingeniously elaborate machinery by which the law could be defied and the kafir filled up with deadly Delagoa spirit, till his eyes looked like poached eggs and his tongue slopped out of his mouth. They were served through tiny holes like the ticket window of a railway station, so that even if their evidence were taken they could not swear to the person who served them.

The ramshackle one-storied building of corrugated iron that was 'licensed to sell' to whites was barely fifty feet by twenty. Yet it contained a bewildering maze of narrow passages and tiny rooms, that appeared to have exits and entrances wherever there was room for an opening. Dane explained that their object was to baffle the police and facilitate the escape of the kafirs in the very remote contingency of a raid. The kafirs knew their way about as well as ants in the windings of their mound.

By way of illustration Dane gave the alarm by whistling and shouting 'Police!' There was a rushing, bustling and bouncing against resonant iron partitions, as the kafirs were ejected by the four barmen. They fell like sacks on the stoep or off it, few being sober enough to remain erect after the withdrawal of the propelling force. When the missionary walked round the building he counted nearly forty lumps of ejected black humanity, of whom it was safe to say every one was incapably drunk.

'Surely there is evidence enough here to convict the seller of supplying liquor to natives?' Mr Hyslop remarked to his guide.

'Not a vestige. The law requires absolute proof of the sale to and receipt by the native. Could you swear that any one of these kafirs obtained the drink here? Everything points to the reasonableness of what would be Barzinsky's defence if he were prosecuted – that these kafirs came to his place in a state of intoxication, and he promptly and properly ejected them.'

'But I could swear that I saw liquor sold and drunk by kafirs. I counted eighteen tots passed through that little window,' the missionary objected.

Mr Dane smiled.

'I'm afraid you would not come out of a cross-examination very satisfactorily. What would you say when the solicitor for the defence asked you if you drank or otherwise tested the stuff to prove that it was liquor?'

'Of course I did not do that.'

'Of course not. And what would you say when they produced a bottle exactly like the one you thought you saw used, and proved that it contained lemonade?'

Mr Hyslop admitted that he was not likely to shine as a witness for the prosecution under such circumstances.

'No, you may take it as a fact that it is necessary to get up very early to catch these gentry. A business that shows a regular and steady profit of from five to six hundred per cent is not going to be run on slipshod lines if money can buy the best legal advice and evidence for defeating the law. Every one of these kafirs could be relied upon to swear, if promised a stiff tot, that he got drunk at any place Barzinsky liked to mention. The police know this, and naturally hesitate about taking action unless they can catch the seller in the act.'

Dane led the way beyond the glare of the occasional electric lights towards the open veld – the extensive unoccupied area of the mining property that would in due course be covered with vast heaps of rock brought up from the mine beneath, or the mountains of fine sand that was left after the gold-bearing quartz had been crushed by the ceaseless roaring stamps. The night was dark but clear, and an army might have passed unobserved. But Dane had the trained eye of the veld man, and had seen a quarter of a mile away what he sought – solitary figures moving slowly across a ridge where they stood out for a moment against the faint glow of a distant mine.

Suddenly there was a rush, a scuffle, and the sound of breaking and jingling glass. Dane had collared a native carrying a sack, and was laughing merrily.

'Come here, Preacher,' he called between his chuckles.

The preacher hurried up, and saw by the light of Dane's pocket electric flasher the tall form of Bulalie.

Dane held the boy by the collar while he gave him two or three light cuts over the legs with his sjambok, then hurried him off with a kick.

They examined the sack.

It had contained fiteen bottles of liquor, about half of which were broken.

'Don't touch it; keep away or it will burn your boots,' Dane remarked, as he took up a stone and completed the destruction.

'Listen!'

The dull thump, thump of feet on the veld indicated that the Peruvians who had been dealing out liquor from a hollow fifty yards away had taken alarm and were in full flight.

Dane walked leisurely to the spot. A strong whiff of methylated spirit was borne on the light breeze.

'They've smashed their stock. We've spoilt a good night's business,' Dane said. 'I should say they've broken three dozen bottles – say nine or ten pounds' worth; but I dare say they had sold as much. It costs them tenpence a bottle wholesale and retails at five to seven shillings, so they can afford the sacrifice.'

Dane explained that the party they had surprised were poachers on the preserves of the licensed sellers, and were probably white men of the 'bar-loafing persuasion,' who were either acting for themselves or, what was more probable, as agents for others. There would be a pretty row Dane suggested when they met their principals and tried to convince them that they had really lost their stock and were not trying to defraud their employers.

'What will Bulalie say?'

Dane laughed.

'Whatever he says will have to be accepted. He doesn't stand any nonsense.'

They returned to the compound. The signs of a vigorous debauch were numerous. A fight was going on in one of the sleeping quarters. Four or five of the combatants had been knocked out early in the *mêlée*, and were lying about the floor bleeding from ugly wounds from stick strokes. Half-a-dozen not yet disabled were blindly attacking friends and foes with the impartiality that comes of double vision, and a touch of repulsive grotesqueness was supplied by a group of six or seven on all fours lapping like dogs at a puddle of liquor and broken bottles.

Dane rushed in with his sjambok, and distributed stinging twining lashes on naked backs and legs, while with his left fist he knocked over every native within range by well-placed blows in the neck.

By his instructions four of the more prominent fighters were seized by the police boys, handcuffed with amazing celerity, and dragged, pushed or carried to the compound lock-up, where they were accommodated in the stocks and left to accumulate aching limbs, back and head until the morning, when the folly of excess would be brought home to them by a dozen on the bare back from a lithe sjambok guaranteed to produce the maximum of agony with the minimum of external evidence.

'No water, mind you,' Dane observed peremptorily to the police boy in charge of the lock-up.

Mr Hyslop asked what the order meant.

'I keep them thirsty when they're in the stocks. It's as good as fifty with the cat after a dose of liquor. They'll be half crazy by daylight. Then I give them a bucketful and the fools drink till they're nearly bursting and can't move. The worst of it is it makes them unfit for work, otherwise I should try it oftener. Six hours in the stocks without water will break in the toughest brute. I've seen a big six-footer howl for a drink like a thrashed dog.'

'Do your directors approve of this?' Mr Hyslop asked, aghast at the callous frankness.

'I don't know whether they approve; I don't ask their opinion. I'm responsible for discipline in the compound, and if I flogged for everything, I should not have time for anything else. Kafirs are not much impressed by the sight of a flogging; they rather admire a boy who will take twenty-five without squeaking; but when they see him doubled up and groaning after a few hours in the stocks, they think there is something in it. But as I said, that punishment makes a boy unfit for work for too long, and we can't afford to lose his services; so I have to prescribe that physic very carefully.'

'And all this misery and suffering is brought about by that accursed liquor?' the missionary queried.

'Practically, yes. And it might be prevented if the trading section of Johannesburg would consent to the introduction of the compound system.'

Dane had made a convert.

That night before retiring David Hyslop wrote an impassioned letter on the liquor traffic in the compounds, and urged the immediate adoption of the Kimberley system of segregation.

It was published by an important daily journal, widely read and commented on, and its author marked down as an emissary of the mining houses and an enemy of the struggling storekeeper.

'Clever chap, Sid Dane!' was the comment of the mining clique.

CHAPTER XXIV

THE BACKSLIDING OF BULALIE

An unpleasant growing suspicion that Bulalie was avoiding him became a certainty when David Hyslop, arriving at the compound by appointment intent on a serious talk, was more pained than surprised to see his erstwhile hope and pride running for cover behind a tailings heap.

Careful enquiry and observation had more than partially confirmed the sweeping indictment of the boy by Fraser, and the missionary determined on a vigorous effort to bring Bulalie to a sense of his condition.

But it was easier to plan than to perform. Bulalie was a past-master in the art of evasion. If cornered, as he now and then was, he would avert the impending lecture by declaring that he heard Baas Dane calling him, or manifest an unwonted alacrity in rushing off to perform the duty charged upon him.

It was also very evident that the boy had a great liking for and admiration of Dane, wherein he was in line with most of the natives under the authority of the bluff, blustering, even brutal compound manager. Since he had had opportunities for studying Dane, the missionary had ceased to marvel at the strange devotion and loyalty the man commanded, for he was of the masterful type which the raw native instinctively admires and bows down to.

Scores of theories and more or less convincing explanations have been adduced by those who take the trouble to discuss native idiosyncrasies to account for the well-recognised fact that the kafir prefers the forceful, domineering master to the soft and considerate 'friend and counsellor.' It is a fact on which the illiterate and unthinking base and justify their ill-treatment of the native; the judicious see in it a survival of the pristine worship of the strong.

But whatever the reason, Mr Hyslop had long since come to the conclusion that one of the chief causes of his own failure to make his influence felt by the natives was his inability to assert that unrelenting, ruthless mastership which the kafir expects from a white man. He would never admit in discussion the stock Colonial contention that the kafir has no sense of gratitude, but to himself he regretfully confessed that the native equivalent to that virtue was a very feeble imitation of the real thing. Nor could he honestly assert that the deference to the brutal master was altogether the result of fear, for he knew that Dane and tyrants like him are spoken of in the kraals with respectful admiration long after their authority and sjamboks have ceased to be felt. It filled him with a pained yet justifiable jealousy when he recalled that Dane was often referred to by a name that implied manliness and courage, he by a sympathetic, almost contemptuous appellation which might fairly be translated the man-like-a-woman of whom you need have no fear.

Now and then he tried to mollify himself by the reflection that Bulalie's objection to face him was prompted by fear, but second thoughts dismissed the notion. It might be that the boy's conscience asserted itself at the sight of the man who had first taught him how to recognise the inward monitor, but it was more than probable that Bulalie was obeying an order from his baas not to listen to the preacher.

The only way to secure an interview was by assertiveness. The missionary left a message not likely to be intercepted by Dane, to the effect that unless Bulalie had speech of the missionary the money he had sent to Natal would be lost.

Bulalie put in a prompt appearance at the rendezvous under the wall of the dam.

'Have you brought my money?' was the boy's opening question, after a greeting as awkward and constrained as it once was joyously free.

'I shall not talk of your money till I have spoken on other things,' the missionary answered firmly. 'Sit down on the stone and listen.'

Bulalie obeyed sullenly.

'Tell me truly, Bulalie, why do you do this great wrong – break the law and cause the boys in the compound to get drunk, so that they become ill and get the sjambok?'

Bulalie looked up with genuine surprise in his big eyes.

'I do no wrong, baas. They give me the money – five shillings and sixpence for a bottle, and I buy it for five shillings. They could not get it without me, Other boys would keep the money and say the police took it.'

'Yes, I know, and believe you are honest with the money; but it is wrong to help them to get drunk.'

Bulalie gave the kafir equivalent to a shrug of the shoulders.

'If they drink too much, of course they are sick, and sometimes get the sjambok; but I do not make them drunk. It is not wrong to drink puza if the police do not see you.'

The missionary tried to convey to the boy that the presence and interference of the police was *prima facie* evidence of the act of smuggling and drinking liquor being wrong.

'Do you not think when you go crawling through the grass, and hiding in the dongas and spruits, that you must be doing wrong? Men do not hide when they are doing right.'

'What? Ow! Baas, when I go to find a buck I go quietly, crawl through the long grass and lie low, that the buck may not see me. Is that wrong?'

'But you go to find a buck that you may stay your hunger.'

'When I bring puza into the compound I make money and buy food to stay my hunger.'

The missionary allowed the boy to chortle over his dialectic triumph. He endeavoured to impress him by a suggestion of the legal penalties.

'The baas and the police are good friends. They won't take me, because I am Baas Dane's head boy,' was the astounding retort, given with the emphasis of assurance.

'Then, if that be so, why do you work at night and not boldly by day?'

'Because the police do not wish to see me.'

The next line of persuasion attempted was the racially sympathetic. Why did Bulalie help to take into the compound liquor which he knew was as poison to many of his brethren?

The boy refused to accept the doctrine of universal brotherhood. Many of the worst drinkers were, he said, Shangaans, Magatese, and kafirs of many strange tribes, who were not his brethren. Besides, they were bad and quarrelsome, and if they died from the poison there would be more room for natives of his own tribe.

'But they may die also.'

'If I take hold of a snake by the head I expect to be bitten,' was the philosophical comment.

Bulalie's always cute, logical perception had been sharpened under the tutelage of experience and white example. It was not to be dealt with in a scratch debate. The educational process begun so well at the Mission Station must be resumed at leisure.

'Bulalie, I am taking a house. Will you come and live with me, as you did at Blue Krantz?'

He put the question hesitatingly, and awaited the reply eagerly. Bulalie laughed his old-time merry laugh of mingled surprise and incredulity.

'How much will you pay me?'

The spirit of commercialism had entered into and possessed the boy's soul.

'Four pounds, which is much more than Baas Dane pays you.'

Bualalie laughed and shook his head.

'Four pounds! Ow! I make more than that in bonsellas; but I should be only a kitchen boy, as I was in Maritzburg, with the police always waiting to catch me for being out after the "hamba kyah" bell had rung. No, baas. I am a man now; I am no longer an umfaan.'

The tone and manner of the refusal grated. The missionary made one more effort. He appealed to the sentiment of the old days at the mission.

'I could teach you to write, Bulalie. You remember how much you wished to learn?'

The answer was crushing.

'Baas Dane says writing no good. Plenty kafirs know how to write; they always get into jail. Jail is full of mission kafirs.'

It was a stereotyped colonial flippancy, but it sounded terrible in the mouth of a native who spoke it as if he understood and meant it.

'Then you believe what Baas Dane tells you rather than my words, Bulalie?'

Bulalie hesitated, as if fearful of hurting the feelings of his old baas. He answered slowly, apologetically.

'Baas Dane is good. He shows me how to get much money. You only gave me five shillings sometimes.'

The brazen ingratitude stung.

'But, Bulalie, are you not now head boy because I made you fit?'

'No. Baas Dane says always mission boys are all dam thieves. I told him I was not a mission boy. He says you will steal my money. Have you brought it? I must have it.'

The first impulse of the missionary was to go to Dane and tax him with having slandered him; also to question him on the matter of the remittance. Bulalie had declared that the amount he had handed to Dane was one hundred and thirty pounds, but thirteen pounds less had been sent on. He knew, however, that Dane would deny everything, and he was not disposed to provoke a quarrel on a statement by a kafir.

Bulalie was partially reassured as to the safety of his money, and its return arranged for.

That evening the missionary called on Fraser, and related to him the whole of the circumstances of the remittance and the suggestions of Bulalie.

Fraser listened attentively, then spoke gravely.

'I think you will be wise to wipe that transaction off the slate at once. Hand over the money, and be sure that you get a full receipt.'

Mr Hyslop was uncomfortably impressed by Fraser's manner.

'Do you anticipate any trouble?' he asked.

'The Rand is a funny place. You can never be sure that the most innocent matter isn't going to rise up in judgment against you. You are a man with a mission – a moral reformer. They always come to grief here; it's only a matter of time. Just now you stand well with the mining crowd, as you have given them a leg up on the compound business. Between ourselves, that was a very foolish letter, as it more or less commits you to the championship of a cause you know very little about. I don't think you would have been so enthusiastic in recommending that the boys be compelled to make their purchases on the mine property if you had known that that rowdy, thieving cookhouse and store near the Yankee compound is secretly owned by Dane. People are asking what you got for the testimonial.'

'What a nonsensical notion!' Mr Hyslop interjected.

'Not so nonsensical as it may seem to you. People naturally ask how you live. You are not connected with any church, and parsons with private means don't spend their time wandering about compounds and mine properties. The natural inference is that you are here for some purpose, and as you have written a gushing letter in defence of the compounds, it's clear as anything that you are paid by the mining companies.'

'You are painfully logical,' was the comment of the missionary. 'But how does this bear on the matter of Bulalie's money?'

'Only in this way. You have shown your hand as a reformer, or agitator, or whatever you like to call yourself. Unless I have misread you considerably, you will be rushing into print again presently, as your knowledge grows, and I don't think it will be on the side of the mine angels. In due course you will be in the black list as a dangerous agitator. As you are not the sort of person they can square by giving a job, they will just squeeze you out by assailing your character. How would it sound to have it said of you that you were a discharged and discredited missionary, who had to be superseded because of fanaticism, and that you had borrowed money off one of your converts, who only got it back after several pressing applications and threats of prosecution?'

Mr Hyslop turned hot all over at the thought.

'They would never dare to suggest such a thing,' he answered weakly, for the memory of certain things said about him in Natal passed over his mind.

'Don't give them a chance. Get that money; pay it over, and be careful to get a complete receipt.'

'I will do that. But surely my explanation of the business would be sufficient answer to any suggestion of the kind you hint at?'

Fraser's tone implied pitying surprise at the depth of his friend's ignorance.

'Man, but you are a child in some things. Don't you know that the public never trouble about explanations? They only notice the original charge, and that they generally get upside down. Mind ye, I'm talking of Englishmen, not my own countrymen. They read, and read intelligently, and have the patience and the desire to know both sides of a controversy; but your Englishman just reads the headline: "Serious charge against an ex-missionary," and wants to know no more. He notices that you are "ex", which means, he thinks, something disreputable – dismissed with ignominy – and that sort of thing, and that serious charges have been made against you. That's enough for him. The liquor crowd here are clever. They know it is easy to besmirch a man's reputation, especially if they take a highly moral ground, as they generally do.'

Fraser proved a veritable Cassandra.

The missionary took steps for the return of Bulalie's money, but was met by delays and objections from the co-trustee. Bulalie importuned angrily, and went to a law agent, who wrote the missionary a letter of demand couched in language more offensive than professional, and betraying evidence of having been written with a view to future production. In spite of his assurances of *bona fides* by showing the correspondence with the solicitor acting as co-trustee, the missionary was served with process, and only escaped having to appear in court by the arrival of the money.

'He has won one point in the rubber,' Fraser remarked.

'Whom do you mean by "he"?'

'Sid Dane, acting on behalf of principals – "q.q.", as we express it on the Rand. You must be like Agag – walk delicately. They are keeping you under observation.'

A week later the Rev. David Hyslop was looming large in print.

A Kafir on the New Yankee was severely maltreated by a brutal miner. There seemed no reason for questioning the facts, which were corroborated by four independent native witnesses. As Dane refused to take any action, the missionary secured the services of an ever-ready law agent, and the miner was duly summoned to the magistrate's court.

He admitted the assault and pleaded justification. The four witnesses whose statements had induced Mr Hyslop to intervene declared under cross-examination that the boy assaulted had used a peculiarly offensive expression to the miner, which the defending solicitor declared no white man could bear without justifiably and rigorously resenting.

The magistrate, in fining the defendant the minimum penalty, made some caustic comments on the indiscreet encouragement of native insolence given by such proceedings as these, and evoked a burst of applause from a crowded court by expressing his personal but not official opinion that the prosecutor had been incited to lay the charge by a professional agitator, whom he regretted he could not make responsible for the costs.

The subject of the castigation winced, and confirmed Fraser's diagnosis of his character by rushing into print with a letter justifying his action, and broadly accusing the white miners of the Rand of 'a brutality and tyranny not equalled by colonials.'

In one sentence he made an enemy of every miner and Natalian on the Reef, and clinched the suggestion of the magistrate that he was an agitator among the natives.

Fortunately, perhaps, for him, the editors of the Johannesburg papers exercised a liberal editorial censorship over the letters that David Hyslop now began to issue with the industry and long-winded extravagance of the correspondent with a grievance.

His charges and fulminations lacked that conclusive convincingness that should be an essential in warfare with a vigilant enemy, and more than once Mr Hyslop was saved from being severely called to account through editorial excision and suppression. This, of course, he interpreted into wilful bias and corruption on the part of the Press, and contrived to get an important London journal to give him space for a wholesale denunciation of the Rand and its people, and a reproduction of the passages 'deleted by corrupt and cowardly editors.'

'I'm afraid you've lost your balance,' was the frank but friendly comment of Fraser when the missionary went to him for sympathy and advice.

'I told you you'd be rushing into print, and you've done it, and finished yourself. You are the angry man who loses his temper in a discussion. He always comes worst out, though he is generally right at first.'

'No doubt I am rather strong in my expressions,' Mr Hyslop conceded. 'I feel strongly. The gross injustice, the universal conspiracy to regard the native as an animal − a mere beast of burden, without soul or feeling − outrages me. It is bad enough in Natal, but there the laws are very considerate of the native. Here they are all of the kind made for the repression of convicts, and what maddens me is that every white man supports and approves them. The greatest atrocities perpetrated on the natives are by Englishmen. I suppose if I said that in England I should be denounced as a renegade and defamer of my country, but you know it's true. I wonder how many people at home are aware that the black labour of the mines is obtained by a system precisely identical with the "blackbirding" in the Southern Seas? True, the boys are not kidnapped or brought up on the chain, but eighty per cent of them are induced to come by lying promises, and once here they may as well be in prison, for they can't escape.'

Fraser laughed.

'You are new to the thing, and it shocks you. You surely know that the kafir can only be induced to work by compulsion or special inducements. If the mines relied on voluntary labour there wouldn't be much of an output. Of course, the kafirs have a rough time; it's part of the conditions. After all, I don't know that they are any worse off than the white men who have to pig it in a tin cubicle or spend their time and money in a filthy canteen. And if it is going to be a matter of comparisons, what about your white slaves in the East End of London? Wouldn't they consider a kafir's life paradise? Food and quarters, eight hours' work a day, and sufficient pay to make them independent for life in three or four years, if – '

'If their Christian employers did not prevent it by providing every facility for ensuring damnation for their souls and bodies,' the missionary interrupted vehemently.

'You know,' he went on, 'that it is to the interest of the mineowners that the kafir should squander his earnings. It is the only way they can ensure keeping his labour. Don't talk to me about benefiting the kafir by giving him well-paid employment. His benefit is the last thing any white man thinks of. All he wants is the boy's labour, and if he can't get it by fair means he will get it by fraud. The white man is the black man's curse.'

Mr Fraser laughed heartily.

'You are very complimentary to me,' he said. 'You are paraphrasing my own speech to you on this subject. I suppose it sank in and got so well amalgamated that you thought it was your own idea. Never mind, I won't object to infringement of copyright. I'm rather glad you have taken credit for the authorship. It wouldn't do for me to be identified with such heresy. But why this sudden conversion?'

'It is not sudden,' said the missionary. 'The process has been slow. A man may have a disease and suspect it for a long time before he will accept the reality; even then he hopes for a cure. I recognise that spiritualising the native is a wasting disease, and that many of the symptoms of progress are only delusive, like the mid-day rally of a fever patient. Still, for all that, I have not given up hope of a permanent cure.'

Fraser was silent for a while. He began to clean his pipe – always symptomatic of careful thought, preluding a thought-provoking utterance.

'Has it ever occurred to you,' he asked slowly, punctuating the sentence with little stabs and thrusts at the pipe bowl, 'that you have been physicking the wrong man?'

The missionary looked at Fraser inquiringly. Then the scene in the church at Maritzburg was before him.

He heard himself uttering the words that gave such bitter offence in that never-to-be-forgotten sermon: 'The missionary would have greater scope for his labour among you than among the natives – you, their masters and evil exemplars.'

'I think I know what is in your mind, but to purify the source of the disease would be a greater task than to render the possible victims immune by inoculating them with the virus of clean living.'

'I rather like that medical simile,' Fraser said. 'I'll follow it up. You have been treating patients for the cure of a certain contagious disease. You have now discovered the source of contagion. You cannot remove it or cure it. There is only one thing that approved medical science suggest.'

Fraser looked at the missionary as if expecting him to supply the answer, but it did not come, but instead:

'Well, what is that?'

'Segregation of possible victims.'

'Which, being interpreted, meaneth?'

'Keep the native in his kraal unspotted from the world.'

The missionary sat watching the smoke from Fraser's pipe and thinking hard. At last he spoke.

'No; simple, but impossible under present conditions, and if possible cowardly. Sooner or later the native has, whether he likes it or not, got to risk infection from association with his "superiors." I have had my doubts, so far I have had nothing but failure. I still believe in the efficacy of the leaven, though I begin to think my later suggestion as to inoculation is more immediately practical. If I could but get the chance to inoculate one subject thoroughly, according to my own ideas of thoroughness, I should be content to abide by the result.'

'Here is a suggestion. Take Bulalie to his kraal and resume the treatment. If you can make him vice-proof you will deserve all and more than you are ever likely to get in the way of reward and thanks.'

That this consummation might be attained was the subject of the missionary's earnest prayer that night.

CHAPTER XXV

A HEATHEN DEATHBED

There was a tribal fight going on between the natives of the New Yankee and the Belmont.

It began as all of these blood lettings do, as the aftermath of a liquor orgie. Some two or three hundred bottles above the average had been smuggled into the compound early on Sunday morning. By eleven o'clock ten or twelve boys had been qualified for the mine hospital, and reinforcements were coming in from the adjacent mines, mostly drunk, and armed with bottles and iron bars.

The gravity or otherwise of a tribal fight on the Rand is purely a question of the point of view. Like a 'scrap' between two schoolboys, it is either 'a disgraceful and degrading exhibition of brutality' or 'a display of manly pluck and endurance calculated to bring out a boy's best points and a safety-valve for bad blood and temper.'

Mine and compound managers are as a rule disposed to take the broader view, and if they assert their authority, it is in the direction of checking abnormal expansion rather than stopping the fight. It is true that now and again the casualty list includes two or three fatalities, and forty or fifty more or less seriously injured, but it is also true that the carnage never becomes noteworthy until the representatives of law and order take a hand. Their efforts resemble those of an active fire brigade at a small conflagration – they extinguish the flames, but deluge and destroy the furniture.

Sid Dane was of the section who believe that it is better to allow the combatants to 'fight it out.' He had managed several big fights rather skilfully, and when this trouble started he put a loaded revolver into his side pocket, took his heaviest sjambok, and placed himself in a good position both for sight, safety and retreat. He was no coward; the Natalian who is afraid of a kafir, even on the warpath, is not common, but he realised the folly of arguing with savages in a rage.

He did one thing, however, which seemed either unnecessary or purposeful. He sent Bulalie to tell the Rev. David Hyslop that there was trouble in the compound, and that he might be useful in helping to quell it.

It was past noon when the missionary arrived on the mine. The fighting had become sporadic. A party of Zulus, armed mainly with iron and steel rods and drills, had pretty well rounded up the Basutos, who, as mountaineers, had taken naturally to the vast heaps of excavated rock, and were using the ample supply of ammunition to keep back the frequent charges; but the New Yankee boys were winning and gradually driving the Belmont Basutos off the property.

Presently there came a sudden recrudescence of the flagging fight, as a smouldering grass fire will break out into a gush of flame. There were wild charges, sharp encounters between parties of half a dozen or less who skirmished among the scattered buildings, volleys of rock, bottles, and any and every article that could be raised and hurled. Victims lay about or crawled to cover. One big Zulu lay in the open between two contending parties. He was on his face, and made several ineffectual efforts to get on all fours, preparatory to standing erect. As he always fell back upon his side and vomited blood copiously after each struggle, it occurred to David Hyslop that this was a fit subject for first aid and ambulance work.

Calling out, 'Don't hurt me; I'm the doctor-preacher,' he very courageously walked into the very centre of the fire zone. He reached the Zulu, and was leaning over him when there was a rush of two New Yankee boys, armed with knobkieries. When they reached the missionary a tall figure suddenly confronted them, holding an assegai at the point. It was Bulalie, who, by virtue of his position as head boy, was permitted to carry the forbidden weapon. He stood facing the raiders, holding them back by threat of throwing, and in hurried broken English he uttered a warning:

'Baas, go away, quick! Liquor men pay boys to kill you.'

David Hyslop took in the situation rapidly. He had been marked down for 'wiping out' by the illicit liquor gang as a reward for his persistent and successful exposures of their methods. He had been often warned of the danger he ran. Now it had come.

He rose, glanced rapidly at the enemy, the disposition of the forces and the lay of the land, then backed towards an iron building, twenty yards away, from the window of which a group of white men were looking on at the fight. He had a vague hope that they would come to his assistance, for he was unarmed and helpless.

The rush of the two kafirs, the interposition of Bulalie, and his own retreat had all happened in one quick palpitating flash.

There came another wild rush of naked, arm-flourishing kafirs towards him; five, six – more, and they were beating and striking at Bulalie, who was retreating backwards, keeping his assegai at the point with his right hand, while in his left he held a short fencing stick, with which he cleverly warded off or broke the force of the blows aimed at him.

'Run, quick, baas!' came the alarm, as a gang of boys suddenly appeared on the left flank and ran to cut off Bulalie's retreat. Hyslop turned to run. At that moment a kafir was on him, and a swift but ill-aimed blow from a heavy iron bar glanced down his back. One spurt, and he was at the door of the tin hut, which opened to receive him.

'The head boy is finished,' one of the miners at the window remarked.

Bulalie was lying on his side, his left arm under his head, his right held to his back.

The attackers had passed on and were absorbed in the crowd storming the rock heap still held by the Basutos.

'I must go to him; he saved my life,' the missionary said, when he glanced out at the window.

'You're right there. Those chaps meant finishing you. I wouldn't advise you to go out yet,' one of the men said.

David Hyslop did not stay to argue. He went, and regardless of the stones falling and whizzing past, knelt beside Bulalie.

'Where are you hurt?' he asked.

'I don't know, baas. I can't feel any pain, nor my legs and feet.'

David Hyslop passed his hand over Bulalie's body, and within a minute knew that a spinal injury had deprived the boy of the use of his lower limbs, preparatory to complete paralysis of the entire body.

They carried him to the compound hospital – a plain iron building, different to the others by having a wooden floor and matchboarded walls. The beds were canvas stretchers, and of the two hundred possibles, one hundred and twenty were occupied, mainly by dysenteric and typhoid cases, for they, like the poor, are always with the mine doctor.

He was busy, with a couple of white orderlies, dressing the wounds of an ever-increasing crowd of victims of the fight that was now reduced to a disconnected series of encounters by parties of a dozen or less. The police were now able to take a hand in safety, therefore the casualty list was swelling.

Bulalie was made comfortable on a stretcher in a quiet corner, and David Hyslop patiently awaited the result of the doctor's examination. It confirmed his own diagnosis – fracture of the spine, recovery a thousand to one chance. A lingering death, owing to the magnificent physique and organic healthiness of the patient, more than probable – at least seven to four on. Dr Burdett was a steward of the sporting club, and owed his popularity among the miners to his reputation as 'a good sport'. He was the actual doctor known to fame for having played cards with a dying patient – double or quits for his attendance bill, and, winning, refused to claim the stakes because his opponent was 'a bit out of form', and would probably have won had he lived ten minutes longer.

Bulalie rallied somewhat next afternoon. David Hyslop was sitting by the bed, having been in close attendance.

The boy looked at him and smiled, as if amused at the notion of being weak and helpless. The missionary inquired how he felt.

'Why do you look so serious, baas? Do you think I shall die?' Bulalie asked cheerfully.

'You are very ill, Bulalie, but you may not die. Would you be sorry if you knew you were going to leave the sunshine?'

'I am not yet old, why should I die? I am strong. If the Basuto witch doctor who used to find lost cattle in the big kraal came, he would soon make me well. I can pay him more money than ever he was paid. Send for him, baas. Tell him Bulalie is sick; that his legs have been bewitched by a Basuto scoundrel. Tell him I can pay for a black ox if he must slaughter one.'

'Bulalie, Bulalie! what foolishness is this!'

It was the wail of a pained, heart-bruised man. Was this the reward of his careful, prayerful sowing of the seed?

Bulalie shook his head feebly.

'White muti no good, baas; white doctor don't know kafir. The sick boys all die when they come in here.'

It was not quite true, but painfully near accuracy. The missionary was silent. He could not evolve a telling repudiation. Experience had taught him the folly and danger of ill-considered replies in a serious discussion, so he said nothing for a space.

Bulalie broke the silence.

'If I die, baas, you must write a letter for me. It is the letter I have wanted to write for long. But we will wait till the witch doctor has come.'

'But, you know, Bulalie, the police will not allow a witch doctor to come into the compound. You trust the white doctor; he has made many well again.'

'Then I shall die.'

He spoke with dogged, almost obstinate insistence. The missionary was almost glad. Of course the boy would die. The bold, uncomplaining spirit augured a humour for appreciating plain speech.

'Bulalie, when the old man of the kraal knows he is going to die he always tells those who will stay behind what he wishes them to do when he is gone. You say you are going to die. Have not you anything to say to me?'

He spoke quietly, but with no suggestion of alarming forewarning.

Bulalie lay silent, watching the missionary fanning away the flies that swarmed round the bed.

'I come alive again after I am buried,' he remarked, as if thinking aloud.

The missionary seized the opportunity he had longed for. He began to expound the puzzle of all puzzles to the kafir mind – the immortality of the soul.

Bulalie listened with languid interest. Several times he began to interject a question, but the missionary, fearful of being diverted from his objective, allowed no opening. At last he had finished; he had driven home one point – that death was not the end.

'Then, if I do not die after I go away, my father will not kill me?'

Mr Hyslop looked closely into Bulalie's face. Was he becoming delirious?

'Why should your father kill you?' he asked, soothingly.

Bulalie looked steadily in the face of the missionary.

'I am going to die, baas; you know it, because you know all about muti, and the doctor told you I should die.'

There was niether fear nor repining in the tone. For a moment the missionary envied this magnificent heathen courage. Why was it that it was only the Christian who feared death; who spoke of it reluctantly, with bated breath and awesome tone, but preferred not to speak of it at all?

The words of Bulalie seemed a challenge. He took it up.

'Yes, Bulalie, the doctor did tell me you will die.' Then he added: 'But perhaps not for a long time.'

Bulalie's face was impassive. He was watching the buzzing flies.

'Shall I see Bacheta?'

'I hope so.'

'And my father?'

'Yes, I hope so, Bulalie.'

Bulalie remained silent for several minutes. Then he made an effort to turn his head to the adjacent bed, where a native was sleeping. The missionary interpreted the action.

'No one can hear, Bulalie, if you speak low.'

'I killed my father.'

The statement was made with matter-of-fact coolness. The missionary was satisfied that the boy's mind was wandering. He leant over him and bade him sleep.

'I will come again when you wake.'

'No, baas, stay. Tell me what I shall do. I killed my father because he was going to assegai me. The police said that Sebaas did it, and they took him away to hang him, but they kept him in jail instead. I know all about it, but I have never spoken before lest they should hang me. But you are wrong, baas; my father cannot live again. The pot smashed his head where it always kills. No, he is dead, and I am glad, for I should fear to see him again.'

The speech, allowing for the halting utterance, was clear and intelligent; and yet the listener could not quite dismiss a suspicion of delirium.

'If this be true, Bulalie, you must have it all put down in writing, so that Sebaas may be set free.'

'If I am going to die I will do that,' the boy said, after a pause.

The missionary took out a bulky notebook he always carried. Bulalie watched him.

'Now I know I am going to die, baas,' he said. 'You know it, do you not? Yes, Sebaas must be brought out of jail. Ow! But if I do not die, baas! They will hang me. But you will not tell the police till I am dead, will you?'

It was David Hyslop's turn to pause long before answering.

If Bulalie did not die! There was just the chance of a partial recovery – a possibility that this magnificent human form might linger for a year or two a helpless cripple. If he did, and if the terrible story proved true, what was his duty as the holder of a secret that, if divulged, would ensure justice?

He was relieved of the agony of having to make answer.

'Tell them, baas. I do not mind being hanged. It is not painful, like lashes. Tell them to let Sebaas go and hang me.'

David Hyslop was moved. His heart prompted implicit belief in this heroism, but he felt certain that the story was only the phantasy of a disease-excited brain.

'I will go away and write it all down, Bulalie. Then I will bring Baas Dane to hear you say it is all true, so that he may put his name to the paper. Shall I do this?'

'Yes, baas; but be quick, or I may die.'

Mr Hyslop went to the doctor, and requested him to test the boy's rational condition.

An hour later Dr Burdett reported.

'His brain is quite clear, but collapse may come any moment. I give him twenty-four hours at the outside.'

David Hyslop returned to the bedside.

'Bulalie,' he said, 'tell me all the story. I will write it down, and you shall keep it. If you die, then I will give it to the police, and Sebaas will be let go. If you get better, then no one will know, for I shall say no word.'

He felt he might make this promise with a clear conscience.

Bulalie told the story of the parricide – truthfully, without reservation or extenuation – and the missionary reduced it to writing and read it aloud carefully.

Then, in the presence of a white ward orderly, Bulalie laboriously but proudly affixed his signature in a large, schoolboy hand.

'If I see my father, he will be pleased when I tell him that Sebaas is let out of jail. He liked Sebaas as his own son,' Bulalie said, when the orderly had gone out of hearing.

The missionary took up the cue, and expounded and expatiated on the doctrine of reparation for evil. In the old days at the mission Bulalie had manifested an intelligent appreciation of this phase of Christian conduct, after Mozulikase had been persuaded to perform Bulalie's work for him for a month by way of expiating an assault.

The relapse feared by the doctor set in shortly after the signing of the confession.

The missionary accepted the bed offered him by Sid Dane, and lay down after making arrangements to be called if the crisis arrived.

Next morning found the boy alive, but sinking. His face showed the passive, languid indifference that, despite popular and conventional belief and desire, is the external sign of approaching death in a vast majority of cases.

He recognised and acknowledged the presence of the missionary by a feeble smile, but when asked a question made no effort to reply.

The doctor administered a stimulant. In a few minutes its effect became manifest. Bulalie spoke, feebly but clearly. He mentioned names.

'Are they your brothers? Do you wish to say something to them?'

A flicker of annoyance passed over the boy's face.

'No, they are mine boys who owe me money. Their names are all in my book. You were good to teach me to write figures, baas. They can't now say they do not owe. It is in the book.'

'Is that money for liquor?'

'Yes.'

The missionary discoursed on the wages of iniquity, pointed out that the present condition of Bulalie and the sufferings of the twenty or thirty kafirs around were all the fruits of the abominable traffic. He advised that the outstanding debts be forgiven.

'Then the scoundrels will have more money to buy liquor, and I shall get no bonsella, because I shall be dead,' was the businesslike reply.

David Hyslop was saddened, disappointed. He would give much to obtain one sign of genuine Christianlike contrition. The boy's offer to give himself to the hangman that Sebaas might be freed was a step in the right direction, but its value as a sacrifice was minimised by Bulalie's consciousness of approaching death.

'You said something about a letter,' he said.

Bulalie's face brightened.

'Yes, you send it, baas, and if I see Bacheta I will tell him that I wrote the letter. He does not know that I can write.'

'But, Bulalie, would you lie to your dead friend?'

'He doesn't know I can only write figures. I will write some, and put my name, and he will think I can write. But he had a hole through his chest; I don't think I shall see him, so there will be no need to lie. But I should like him to believe I can write.'

The effort of speech brought a period of exhaustion. It was an hour before Bulalie again spoke.

He recovered consciousness just as the orderlies were carrying out the body of one of the victims of the fight who had succumbed to a smashed skull.

He knew what the stir and commotion meant.

'He is a Shangaan,' he said contemptuously. 'If he had been a Zulu we might have travelled together.'

'What about the letter, Bulalie?'

The boy's face brightened.

'Yes, Bacheta would like me to send it.'

He dictated a brief but intelligible description of the hiding-place of the tin box of diamonds in the donga by the Vaal river. It was word for word the account of Bacheta. Bulalie remembered it not alone because of its importance, but because a kafir never forgets a topographical detail once impressed upon his memory.

The missionary took down the details, making no great inquiry as to their full significance. He was used to receiving communications of a cognate character. They were generally trivial, or important only in the estimate of the dictator.

He waited until Bulalie had time to recuperate under the influence of a stimulant, then asked him if he had any message to send to his brothers in the kraal.

Bulalie seemed to be making a supreme effort to bring all his faculties under control. He could not move, but his voice was clear.

'Yes, baas, tell my brothers they must listen to your words because they come from their brother. Tell them Bulalie has seen all the white men's works, and that they are foolishness. Baas, take all my money from Baas Dane, and keep it. Do not let my brothers know you have it or the law of the kraal will make it theirs. Keep it, baas, and if they are wishful to go among the whites to earn money give them some that they may stay in the kraal, because they are better there. Tell them that puza is foolishness and white ways, and that to listen to the words of the white men who would take them from their kraals is to listen to the evil things of the night.'

Bulalie paused, exhausted.

David Hyslop sat throughout the hot afternoon watching the passing of Bulalie.

He was conscious and half ashamed of a sense of bitter disappointment at unrequited effort, of unconsidered grief, of unesteemed self-sacrifice. He had with pardonable egoism hoped that Bulalie would express, however incompletely, some sense of services of unobtrusive care, leave some sign or word that the labour had not been in vain.

When the boy again opened his eyes the missionary spoke.

'Bulalie, are you glad that you have known me?'

It was a direct application for a testimonial, but it was not for himself he sought it, it was for the cause.

Bulalie smiled.

'You have been my brother,' he said, then came the crowning guerdon. 'Keep my money for yourself, you are better than my brothers.'

'No, Bulalie, I may not do that. I will do for them what you bade me. But will they believe me when I tell them your wishes?'

Bulalie looked sad and thoughtful.

'They would if they knew as I do that you are the only white man whose words are always true. Tell them I said that you are the preacher who never lies.'

'I am content,' David Hyslop whispered as, half-an-hour later, he gently pressed down the lids of the eyes that were fixed upon his, and drew the blanket over the black but comely face.

CHAPTER XXVI

REGENERATION

David Hyslop wrote to his wife an account of the passing of Bulalie.

'All is ended now, the hope and the fear and the sorrow, all the aching of heart, the restless unsatisfied longing, all the dull deep pain, and constant anguish of patience, and yet I am content. True my darling hope was never realised in him, true I am unable to say as I would that I brought him out of the clay and set his feet upon a rock; but I have this glorious painful knowledge that I inspired him with a love for his teacher that prompted him to give his life for mine.

'It was not till I collected the scraps of the story days afterwards that I knew Bulalie had overheard the natives saying the preacher was to be finished at the wish of the illicit liquor gang. He was searching for me to warn me when the attack was made, and it was in convoying me to safety he received the blow that killed him. He died a splendid heathen performing a Christian act.'

When David Hyslop examined the effects of Bulalie they found he had amassed nearly two hundred pounds. The knowledge of the source of the treasure saddened, but out of evil good might come, if the money were put to some such purpose as that indicated by the dead owner.

The precious address of the baas of Bacheta proved to be a dirty scrap of paper torn from the edge of a book page. On it in large characters, partly script and imitation print, were the words: 'Jack Hodson, King's Kraal, London.'

The missionary set about enquiries. It was not difficult to trace a man who had been a prominent figure in a mining camp, and Jack Hodson was discovered in Johannesburg in the condition of optimistic impecuniosity with which all pioneers are familiar.

Mr Hyslop advanced the money necessary to take the grateful miner to the Vaal, and was as gratified by learning that the quest proved fruitful, and John Hodson was once again 'flush'. With the generosity of the old-time digger he insisted on the parson standing in, and gave him the alternative of accepting a couple of hundred pounds, or seeing the notes used as a pipe light.

Hodson, who had recovered three thousand pounds worth of stones legitimately his own, carried David Hyslop off to Maritzburg, where they ascertained the fate of Sebaas.

The boy had been convicted of the murder of old Tambuza, but owing to the existence of an element of doubt he was given the benefit of it, and sentenced to imprisonment for life.

The operation of reviewing the case was long and expensive, but David Hyslop spared neither time nor the money which Hodson pressed upon him, and within a couple of months Sebaas was liberated.

'And now,' David Hyslop wrote to his wife, 'I feel that my labour has not been in vain. On the pleasant farm I have taken within a few miles of the old station we can resume the work of regenerating the native by precept and example according to ideas enlarged and improved by the experience of suffering and disappointment, free from the narrow control of superiors who lack the opportunities for knowing what to avoid that have blessed my labour . . . My failure has been apparent, not real. The leaven has not leavened the whole, but its potentialities for good will be greater than ever.'

'Therefore, brethren, be steadfast, immovable, always abounding in the work of the Lord; forasmuch as ye know that your labour is not in vain in the Lord.'